SHADOW STALKER

Revenants Book 2

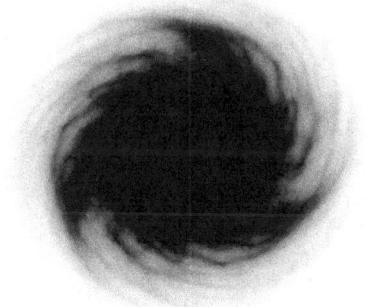

Elissa Daye

This is a work of fiction. Names, characters, places, and incidents are products of the author's imagination or are used fictitiously and are not to be construed as real. Any resemblance to actual events, locations, organizations, or persons, living or dead, is entirely coincidental.

World Castle Publishing, LLC

Pensacola, Florida

Copyright © Elissa Daye 2020

Paperback ISBN: 9781953271242

eBook ISBN: 9781953271259

First Edition World Castle Publishing, LLC, December 21, 2020

http://www.worldcastlepublishing.com

Cover: Melissa Davis

Editor: Maxine Bringenberg

Chapter 1

When all is lost, there is still hope. That's what everyone always said, but sometimes the hole was so deep that climbing out was damn near impossible. Years ago, hope might have existed for her, but in this day and age, the lackluster emotion was something that Caylin pitied in others. Hope, no. There was no hope. Only chaos and destruction, and mankind seemed to be the root cause of it all.

Every year darkness seeped into her veins like a bitter oil, corrupting every inch of her waking moments. Caylin couldn't seem to shake it no matter how hard she tried. Running from place to place in an attempt to find something brighter on the horizon had only made her life that much more difficult to swallow. She now lived her life hidden among the shadows that ransacked the world around her.

The black abyss echoed in her ears like remnants of a past she was desperate to extinguish. Ignoring it seemed like the best laid plan, but the effort required for this process took its toll so quickly. Everything that seemed bright in the world turned to shades of grey, dulled by the limitless humdrum of malcontent. Her life was no longer her own, for her path was woven from the madness and misery before her. Her world was growing darker by the minute, and Caylin seemed to be the only one to translate its message. Death, decay, corruption.

What one person thought was depression, Caylin knew it was something else entirely. She'd seen the madness work from its creation to completion with every day she walked on the streets. The shadows rose from the cracks in the ground, where water spewed, and mist repelled. They brought with them an energy so vile that the human body had no way to fight it. Caylin shuddered as she remembered the last time she'd seen the shadows rise into a prostitute named Shana. The poor woman had gone mad almost instantly, scratching her skin with her sharp nails and ripping her hair from her head. Her pimp had tried to calm her down, to remind her not to break the merchandise, but she had gone after him instead. Caylin still remembered the way the blood had pooled around her when she lay dead on the ground from the bullet he had put in her head. Caylin had been too late to stop it. The guilt ate at her even now.

Evil incarnate. It filled the cracks and magnified the shadows' world everywhere she had stepped for as long as she could remember. Was she immune to its icy lips? Apparently not, for its aftermath plagued Caylin when she wished for nothing more than absolution, for some sign that her blind faith that humanity would rise up against the shadows and do what was right to bring hope back to the world was justified. Instead, they had fallen prone to the darkness and let it control their base impulses. Crime rose, murder multiplied, and despair festered as the rich continued to ignore the root cause of injustices around them.

Caylin knew her time on Earth may appear short to others, but for her, this life was one of many, something she'd learned at a young age. She'd yet to recover every memory from those before, but her purpose had grown clear with every year. She hunted the shadows that dominated the chaos of the living around her. It annoyed her to no end that someone would even think to stop her in her dreams, let alone the real world.

This madness was like a reckoning that grew heavier each day, building as it encompassed one circle at a time until it exploded into mass chaos. Every year it pulsed around her world like a flock of locusts, devouring every inch of sanity right before her eyes. If only its victims had been able to see its path before it crushed them like puny little bugs under heavy trodden feet.

Neglect, ignorance, spite? All of these things seemed the same to her in the end. The darkness around her seemed to feed on it. With her power came visions that she could not seem to avoid. Caylin's sight made it impossible for her to ignore the way the world was slipping away around her, her curse for being born under the phoenix sign.

Caylin watched a couple teetering from the doorway of an all-night bar. They seemed oblivious to the dangers lurking in the shadows around them. She shook her head in disgust when one of them bent over and emptied her stomach, where the street met the curb. They continued on without noticing her in the doorway.

Lucky fools, the ignorant sheep that trampled the sodden grounds around her. Caylin had no such luck. She could see the darkness rushing into the living around her as it enslaved her city of lost angels. Caylin knew if she weren't careful, they would be coming for her soon, a sacrifice to the beasts that harkened behind her.

Creeping from the darkened doorway, she walked quickly down the alley behind her. Caylin found the perfect spot to stop and set her bag down on the ground. Pulling out her candles and crystals, she took a deep breath and said a small blessing in her mind before placing the candles and crystals in the correct order on the cement before her. She knelt at the makeshift altar, lighting each candle carefully. Each one had been scrimped and saved for with whatever money she happened to earn on the streets, doing things no man or woman should ever have to do. Caylin had forgiven herself long ago, but she knew she would never find absolution in someone else's eyes. Pulling her long blonde hair behind her head, she rolled it into a tight bun and used her pencil to keep it in place. Caylin closed her green eyes and spoke from the heart.

"Goddess, long may you reign and protect those that do not bear false witness to your love. If tonight they take me away, I shall live again. This, my promise. That the sacrifice of my life in your service would end my suffering until my soul is needed once more. May I remember my life before and discover a way to fight the evil that has caused my world to burn."

Caylin knew they were coming. She'd felt them waiting for her outside, watched their black trail of smoke as they gathered from the grates below her feet. That was why she had made a quick detour to this alcove below the bridge. At least here, she could draw them away from the rest of the people roaming the streets at night. Their power was growing stronger each day, and she couldn't seem to lose their trail. Did they find her, or was she seeking them? Caylin didn't know the answer for sure, and that bothered her. Trouble always seemed to find her.

The lights before her extinguished as a silent wind ruffled against her face. The seething cold of its touch took her breath away. Caylin gathered up the candles and let the wax drip to the ground before shoving them in her bag. Shutting her eyes, Caylin waited for the shadows that wanted to take her away. She reached behind her back and pulled the sword from its sheath. Asodio, the beautiful athame that Remie had given her to protect herself while working, was sharp and ready. Remie, he was an entirely different story. Brave, beautiful Remie, who walked the streets much like herself, but taught her other ways to survive it. She was forever thankful to him and the protection he had provided for her and the other girls.

Caylin rose as the first shadow came rushing at her. "Bring it!" She focused her energy into the blade, and its purple glow threatened the span of the darkness around her. Spinning around, she sliced the light into the shadow, and its disconnected halves fell to the ground. Another one came, and the athame ripped it apart with one swipe. The last one seemed to be weighing its options. When it tried to rush from the area, Caylin raced after it and ran it through with Asodio. The sharp, pitched shrieks as it dissipated before her were painful to her ears.

Sheathing Asodio, Caylin pulled the pencil from her hair and let the strands fall across her face. If anyone had told her when she had left home at fourteen that she would be vanquishing shadows by the time she was twenty-three, she would never have believed them. While she'd had an affinity for the occult, having discovered early on that she could see lives that existed well before this one, Caylin had never known how much magic ran through her veins. She had known it was there but had very little control over it. It wasn't until she'd found Remie that Caylin had learned how to harness the energy within to do so much more than she ever imagined.

When she retrieved her bag, she heard the tinkle of shattered glass inside. "Damn shadows! They ruin every fucking thing."

She reached inside her bag to check over the damage and winced as her skin sliced against one of the jars. "Freaking fuck-tastic."

Even though the madness surfaced from the ground up, Caylin knew the darkness wasn't isolated to just the magic beings below. Shadows were everywhere, in every crack and crevasse, hidden beneath the skin of people who had no qualms about destroying what little beauty was left in this world, and Caylin despised each and every one of them. She didn't quite know yet how she would destroy enough of them to make a difference. Remie assisted from time to time, but for the most part, it was just Caylin. Her role was clear to her if to none other. She was a Shadow Stalker, reincarnated each time to restore the light wherever shadows dared desecrate. Tonight, Caylin-3, Shadows-0. Swinging her bag around her back, she made the trek back to her apartment to log her night into the journal, where she recorded all her encounters.

Chapter 2

Caylin rapped her secret code on the door and waited for the three knock reply. Stepping back from the entryway, she glanced around her to make sure she wasn't being followed. The door swung open, and Caylin was ushered inside.

"You're late." Remie locked the door behind her and peered outside the tiny window next to it. Tonight he had swept his black hair behind his neck. His dark, brooding eyes were scanning the street outside.

"Relax, Remie. No one followed me." Caylin smirked at him. Remie was always cautious where dark magic was concerned, and there was none darker than the shadows that rose from the ground.

"What took you so long?" His tone would have been irritating had she not known how much he truly cared about her safety.

"Were you worried about me, Remie? Isn't that adorable. Asodio and I had a date with some black devils."

Devils that she knew Remie knew well. Remie walked between all worlds like the shadows she fought. He had found her years ago and swept her up from the dangers of the streets. Remie had sensed the magic in her and took great pains to help her bring it to the surface. His teachings had saved her from the life of prostitution she had been sucked into. He gave her other skills to help her survive. Thievery was perhaps not the most honest pursuit, but she never took more than she needed from her victims, and only what they could afford to lose.

Caylin chose her targets well, though. With her ties to the prostitutes who walked the streets late at night, Caylin knew who deserved to lose more than just a little.

"Shadows again?" His right eyebrow rose curiously. He shook his head in disgust and turned from the window. "Why didn't you call me, Caylin?"

"Because I didn't need your help, Remie." Caylin shrugged off his concern and moved onto the stairwell that led upstairs to the abandoned apartments where they lived. This was the Ghost District, a housing development that had been abandoned for several decades. When the city had deemed the buildings uninhabitable, they had turned their backs on them and watched as they became mere skeletons, and the wayward rebellious streets had taken them over as their own. The Ghost District was a dangerous place for a wholesome girl to shelter herself. It was a good thing Caylin had abandoned any hopes of regaining her innocence. Instead, she let her exterior harden like a cement shell and learned how to give whatever was dished out to her. Those who lived in her area had learned a long time ago to stay away from Remie's building.

"Someday, you're going to need more help than you realize, Caylin." Remie's eyes were soft, yet cold as if he knew something he would not share.

"I doubt it. Asodio and I are well matched." She put her hand on the sheath and gave him a cold gaze.

Caylin didn't like anyone telling her what she should do or how to handle her business. The shadows, they were hers to deal with, her burden to bear, and she did so without blinking an eye. While other people her age might be finishing up college and starting the next phase of their lives, Caylin was resigned to her life. Darkness surrounded her wherever she looked, and she had become comfortable with its cold blanket.

Remie followed her up the stairs quietly, as if he were in deep reflection. "Did you eat?"

"No." Caylin reached inside her bag, forgetting about the shattered glass, and felt it slice into her finger again. She let the bag slide to the floor and instinctively brought her finger to her mouth. "Damn it!"

Remie pulled her hand to his and shook his head softly. He closed his eyes, and a soft glow of light leapt from his fingertips. Caylin felt his energy seep into her skin and took a deep breath in. She felt the ebbing flow of blood slow, and her skin tingled painfully as the cuts started to seal over.

When he was done healing her, he shook his head at her. "You should be more careful, Caylin."

Caylin jerked her hand away from his and shook her head. "You're not my master, Remie."

"No, but I am your teacher." Remie ushered her into the doorway and gestured to the table.

"Don't be bossy, Remie. It's not becoming." Caylin's brows darkened as she remembered where she had been all those years ago. Having run away from home, Caylin had landed on the streets unprepared for the challenges ahead of her. No one could have predicted her current circumstances — except for Remie, perhaps. He always seemed to know everything, which was damned annoying at times.

He was a very resourceful man who walked between all worlds, like the very shadows she fought. Remie had taught them all the skills that kept them fed and away from strange men's beds. Remie detested prostitution and had made it his life's goals to arm the women of the streets with another profession that would help them survive. Thievery may not be the most honest profession, but none of them took more than their victims could afford, often so little it would never be noticed.

"Eat something, Caylin. You're almost skin and bones." He waved his hands in the air above the table, and two bowls of soup appeared.

"Show off!" grumbled Caylin. She had no idea how he made things appear out of thin air. Maybe he whisked them away from some unsuspecting person's house. As she imagined the disbelief that the person felt, a giggle rose in her throat. She took Asodio off her back and placed it by the wall nearby before sitting down to eat. Caylin quickly swallowed the sound before it could be released from her lips. Laughter wasn't something she experienced. Not any more.

Remie winked at her as if he had read her mind, but he did not give a voice to her suspicions. "So, how many shadows does that make this month?"

"Thirty-two and a half," Caylin answered absently as she shoved a spoonful of soup into her mouth.

"A half?" His eyebrows rose curiously.

"Well, I cut one in half just as it tried to teleport away. I'm afraid the bottom half made it back down to its origin. Wherever that is." She continued to eat the soup, wishing she had some bread to sop it up with.

"Almost forgot." Remie snapped his fingers, and a bowl of bread appeared on the table.

"Okay, now you're just showing off." She let out an angry huff.

"We all have our gifts, Caylin. It's how we use them that

makes the difference." Remie smiled mischievously.

"Right. That's what all men say." Caylin made her usual slam against the male race.

Remie seemed to take it in stride as usual. "I've always said if you want to know a real man, you have only to name the time and place."

Caylin ignored his wink and clutched the spoon tightly in her hand. She let out an exasperated sigh and rolled her eyes. "It would never work between us, Remie."

"Why's that?"

"I'm emotionally unavailable, and you're…well, you're…." Caylin struggled to find the right words.

"Not worthy of you." Remie smiled softly.

"Why do you always say that? Who am I compared to you?" She shoved her soup away from her and looked away from him. Emotions swirled inside her. Asodio seemed to pick them up, as the sword glowed bright blue in its resting place. Closing her eyes, she tried to smooth the waves rippling inside her. The best defense was to never let someone see how much they affected her. She did care for Remie, but she was not attracted to him the way he deserved. She was essentially a shell of a person where men were concerned. Having been used and abused so often on the streets, she found little worth in her sexuality.

"I know you think you're damaged irreparably, but someday you will find the beauty inside yourself again, Caylin. I hope I'm there to see that day." Sadness reflected in his eyes. He truly cared for her, even though Caylin would never return the affection.

Caylin sighed. "You'll probably die first."

"Doubtful." There was a merry twinkle in his eye. "I plan to live forever."

Caylin shook her head. "You probably will, you old cantankerous fool."

"Ouch! Such words. And I thought I was making progress too. Perhaps it's time for this old fool to shove off." His words had a hidden meaning that Caylin did not like.

"You're leaving?"

"I've outlived my usefulness here, really. You don't need me anymore, and…. Well, I grow tired of the same old thing every day and night."

"I see. And all the women who've come to rely on you?" Caylin felt a bitterness enter her at the thought of him leaving his home.

"Are all self-reliant now, Caylin. Besides, they have you to look out for them." Remie nodded at her in emphasis.

"I'm nobody's savior, Remie." At least she did not feel like one. She preyed upon others the way they had done to her. So what if her victims were not innocent? There was nothing pure about her. Not for quite some time.

He was right in one thing, though. Caylin did protect the women who walked the streets. No one else would. Caylin chose her targets well, often choosing the most physically violent men to take her anger out on. While Caylin no longer had to be one of the women displaying her goods to the world, there was still a sisterhood, a kinship with them that she would never lose. When a woman came back battered and bruised, Caylin was there to settle the score. A dark angel to those that had fallen around her. If she attacked them physically, they would have retaliated on the women they had hurt, so Caylin followed them around and found their patterns. When she had enough intelligence about her perpetrator, Caylin struck. Whatever she scored from them, she split with the women who had been mistreated. It didn't make up for the brutality, but it did make their lives a little more bearable.

"You are more than you know." Remie watched her carefully.

"Perhaps. Will you go?" Caylin pushed aside the needy feelings that were surfacing. She had survived before Remie entered her life. She would continue to do so once he'd left.

"Not yet, but the day will come." Remie stood up and walked away from the table. He sat down at his desk, where he journaled each night.

Caylin watched him work and admired the shape of his head as it bent down to his task. He was a beautiful man—if only she could muster the right affection for him. Remie would make sure she was happy, but somehow Caylin knew that would never be enough. It was as if her soul knew where to align itself, and while Remie was the perfect ally, he was not the lover her heart would seek out if it ever sought anyone. She looked away from him and suffered her melancholy in silence for a moment.

She dumped her bag onto the table and shook her head at the shards of glass that tinkled together. Caylin concentrated on the pieces in front of her. As she did, the tiny shards rumbled on the table, as if the force around them was disturbing them. Putting her hand on her temple, she squeezed her eyes shut, then opened them. Pushing every ounce of her energy into the clear glass in front of her, the pieces started to lift from the table. Willing them to come together, Caylin took in a deep breath and focused harder. The broken glass slid together slowly. Like a jigsaw puzzle, some had to be manipulated to find the right spot. The shards rotated in the lamplight, and glints of light shimmered on the wall.

When the pieces were all in place, Caylin held her hands out over them and sent heat from her fingertips. A golden light swarmed from her skin and wove itself around the injured jar. The cracks absorbed the heat and started to melt back together as the light turned bright red. She took a deep breath, and a cool blue mist of light left her lips as she blew on the glass. The glowing red glass disappeared as a frost covered the entire thing.

Caylin sat back and admired her handiwork. If only everything in life were this easy to repair. She turned to find Remie looking at her with pride, and she shrugged her shoulders. "I didn't feel like buying another."

"I can understand that one. Not like we have a Target anywhere near here." He smirked at her momentarily before a tenderness filled his eyes.

"Right." She shrugged off his attention, fleeting though it was because already Remie had returned to the task at hand. She sighed quietly and pulled out her journal too. They would fall into their nightly routine, and Caylin was glad of it. Before long, she would find her room and spend the rest of the night trying to evade sleep.

Chapter 3

Darkness surrounded her like a bitter twilight as beams of light broke through hazy clouds of putrid black smoke. Caylin struggled her way through the murky world before her. She knew this place well, the land of her dreams. She'd been traveling here for as long as she could remember, and it never made any sense to her. With the frequency with which she had the dream, sometimes she wondered if it were real, but the shadowed world could have only been one of her own creation.

Getting back to the beginning of it all, the root of the darkness that coursed through her bones, wasn't something Caylin wanted to do even in her dreams. It was sickness, a disease that started like a small wave and ended with a typhoon of emotions that covered every inch of her body with its angry remorse.

Tonight was no different. There were no walls, windows, or doors. Everywhere she looked was a wide expanse of space filled with the kind of energy that corroded her soul. This was more intense than her waking world. While mankind was dripping in its own shades of evil, this place was saturated in it. The dream world was untamed and unpredictable.

Caylin traveled down the road before her, as she did every

night. The road changed each time slightly as if the scenery was not predetermined as she had once thought. It was the journey that was tedious. Tonight she walked until she came a to fork in the road. Choices—she hated making choices. Caylin let out a disgusted breath. It seemed like no matter what she chose, it was always the wrong decision.

"Why can't the road stay together?" She blew her hair out of her face and scrunched up her nose in annoyance.

Which way should she go? The path to the right was covered in debris, almost as if a tornado had ripped through the area and cast its contents onto the world below. Caylin did not feel like climbing over the mountain of trash, sticks, and sharp glass before her, but the path to the left was pitch black. Taking a small step to the left, she held out her hand, and it seemed to almost disappear before her. She brought her hand closer to her face and could finally see it again.

"Hmm…looks like I'm screwed either way." Caylin had lived the past few years in the cover of the night, though. She would take her chances with the darkened path. While this one appeared safer, Caylin knew things were not always as they seemed. Even in her dream, she carried Asodio on her back, ready to spring into action at a second's notice.

Caylin walked a few steps and felt her shoes slide in something wet and sticky. She shuddered. "I'm not sure I even want to know what that is."

Pulling Asodio from her back, she used its light to illuminate the path before her. She had not wanted to do this at first, because her dream world was often filled with creatures that seemed attracted to her magic. The road before her was paved in blood, or at least she imagined it was, seeing as how the area around her was shaded in greys and monotone colors. Bright, vivid primary colors were non-existent here. This land was hopeless, much like the rest of her. Why would it be bright and beautiful?

"Well, at least these shoes will be clean the next time I wear them." She grinned to herself. The benefits of her dreams were that she woke up, and everything was just the way it was before she went to sleep. If only every foray into the wild had the same results.

As she traveled, Caylin saw small black weeds that came up from the ground. She moved closer to inspect them and realized these were not what she thought they were. They rose from the ground in black oily pools and reminded her of large patches of seaweed at the bottom of the ocean. Instead of a green gooey substance, they were somewhere between liquid and smoke.

When she stepped closer to one of the growths, she heard a woman's voice sobbing uncontrollably.

"Hello?" Caylin whispered to it.

"It wasn't supposed to end like this," the voice answered.

"Like what?" Caylin replied. The creepiness of the situation was not lost on her.

"Death, doom, decay...."

"What?" Caylin shrugged off the uneasily feeling. Why did this voice seem so real to her? For some reason, Caylin knew this was not like her other dreams, but she had no proof. Any minute now, she would awaken, and her life would be the same way it always was. But this time, it was more real.

One thing she knew for sure — these things before her were not what they seemed. She moved closer to a few others and heard other voices wailing in pain and despair. Caylin realized these smoky things were once living. Now they were nothing more than waving shells of their former selves. The black masses were the inky souls that had been stolen from the living world.

Did this mean Caylin was convinced this was not a dream?

No. She was asleep. She knew that for certain. But there was a little bit of truth to what she was seeing. She had witnessed souls being siphoned from human bodies before. The shadows that haunted their world were constantly sucking the life from mortals. Caylin really did not know why she felt the need to protect the world around her from these evil entities, but she did. Perhaps it was the centuries of magic coursing through her veins.

Kneeling down on the ground, Caylin closed her eyes and said a silent prayer for the souls beneath her. If she had the ability to set them free, she would, but Caylin was not even sure what good that would do while in the dream state. She rose from the ground and forced herself to push on down the road.

As she walked down the path, Caylin found herself moving toward what looked like a city. Cement buildings crawled up from the ground like icy cold talons. Their jagged edges were not like the structures in her own world. They did not have the usual boxy shapes — instead, they were made with sharp, angry angles that made her wonder what creatures could possibly call them their homes. While there were visible windows, Caylin did not see any doors to enter them, not that she wanted to go inside any time soon.

The road split, and intersections were now visible. A slow hum passed over her, and Asodio started to glow on her back. She felt its warning course through her. Caylin stepped into the alley and pushed herself up against the wall. Moving her head slowly around the side of the building, she looked out into the streets. Far down the road, she saw long gangly black shapes making their way slowly across the broken pavements.

"*Shadows.*" Even in her dreams, Caylin despised the malignant creatures. She pulled Asodio from her sheath and prepared for battle. By now, they would have found her, but they seemed to be focused on some point in the distance. She did a quick count and found there were at least twenty random shapes moving down the road.

"I wonder...." Caylin stepped from the alley and crept closer to one of the shadows. She was surprised to find it did not even notice her. "That's unusual."

Caylin put her sword away, slightly confused by their lack of interest in her. By now, they would have attacked her, even though she was in a dream state. They always attacked. It was in their DNA, if they had DNA. That was a question for another day, though. Right now, she wanted to know how close she could get to them. If she could walk close enough to follow them, Caylin would be able to determine their destination. She slipped in right behind them and kept her distance just in case. She was concerned that an attack might make her so defensive she would jolt awake. Caylin was not ready for her dream to end.

Maybe her dream would give her some kind of clue about how to deal with them in the real world. Sometimes her magic worked like that. That was how she had found Remie the second time after he had released her from her hellish prison and sent her on her way. It was as if her soul was searching for him because every dream seemed to be filled with his face. She had not understood it at the time until Caylin had seen him in the subway, perched near the benches on the back wall, where the light flickered over him. Its glimmering effect highlighted his mysterious nature as he seemed to be half in shadow and half in light. That really did define him too, for Remie's goal was to do good, but his actions were often tainted with immoral tendencies, hence his propensity for thievery. A Robin Hood amidst the urban decay, Remie was a hero to none. Her lifeboat, perhaps, but never a savior. Nevertheless, she would not trade his friendship for anything else in this lifetime.

Caylin followed the dark figures as they marched over the ground. She was surprised that their bodies had more of a human shape than the ones in her world. They usually floated over the ground slightly, making them even more haunting, but seeing their fully formed legs walking sent a slight shiver up her spine. It was as if they were evolving if that were even possible. With magic, dark or light, she imagined anything was possible. All she knew was that the shadows were plaguing her world, and she felt hell-bent on stopping them. Did anyone task her with this? The universe, perhaps. Sometimes she wondered if there were others like herself, but she knew that would not make a difference to her. Caylin was a perpetual loner. Aside from Remie, she kept to herself. She never had fit in with others.

As Caylin moved forward with the crowd, she saw a large grouping of fir trees ahead. Like a sanctuary of life amidst the bitter remnants behind her, Caylin was surprised to find it stretched out before her. It reminded her a little of Central Park in New York. Its wide expanse was like an oasis in a shriveled desert. "Odd...."

These dream worlds were not known for any shadow of life. Not like this. She imagined it must be a cover for something else entirely. Caylin was not disappointed, for as they moved past the tree lines, the trees turned to mere skeletons of their former shells. Creepy limbs extended into twisted thorny spires that, at some angles, looked like dangerous claws. The trees started to thin, and a small clearing appeared. Dozens of shadows surrounded a tall object before them. It looked like a prism made of some dark rock, much like obsidian. For some reason, Caylin was just as compelled by the structure as they were. It was almost as if it called to her.

Caylin stepped closer to the large group of beings. As she neared the prism, her head started to hurt. She could not tell if it was the prism or the shadowy beings around her that triggered the pain. Perhaps all of it changed in the dream world.

Caylin slid between the last pair of shadows and looked up at the prism before her. It was as tall as a building about four stories tall. It reminded her of an obsidian obelisk, like something she would find in the hot deserts of an older time. She looked closely at it and saw it was filled with a black smoky substance that swirled inside it, shifting and shaping into orbs that dissolved into oily pools.

Caylin put her hand up and was about to touch the prism when she was shoved out of the way. "What the hell?!"

"You're welcome." The intruder's voice was filled with grit as he glared at her.

"Welcome? Are you fucking kidding me?" Caylin brushed herself off and pushed up from the ground. She was about to give him a piece of her mind when she realized her reality had changed. The shadows that had been ignoring her at this point turned to face her. Red light glowed from their faces, like wicked eyes that were memorizing every inch of their prey before they attacked.

"What the hell?" This was new. Again, she was reminded how much the shadows had morphed into mortal forms.

"They were luring you here." His face was covered with a stubble that made him appear rugged. Handsome? Perhaps, if she were the type of girl who cared about sexual appeal. Her desire had fizzled out a long time ago.

"I was this close to figuring it out."

"Right. And when they sucked you into the deathly vortex, what then?" His brown eyes glared at her. Apparently, he did not like the fact that she was unappreciative of his rescue.

At that moment, Caylin realized that arguing the matter further was foolish. The shadows were now moving toward them. Their attack was imminent. She was about to arm herself when the man pulled out a wand. She laughed at the puny instrument. "What, are you going to beat them over the head with a stick?"

He smirked at her and shook his head. He murmured a few words she could not understand, and everything faded away from view as a bright light permeated the area. Before long, even he had disappeared. When the light faded, her dreams turned off, and her dream state was filled with a gentle peace that she had never felt in this lifetime. She tested the warmth around her and was reminded of the chocolate colored eyes that had been soft and firm at the same time. Caylin was not sure what to do with the peace.

There was something about him that disturbed her, and she could not put a finger on it. He could have been the type of man who would have haunted her dreams if she had not been jaded by her past. She was living proof that darkness could change everything you were. She liked to think this lifetime had not started that way, but as far back as she could remember, sadness followed her. From an early age, Caylin had learned how unimportant she was to the world around her. It was dumb luck that she had survived her childhood with the amount of neglect she'd received from her parents. When her mother had left her father, Caylin thought that would change, but it never had. It was a dog fight to survive with the barest scraps of affection tossed her way. Even her teachers had trouble connecting with her. Caylin had simply given up on any kind of human relationship.

Caylin had tried to find her voice when she was a young teen. She'd seen the darkness growing to epic proportions.

When the fourteen-year-old had attempted to tell her mother about the madness inside the small town where she'd grown up, her mother had treated her like she had lost her mind. Caylin had overheard her talking to what must have been her tenth boyfriend that year. He had suggested that her mom lock her in the nuthouse and throw away the key. Before long, he had finagled his way into every inch of her mother's conscious, until she had made a phone call to have Caylin admitted. Having overheard this, Caylin had packed a bag with as many clothes as she could and left her home behind. That was an end and a beginning at the same time. An end to what was left of her childhood, and the beginning of a first-hand knowledge of how the streets could rip your soul from your body.

The darkness of the streets, the sickening way the men lusted over her youthful body, was something Caylin would never be able to fully digest. Part of her had splintered off, stealing away the rest of her hope and leaving her with nothing but trepidation, making her feel sick in her current state as the peaceful dream he had cast rippled over her. She shuddered and crossed her arms around herself. She didn't want to feel his energy here. She didn't trust it. And she would never trust him if he, in fact, did exist.

As Caylin continued to sleep, the protective bubble the man had cast around her starting to erode as if some force were pushing against it. Had he been right? Were they targeting her? Was it easier to do so in her dream state than when she was wide awake? Caylin reminded herself that this was *her* dream. She squinted her eyes and pushed against the intrusion, but a loud cackle echoed around her.

You can run, but you can't hide…. The voice made her shiver slightly. Its tone was grating. *Soon, you'll beg for my touch….*

"Never!" Caylin was repulsed when an image of a dark

figure entered her mind. Its form was like the shadows, but he was completely solid. He ran a finger down her spine, and a shiver ran up her back. When his hands reached around her neck and pulled her against him, she choked back a sob. "Stop!"

Never. Not until you're mine. When he turned her in his arms and brought his face down to hers, Caylin saw the burning lights behind his eyes. His lips touched hers, and she fought back a sob, but then realized the sound was not coming from her. Her mind was suddenly filled with hundreds of voices, each in obvious despair as wailing screams bounced around her head.

Caylin pushed away from him and screamed so loud the image of the man before her burst. Anger filled every inch of her. Whatever this thing was, it wanted her to give in to the darkness. Caylin refused. When his anger shook the world around her, Caylin said a little prayer and squeezed her eyes shut. When she opened them, the man who had come to her rescue before, was standing in front of her.

"Why are you here?" Her voice was barely a whisper.

He did not answer, even though she could tell he wanted to. He gave her a sad smile and held up his wand. Before he could wave it, she held up her hand.

"Wait!" Caylin knew he was about to tip the scales again.

"Yes, Caylin?" His voice was gentle, a conundrum from someone as hardened as he appeared.

"How do you...?"

His eyes—she could not get over the haunted look that seemed to fill them. "Rest now."

He waved his wand before she could say anything else. She fought the annoyance that grew within her. How dare he try to control her? Before she could voice her anger, the world started to disappear, and Caylin fell into a much deeper sleep.

Chapter 4

Caylin jolted awake in her bed. "What the hell?"

She put a hand to her head and tried to still the loud pounding, as she often did in the morning, but when she looked at the clock on the nightstand, she realized her sleep had lasted much longer than she intended.

"Shit!" Remie was going to be worried if she didn't check in with him soon. He meant well, she knew that, but sometimes he could be overbearing in his need to protect her. She never understood why he felt the need to watch over her so closely. Sure, her dreams had pointed her to him, but the meaning behind it all had never truly been revealed. That was the way dreams worked sometimes.

She opened one of the pill bottles next to her and popped a few to take the edge off the pain. The migraines were a small price to pay if it meant she could gather more information about the shadows. Unfortunately, Caylin was not sure what intel she walked away with this time. Shuddering, she remembered the dark lips that had seared against her own. The screams echoed in her head, a reminder that something much worse lurked beneath the shadows. What that was, she couldn't be sure of. From her encounter with it, she knew it was a male entity of some kind. She closed her eyes and tried to picture him, and the voice popped back in her head like an icy echo.

Soon, my pet. You'll be mine.

His? Who the hell did he think he was? Caylin bowed before no man, especially one whose soul was so corroded it was no longer recognizable. It pissed her off to no end that he had attached to her in her waking hours.

Caylin walked over to the altar in her room and lit all the white candles. She put her hands over the flames and cupped them together. She used them to bring the smoke closer to her body to cleanse her aura from any potential negative energy that might have attached itself to her. This was something she had to do, considering she spent a fair portion of her time throwing herself into the darkness around her. It came with the job.

"Blessed mother, provide peace and protection. Keep the evil at bay, so I can continue to do your work." Caylin closed her eyes and took a deep breath. The air entered her body like any other person's, except Caylin used it as cleansing energy. The calm, soothing air became a current of light as it flowed from her head all the way down to her toes. It pushed out the dark energy that attached itself to her. When she opened her eyes, Caylin felt more settled.

She sat down at her vanity and looked down at the journal before her. She quickly put pen to paper and wrote about her dream. Caylin wasn't sure if she should tell Remie what had happened. If she did, chances were he would threaten to never let her fall asleep again, but Caylin knew that to find more answers, she would have to fall deeper into her dream world. Finding him was the only way she could erase him from her mind, perhaps even from her world.

What part did he play with the shadows? Did he control them? Was he their master and creator? A god of the underworld who sent his sentries above to erase any kind of peace in our world? There were so many questions, and Caylin wrote them all down. She couldn't help thinking the shadow creature was looking over her shoulders. Turning to look around her room, she saw the flame flickering wildly at the altar, a sign that there was danger nearby.

Closing her eyes, Caylin let herself reflect on the other man in her dream. She still wasn't sure why he was significant, but he seemed hell-bent on saving her. If he truly knew her in the real world, he would know that protection was for the weak. Caylin did not have a weak bone in her body. Nibbling on her lower lip, she admitted to herself that this was an outright lie. She did have one weakness — her need to have someone, anyone actually, care about her. That was why she tolerated Remie's preoccupation with her safety. Caylin never questioned that Remie cared for her. He was the first person in this lifetime who had. Everyone else had either gone through the motions with a fake fervor or hadn't bothered at all.

As she let herself imagine the man, his face appeared before her. His short brown hair was tousled on the top, making him look as if he was too preoccupied to run a comb through it. She could almost imagine running her fingers through it — if she were prone to those kinds of thoughts, that is. Fantasy was a luxury that Caylin never had, but still, his face called to a deeper part of herself.

She shook her head in annoyance. She did not need this. He was just a figment of her imagination. Caylin was sure of that. He didn't really seem to fit the rest of her dream world anyway. He did not appear dark and twisty like the rest of it. Cocky, self-absorbed, and ruggedly handsome. That was a combination that would annoy the hell out of her in the real world.

"What does it matter? He was a figment anyway." Caylin

groaned. Why did one image bother her so much? It wasn't like she actually cared about someone's sexual appeal. Sex had not been all that rewarding to her. It had been a means to an end. She had learned to muddle her way through it. She simply cut herself off from the rest of the world. That had been the only way she had survived it. Maybe that sounded cold and predictable, but that was just the way it was. Caylin had no use for a man in her life.

Boyfriends? She'd never really had one. Did they use women the way the streets did? Probably. Outside of Remie, she had no real positive experience with men. Did that make her cold and jaded? Yes. It did. Caylin did not fool herself that there was a happily ever after out there for her, lined with a white picket fence. There were no rose gardens and lilies anywhere in her future. This life had been predetermined. Her job was clear here: vanquish the shadows that preyed upon those that could not protect themselves. There was no time for anything else. Not if she wanted to say alert enough to attack at a moment's notice.

Speaking of which, at that precise moment, her phone rattled on the vanity before her. Caylin snuck a glance at the text. SOS, Marlow. Caylin sighed. Clearly, the young prostitute had gotten into a situation she could not handle. Was she ready to take on Marlow's problems tonight? Looking in the mirror, she found no savior looking back at her, but the lackluster woman who had certainly seen better days. Shaking her head, she pushed herself up from the table.

"Duty calls."

Caylin pulled her clothes from the closet. Great for hiding in the shadows, the tight black jeans fit her body almost like a second skin. The black tank top she paired with her leather jacket. Caylin gathered her sheath and slid Asodio safely inside.

While she didn't think she would need it to help Marlow, there could be other dangers out there. This she knew better than most people.

Once she was ready to hit the streets, she checked her messages to see if Marlow had given her an address to head to. 402 South Emerson. Caylin sighed in relief. "Good girl."

Caylin replied. OMW...on my way. Now, if only Marlow could hang in long enough for Caylin to get there. She didn't even bother locking her door when she left her apartment. No one ever came into this building, except for the rats. Caylin heard the tiny patter of feet and shivered slightly. Nasty little creatures, but in the grand scheme of things, they were just a small annoyance on the tapestry of her life.

When she made her way out into the street below, Caylin crouched low to the steps. A hum of energy echoed around her. Most would have never noticed, but Caylin was sensitive to the undercurrent of energy. To her, it was like a large helicopter was landing nearby. The waves of rippling darkness smashed against her aura, and her defenses went up. Closing her eyes, she said a silent prayer to the divine and attempted to calm her nerves.

"I don't have time for this shit." Caylin gnashed her teeth together and waved her hand in the air. A purple glow of light raced from her fingertips. It ran to the top of her head and slowly worked its way down her body. This blanketed her aura from the world around her. It would make it harder for the shadows to find her. Not that she didn't want to confront them, she just had other things to take care of first.

Caylin walked down the street, keeping a steady eye on the buildings around her. If anyone or *thing* tried to attack her, she would be ready for it. She passed a few corner bars with their flickering neon signs. There were a few people walking inside, but none of them gave her a second glance. An old man leaned against the side of the building with a large bottle covered in a brown paper bag. He looked as if he had seen much better days, but Caylin did not feel sorry for him. He'd chosen the streets, just as she had. Though the world could be cold and empty when you had no home to call your own, the life you lived was up to you. Caylin had made many mistakes over the years, ones that had shaped the woman she was.

Turning the corner on Riverdale, she saw the late-night adult stores that seemed completely deserted from the front. Caylin knew better, though. It was always the back rooms of these places that were overcrowded with sleazy pimps turning their girls out for an extra payday. Caylin shivered just thinking about the things that happened during those late-night parties.

Pushing on, she ignored the need to go in and break down the door and protect the women inside. She reminded herself that she could not save everyone, and if they needed her help, they would have called for her just as Marlow had. She turned another corner and found the address that Marlow had texted. A warehouse. Interesting. Why would someone bring a prostitute to a warehouse?

Caylin walked up to a window and peered inside. She could see a light glowing further back in the building, but could not make out any people. The rest of the warehouse was filled with large boxes and wooden crates. Drugs, perhaps? If that were the case, getting Marlow out of there would be more difficult than she first thought.

She crept around to the back of the building and tried to open the door. Locked. Pulling her lock picking tools from the inside pocket of her leather jacket, Caylin inspected the lock. She slid the tools into the lock and slid them around inside it until she heard the click of the door unlocking. Sliding the tools back inside her pocket, Caylin slowly opened the door.

"Looks inviting...." She shook her head. The area before her was almost pitch black. Moving along the wall, she put her hand up to guide her. She made her way around as quietly as she could until she could see the dim light to the right of her. As she crept closer, she heard Marlow's voice.

"Please stop." Her whimpers were almost inaudible as if she were close to losing consciousness.

"I paid for the whole night, bitch. I'll stop when I'm good and ready."

"Or now...now's good." Caylin entered the room with her hands on her hips.

"What the fuck are you doing here?" The man spun around, and the whip in his hand flashed through the air. Caylin caught it and yanked him forward.

"Taking out the trash." Caylin smashed her fist into his face and felt a small triumph as a river of blood flowed down his face.

"Bitch!" He wrapped his hands around her neck and squeezed tightly in a deathly vise. Instead of panicking, Caylin felt triumph.

Anyone else in her position would have tried to claw their way out of it, but Caylin waited until the last moment to react. This made him think he had the upper hand. Caylin grabbed his crotch and squeezed so hard the man crumpled to the ground. She smashed her elbow into his face and turned around to face him.

"You're pathetic." She spat on him before her foot smashed into his face. He fell to the floor, and his eyes rolled back in his head.

"What did you do, Caylin?" Marlow whispered in horror.

"What? Him? He's just sleeping now, which is more than

he deserves. Let's get you out of this." Caylin undid the ties on the prostitute's arms. She looked Marlow over and shook her head in disgust. There were long lines of red scratches on her arms, some from where the whip hit her, and others clearly made by the knife that was sitting on the table nearby. "He was going to kill you."

Marlow could not meet her gaze when Caylin put a gentle hand on her face. "Maybe it was my time."

Caylin watched a single tear fall down Marlow's face and closed her eyes. Now was the time for some hopeful rhetoric, but Caylin didn't have any in her repertoire. "You're lucky this time. Stay away from the east end guys, Marlow. They're all like this. Drug dealers who think the world owes them everything. Even your life."

"I know." Marlow's tears now fell full force. She needed someone to comfort her, but she knew Caylin was not the right person to help her.

Caylin reached inside the man's pocket and pulled out his wallet. She took the stack of bills inside and handed it over to her. "Here."

"I can't take that. He'll come after me." Marlow was clearly afraid of the man.

"You can and will. In fact...." Caylin looked around the room and found a painting that looked out of place. She pushed it out of the way and saw a safe was embedded in the wall. Taking Asodio out of her sheath, she willed every inch of her energy into it. She sliced the sword through the air and shoved it into the keypad, which shorted on impact. The safe door swung open, and Caylin reached inside. She split the money inside into two piles. "Here. Take this and get the hell out of this town. Do something better with your life, Marlow."

Marlow's eyes were huge when she saw the money before

her. "What if—?"

"He won't find you. And if he comes after me, I will take care of him." Caylin actually looked forward to it. She'd never killed the living before, but she wasn't opposed to doing so if it rid the world of a cretin like this. And the funny thing was, no one would miss him. A new drug dealer would line up to replace him before anyone knew differently.

"But—"

"Don't worry, Marlow. I'll make it look like he took the money himself. Trust me. I've done it before." And she had. Pinning the loss of drug money on the dealers was one of her specialties.

"Okay." Marlow looked away from her, then turned back again. "Caylin...."

"I know, Marlow. Trust me. I know."

The sorrow in Marlow's eyes spoked to a place inside her that she wished she could toss out. That need to be loved by someone, to be cared for and to feel important in a world that could care less about you was something that they had in common. Maybe that was why Marlow had felt she could trust Caylin. Caylin shook her feelings aside and concentrated on getting Marlow to safety. "Look, you have to go now. I'll take care of the mess here."

Caylin watched Marlow walk away before she started to clean up any sign of her presence. She planted a few things in the room to make it look like a drug deal gone bad and set him in the chair at the desk. When she was done, she looked over her work. "That should do it."

She left the building much as she had entered it, under the cover of darkness. That was something she had learned to utilize early. Many lessons had been difficult to learn, but she still managed. Luckily, perhaps there was a little bit of fortune inside her, for she always seemed to know when to run. A century of magic coursed through her veins carried with her soul with each one of her lives. With this magic came great responsibility. When she was old enough to understand it, Caylin knew she must keep it hidden from the rest of the world, even from her family, which had proved easy, considering how easy it was to live under her mother's neglect.

What did Caylin do to deserve this life? Shaking her head, she pondered the good and evil in the world around her. Unfortunately, Caylin came into contact with very little good. Not when the shadows soaked up every ray of light. As she walked the streets every night, she watched the mass of innocence disappearing around her, as shadows invaded under the cover of night. They stole the souls of those who were too weak to defend themselves against it. Their spirit had been lost long ago. The darkness targeted those who society had written off without notice — the homeless, the ill-stricken, the undesirables. Each one was treated like yesterday's trash.

When she first met Remie, she was nothing more than a girl with a little magic in her veins, with several lifetimes of memories in her head that made no sense. He had changed all of that when he brought her into his fold. When he told her she was special, Caylin had almost laughed in his face. What could he possibly think made her so damned special? No idea. She wasn't much different than your everyday person, aside from her belief that all energy around her could dissolve the light from the brightest heart. The magic inside her made her different, but many times she found herself completely defenseless, sometimes at the most inopportune times. It was not until she made it far away from this earthly beginning that she had come into her own where her powers were concerned. Caylin was not even sure there were others like her. Half of her hoped so. The other half doubted there was anyone else like her left in this world. Perhaps that was the anger inside her revealing its ugly head.

Caylin faced her future each day, with the knowledge that her life might end around every corner, bringing her soul full circle once again. She prayed that her soul would always remember the strength of the convictions she held dear, for Caylin refused to compromise herself. She would find a way to fight the darkness that no one else seemed able to see, even if it meant she had to do the lioness's share of the work.

Chapter 5

As Caylin walked down the street, she found the lights that were normally on were extinguished from the bar windows. Had they lost electricity? Not that it mattered. Traveling in darkness was something Caylin was used to. Nevertheless, this seemed different. Caylin felt the hairs on the back of her neck stand up and knew this was far more than a power outage. Caylin stepped into the closest alley and peered around the corner.

"Where is she?" A man in a long black trench coat held up some kind of shining orb in his hand.

"Hell if I know," the one next to him answered through gritted teeth. "Why did they send us to find her anyway? Don't they know we have better things to do?"

"Shut up, Mannie. If you want to be part of the Craven, you have to follow orders. Don't be a dumbass. You'll ruin it for both of us."

"Right, Mick. And what exactly has joining up with them done for us?" The man was clearly annoyed.

"Mannie! You know what happens if you choose to leave, right?" the man warned him. Caylin saw him hold up his hand under his chin and slide it slowly across.

The man shuddered. "I should never have let you talk me into this."

"Face it, we're stuck now. Where did that bitch go to?"

Bitch? Caylin felt the need to teach them some manners, but she had already dished out a fair amount of discipline tonight. Right now, she really just wanted to go home. But there was that part of her that was curious about who they were talking about.

Caylin followed her curiosity and stepped out of the alley. "Who are you looking for, boys?"

"There she is! Get her!" Mick reached for something in his coat.

Caylin did not hesitate. She pulled Asodio from its sheath and held it in front of her. "Bring it on."

Two on one, those weren't bad odds really, but at that moment, a friendly voice called out to her. "Mind if I join you?"

"Remie! Damn it. I can take these assholes," Caylin bit out through gritted teeth.

"I know, but I was bored." Remie flashed her one of his annoying grins, and she rolled her eyes at him.

"Fine, but I get the fat one."

Remie chuckled. "He's probably slower anyway."

"Who are you calling fat?" Mannie now had a dagger in his hand.

"Isn't it funny how he thought we were talking about him?" Caylin taunted both of them. "How do you know I wasn't talking about him?"

The other Craven, Mick, snickered. "Well, clearly, he's bigger than me, but that doesn't matter because Mannie could take both of you."

"Right. In his sleep, maybe." Caylin sidestepped Mannie's first attack as he tried to slice her with his dagger. She slammed the hilt of her athame against his cheek and tripped him with her foot. When he fell to the ground unconscious, the other man seemed to rethink his odds.

He held up his hand as if to give up, but then pulled some kind of orb from his pocket. He held it up as if he were trying to look deep inside it. Then he pulled his necklace up and spoke into it. "It's her, she's here—"

Caylin did not wait any longer. She swung Asodio through the air and sliced the crystal in half.

The man looked at her in horror, as if she had eradicated his one lifeline. "You don't know what you've done!" His face contorted in pain, and flames started to gather around his feet. In a matter of seconds, he was completely surrounded by fire. The orb he was holding in his hand came flying through the air. When it was about to smash on the ground, Remie held his hand up, and the orb floated up to it.

"This could come in handy." He smirked at Caylin, who was still in shock. The man's last agonized screams were now fading from the air, and all that remained was a small pile of ash on the ground.

"Wow. Remind me to go for the necklace first next time." Caylin kicked her foot through the ash.

"Who's to say there will be a next time? Unless you're moving on from the shadows?" Remie's eyebrows rose as if curious about her next moves.

"I make no promises." Caylin winked at him. Remie was digging for information about her whereabouts, and Caylin did not feel the need to cue him in. He was the one who had set her on this path, after all. What did it matter that she had handled Marlow's problem without him? Remie had often hinted he would be leaving eventually anyway.

"Still…."

"What, Remie? Are you worried about me? If you haven't noticed, I'm perfectly capable of taking care of myself." Caylin gestured to the man groaning on the ground. She picked up his necklace just as his eyes flew open.

"Wait...don't...." Mannie tried to reach for the crystal she held in her hand.

"What do you think, Remie?" She didn't even bother to look over at Remie to see what he wanted her to do. It was not in their nature to kill other mortals. At this point in time, Caylin simply wanted to know who was looking for her. She ripped the necklace from his neck.

"Please, don't —"

"Tell me who's looking for me." Caylin ran the crystal through her fingers, taking in every intricate detail in a matter of seconds. The crystal was clear like quartz but had something trapped inside it. When she tilted it up and down, a smoky black trail moved up and down it.

"I can't tell you...." His voice was near hysteria.

"I see. Well then...." Caylin lifted her hand up as if she were going to smash the crystal on the ground. She never got the chance, though.

A shadowed figure popped up next to her out of thin air, ripped the necklace from her hands, and threw it on the ground. She rolled out of the way to avoid the fire that started before her. As the Craven on the ground became enflamed, the figure gave a haughty laugh. "Newbies...."

"Who the hell are you?" Caylin gripped Asodio in her hands and was about to attack him, but he laughed in her face.

"Ah, the fearless Stalker. About time we met. We've been looking for you." He held up his hand and conjured a red ball.

"Me?" Caylin sneered at him. Clearly, he was not here to make friends. Asodio's glow was a deep purple, as she put all her anger into it. She was not about to let this low life get to her.

"A shame. The Revenant has been looking for you. You could work well together."

This man wanted her to work with the Revenant? Who or what was the Revenant? If he worked with the Craven, Caylin was sure she wanted nothing to do with it. The Craven was supposed to be a hidden magical organization, that in her opinion, wasn't nearly as invisible as they thought. Caylin had seen their kind out and about frequently. She had never actually been the brunt of their attacks, but there was always a first time for everything. "I don't know who this *Revenant* is, but I want nothing to do with him."

"Too bad. Your loss." The ball in his hand grew larger, and Caylin could feel the heat.

Remie stepped in front of her as if to block the attack. He held up his hand and cast a shield of light around her. "I've got you, Caylin."

"Got me? Are you fucking kidding me? Get out of the way, Remie!" Caylin charged at the shield and tried to slice through it with Asodio, but her body was thrown back. Sheathing Asodio, she turned and flew at Remie, ready to spit nails. "You asshole. Stop treating me like a child."

Remie peeled her hands off him, trying to hide a grin. "Look, he's going to destroy this shield. You really need to let go."

The man sneered at them. He released the first ball, and the shield flickered. Caylin looked at Remie and shook her head. "Shoddy work, Remie. He shouldn't be able to get through if you cast it right the first time."

"Well, if you weren't trying to distract me...."

This time the man's attack disrupted the shield completely and the remnants fizzled to the ground. The two of them were still in the middle of their argument when he was about to toss another ball at her. Caylin pulled Asodio out of its resting place and held it up as if to ward it off when another body entered the fray. A large bolt of white light shot across the air and knocked the man on his ass. Before his attacker could get another blast at him, the Craven faded from sight.

"Making trouble again, Caylin?"

Wait...she recognized that voice. Caylin swung around to find herself face to face with the man from her dreams. Many thoughts swam around her head, but the loudest one made its way out of her mouth. "How do you know my name?"

He never answered her. A smug smile was plastered on his face when he turned to face Remie. "I thought you had her under control?"

"Well, I did...until she decided to outgrow my plans." Remie turned away from Caylin.

She could not ignore the guilt etched on his face. "Remie, what the hell is going on here?"

"It's time to bring her in, Remie. No more excuses."

"Griffin, look, she's not ready yet."

"Griffin, is it?" Caylin moved closer to him, with Asodio now grasped firmly in her hand. She grabbed onto his collar, hell-bent on shaking some information from him.

He pulled her closer to him, and Caylin was ready to pummel his face. What the hell was he going to do, kiss her? Caylin looked into his eyes and found a warmth hidden inside.

"Hold on, Caylin."

"What...?"

She blinked in confusion. His eyes were almost hypnotizing. She looked away first and tried to gather her wits, but realized it was too late, as her assumption about his actions was completely off. Before she knew it, the air around her turned, and the world slipped out from under her. They were moving through time and space. The scenery changed over and over. Caylin tried to make out the details around her, but her head started to feel heavy. As she lost consciousness, she fell against his shoulder.

Chapter 6

When Caylin awoke, she found herself propped up on something hard as a rock. She blinked a few times to adjust to the pitch black around her. Where the hell was she? When she heard the shuffling of feet nearby, she reached behind her back for Asodio and cursed inwardly. Where was it? She needed a back-up plan fast. Her fingers crept along the cold floor, searching for her trusty weapon or anything that might work in a pinch. When she felt a small rock, she curled her fingers around it and prepared to jettison it at whoever was creeping near her. Before she could, a small glow of blue light illuminated nearby. Caylin squinted her eyes to adjust to it.

"Caylin?" Remie's voice called to her tentatively.

Caylin was half tempted not to respond, but that lasted briefly. "Yes?"

"Are you in one piece?" His concern was palpable.

Whatever had been going on between Remie and these other people, he did seem to care for her. Caylin wasn't sure what to think. "I seem to be, but I can't find Asodio."

"I have it here. I just want to make sure you're not going to use it right away." His words had a teasing tone, but there was a seriousness buried beneath.

Caylin ignored the caution in his voice and barreled through with her questions. "Where are we? Who in the hell was that man? And how do they know you?"

The air around them was thick with a pulse she could not quite understand. She cast a small ball of light in her hand and took a look around her. It appeared to be a cave of some kind. As she moved her hand around her, she saw dark crystals hanging off the walls in different places. That explained the energy she was feeling. In fact, it was so strong she could barely feel Remie's energy. The stone was sending strong pulses all around them, blocking her senses in a way that made her feel as if her equilibrium was shot to hell. Her head started to pound furiously, the faint traces of energy corroding through her own. Caylin closed her eyes and threw up a shield around her. The purple light ebbed and flowed until it sunk into her skin. This would only last for so long, though.

When Remie didn't answer her questions, she tried again. "One question at a time then. Who the hell was that man?"

"Griffin."

"And why was he following me?"

"That was my fault." Remie didn't seem all that concerned about it, though. He had the air of a man who had other things on his mind, things that he had on lockdown, preventing her from probing into his conscious.

"Why? What did you do?"

"I called for help."

"We didn't need any help, Remie."

"You're tainted."

"Tainted? What the hell are you talking about?"

"You got too close to them, Caylin. He's marked you."

Caylin let out an exasperated breath. "Riddles with you... always a fucking riddle. Your next answer better be completely truthful. Where are we?"

"This is merely a holding place until we can make our way to the Watch Tower." Remie moved closer to her, and the glowing light followed him. It was an orb that he had cast to light the way.

"Watch Tower?" Why did that sound remotely familiar to her? Like the elemental watchtowers called upon when casting a circle, perhaps? Or some religious order that superseded other beliefs on human morality? There was no love lost with formalized religion, where Caylin was concerned.

"The Watch Tower. How do I describe...?" Remie's face grew weary. "It's an organization of some of the most powerful people on this planet. Their purpose is to destroy the evil entities that are wreaking havoc on our world."

"Well, that's awfully ostentatious, isn't it?" Caylin rolled her eyes at Remie. A group of people playing God? Is that what the Watch Tower was? No wonder he hadn't told her about them. Caylin was not the kind of girl who wanted to be fettered to any group. She was much happier on her own.

Remie did not seem taken aback by her words. "I thought so myself. I've learned to trust them."

"So...they are from the Watch Tower. Why do they want me?"

"For the same reason the shadows do. You have a powerful destiny."

Oh boy, here we go. Destiny. Well, that explains absolutely nothing. "That's a crock of shit. I'm not different than anyone else, Remie."

"You are the Stalker. Some people are born to do great things. You were born to destroy shadows."

"Oh, goodie." Caylin rolled her eyes. That wasn't new information for her. She had been taking them out for years now, but what did that have to do with the Watch Tower?

"You have a long way to go, Caylin. The Watch Tower can help you." Remie's face was far more serious than she had ever seen it.

"I do fine by myself, Remie. I don't need a faction of self-indulged magicians to help me."

"We've been keeping an eye on you."

"Oh? Really? When exactly did that start? When I was born? When I lived with the trailer trash, who thought I was expendable? When I was being manhandled on the streets taking whatever scraps I could get to survive?"

"I came when I could." His words were no real defense for his actions. The guilt on his face made that all too clear.

"That's what I thought. Some friend." Caylin felt a sneer forming on her face. She should have learned not to let *anyone* get close to her. Everyone was out for themselves and would only screw her in the end. Caylin's anger was bubbling, gurgling inside her like a geyser ready to erupt.

"It's not like that, Caylin. We didn't know about you until the Shadow Walker had a vision."

"Shadow Walker?" Caylin rolled her eyes. She really didn't care who this Shadow Walker was. Caylin was already making her exit plans.

"From Sector Four. There really is a lot to tell you, most of which should be done at headquarters." He held up his hand, reading her emotions like the empath he was. "Don't go."

"I'm already gone," Caylin nearly spit through gritted teeth. Forget him and that antiquated organization. There was nothing any of them could do for her anymore.

"We need you."

"That's too bad for you, I guess. Now, please give me Asodio." When he did not hand it over, she knew she would have to take matters into her own hands. Caylin walked over, held out her hand, and called for her athame. Asodio was easily located by the purple glow that emanated from behind him. She would have done this sooner, but she had thought she could trust him. No worries. She'd traveled the road by herself before.

"Caylin, what are you going to do?" he asked her when she ripped the sword from its resting place.

"What I should have done long ago. Leave." Caylin put the sword back in its sheath.

"You can't."

"Try and stop me," she challenged him. She put her hand on the hilt of the athame and waited to see what he would do.

Remie held up his hands and his shoulders dropped in defeat. "These crystals are blocking your energy source. It's far safer here than anywhere out there."

"I'm not so sure it's safe here." Caylin felt her anger rising. What a fucking hypocrite Remie was. He had told her their duty was to protect others, something she had thought he was doing. Instead, he was using her — for what? To see how far her magic could get her? To mold her into something, manipulate her emotions for his own personal benefit? Caylin had thought he was different. "You used me just like everyone else. I guess nothing is sacred anymore."

"It's not like that, Caylin," Remie tried to defend himself. His mind was probing into hers, trying to override the emotions clouding her thoughts right now.

She felt the gentle probing and pushed back against it. Caylin trained her eyes on him with a dangerous glare as she put her thoughts on lockdown. Her anger boiled over, and a small tear worked its way out of one of her eyes. She dashed it away angrily, erasing its existence before any more could come.

"But it is, Remie. You should have known better."

Caylin stepped away from the concern on his face. She didn't want his empathy. Look where it had gotten her. Caylin put one foot in front of the other, disregarding the warning he had given her moments before. So what if the shadows came? At least she knew they were her enemies. Caylin knew where she stood with them, and right now, she was furious enough to take down at least twenty of them. She was ready for the challenge.

As she stepped out of the cave, she was not surprised to find herself standing in total darkness. When her eyes adjusted, she was aware of the slight glow from the moon above lighting the way just enough for her to see the shadowed trees around her. Long branches hung over her as she moved forward, reminding her of long spindly claws. As the wind blew through them, they moved just enough to give the impression that they could swipe at her at any time. Caylin took a deep breath and steadied herself. Now was not the time to let her imagination run away with her. There were plenty of real things out there that would be more than ready to snuff her life out without any second thought.

She walked a few more steps before she turned around. "What do you want?"

"You shouldn't have left," Griffin cautioned her.

"You should have left me alone." She put her hand on Asodio, prepared for whatever came next. She was not going to let them take her again.

Griffin did not move threateningly toward her. His eyes were conflicted, just as unreadable as the rest of him. As he stepped closer, Caylin moved back. This was the same man who had come into her dreams, and it wasn't the first time she had felt his energy. Had he been one of the people watching her?

"You need to come with me, Caylin." His words were soft, but his eyes were hardened as if he was prepared for the fight.

Sensing the danger brewing between them, she conjured a purple fireball in her hand, ready to unleash it at any point. "If I were you, I would choose wisely—"

"I'd hoped to do this differently, but you've given me no choice."

Caylin unleashed her fury on him. The ball zipped toward him, and he deflected it with a white shield of light. It rebounded from it and shattered into a puff of smoke. Caylin reached for Asodio but found her movements constricted as a lasso of golden light unfurled from Griffin's hands. It wrapped around her tightly, and she struggled against it. The more she struggled, the tighter it became. Caylin's efforts only made her fall forward. She was about to smash her face head first on the ground below when she was instantly levitated.

Griffin stepped closer and whispered in her ear, "You have a lot to learn, Caylin."

She spat at him, but her aim was off. "Fuck you."

"Not very ladylike." He clucked his tongue at her.

"Bite me." She glared at him and saw his eyes flash dangerously.

"As delicious as that sounds, we have work to do." He made a large circle with his hands, and a green portal opened before them. This time he didn't even touch her. Instead, he pointed to the portal, and she was pulled toward it.

"I hate you!" she yelled at him as her feet touched the portal. That was the only time she saw him flinch. She barely had time to reflect on it as the world whipped around her. She was tossed through the air like debris in the eye of a tornado. Time and space zipped around her, and a wave of dizziness hit her. Her last thought before she lost consciousness was that she was going to kick his ass to next Sunday at her first chance.

Chapter 7

When Caylin came to, she rose kicking and screaming. "Let go of me!"

"Calm down, Caylin."

Caylin struggled against the lasso that held her tight. The more she struggled, the tighter the ropes became. She was still levitating and realized his magic was much stronger than she'd thought. Caylin would have to try a different approach. "Let me down."

"Please?" His eyebrow rose as if to taunt her.

Caylin clenched her teeth together and tried to decide if her pride was more important than getting free from her constraints. Her anger won. "Fuck you."

"That's not very ladylike." He shook his head at her, but a large smile was on his face.

"Being a lady gets you nowhere."

"I see." He looked away from her as if to feign boredom. "I'll let you down when you say the magic word."

She gave him a soft pouty smile and turned her charm up just a notch. "Put me down...NOW!" Caylin's whole body started to electrify, causing the lasso to shake in response. It zapped her lightly as if punishing her for her attack. "Ow!"

"Wrong word," he chuckled.

"Fine." Caylin narrowed her eyes on him. "Please let me down."

"Was that so hard?" Griffin went to remove the lasso, but he did not count on what she would do next.

The moment Caylin fell through the air, she rotated her body, so she landed on her hands and feet, graceful as a cat. Caylin flew at him in a rage. Her fist slammed into his gut. When she went to punch his face, Griffin caught her hand with his own. He jerked her against his body so fast, Caylin was off balance. She tried to pull away, but his arms held her tight. As she stared in his eyes, something inside her stirred, like static electricity that surged between them. Caylin shifted uncomfortably in his arms, still trying to figure out how this man could be that strong. From here, she could feel his muscles bunched beneath his clothing, something she found to be quite surprising.

"Caylin…," he whispered as his lips came down on hers.

Caylin was no stranger to a man's touch or his kiss. She waited for the revulsion to rise up, a remnant of all the black nights that had plagued her mind. Caylin went limp in his arms, trying to find the will to fight. Her heart skipped in her chest, and she couldn't help feeling its traitorous turn. There was something about him, even more familiar than the man she had seen in her dreams. For the life of her, she could not place the feeling that came over her.

Griffin deepened the kiss, and she closed her eyes. White light exploded behind her eyelids, and she was reminded of the peaceful place he had transported her to in her dreams. She had the distinct feeling he was manipulating her. Somewhere deep inside, she managed to bring the anger back to the forefront of her mind. Caylin stomped her foot on his instep and reveled in the growl that left his mouth when he broke the kiss. The white lights disappeared, returning them to the darkness that surrounded them.

"Let me go, you asshole!" Caylin felt her hair start to rise around her. A purple glow emanated from her.

"You might want to let her go," cautioned a female voice behind him.

Griffin released her and stepped back. "Until next time."

"There won't *be* a next time." Caylin was so angry she was ready to spit, like a tightly wound cat ready to spring on its attacker. She watched the two people exchange a look that Caylin could not decipher. "So, they sent a woman thinking you could talk some sense into me?"

"No. I asked to come."

Caylin's hair was still rotating around her. She looked around at her surroundings. They were in a darkened alley that could be anywhere in the world. Caylin was wound up like a bomb waiting to explode. "I suggest you let me go."

"I'm not afraid of you, Caylin." The woman looked at her, almost dismissively.

"You should be." Caylin held up her hand and shot a ball of fire from her hands.

The woman deflected it with a flick of her wrist. "You've got to do better than that, Stalker."

Caylin was still sizing the woman up. She was average height, nothing all that impressive in size and stature, but it was the physical power that was dangerous. It was the pulsing magic that coursed through the woman's veins that gave Caylin a slight pause. "What if I don't want to be the Stalker anymore? You all should just let me be."

"That I cannot do."

"Suit yourself." She put her hands together and conjured

a line of purple flames that moved from where she stood to where the brunette was looking at her in almost boredom.

The woman sidestepped the flame and pointed one finger down at it. An icy frost came from her fingertips, dousing the flames one at a time until they had completely fizzled out. She crossed her arms over her chest. "Is that all you got, Stalker?"

Caylin's eyes flashed open, and she reached for her athame. The purple blaze lit up the darkness around them. She leapt at the woman, who cast a lasso of blue light and ripped Asodio from her hands. Caylin dropped to her knees and growled. "Give it back!"

"I think not." The woman snapped her fingers, and the athame disappeared from sight.

"You! Ahhhh!" Caylin charged at her, prepared to tackle her to the ground.

"Ah-ah!" She cast a shield of white light, and Caylin bounced off it.

"Who are you?" Caylin crouched on the ground and tried to catch her breath.

"Someone who was once lost like you. They found me too. They call me the Shadow Walker. You can call me Lyssa."

"So, you sent them to find me." Caylin drew herself up to her regular height and glared at Lyssa.

"In a manner of sorts. We were already looking for the Stalker. We just hadn't found her yet."

Caylin closed her eyes and shook her head. She just wanted to be left alone to fight her own battles and protect the ones who could not protect themselves. She didn't want some huge destiny. What she was already doing was plenty for her. "Why couldn't you have let me be?"

"We all have a purpose, a place. It's time for you to discover yours. Now, if you're done attacking me, I can bring you to the

Watch Tower."

"I make no promises," seethed Caylin as she cast another ball at Lyssa.

"You're like a caged beast. That will come in handy. But we're on your side, Stalker." As if to prove it, Lyssa brought Asodio back with a snap of her fingers. "Here. You're going to need it."

Caylin flicked her wrist and summoned the athame to her. With Asodio in her grasp, she prepared for another round of attacks. Her anger was cut short by the deep purple glow of the sword. She felt the dark hum ebbing from its metal and knew they were no longer alone. "Shadows."

"Yep." Lyssa prepared for their attack.

The first three came slowly, their legs planted firmly on the ground. Each one held what looked like a blackened icicle that had a slight red glow to it, the same glow that flashed in its eyes. The first one sliced at Caylin, and she blocked it easily with a white shield. The creature shrieked when Caylin sliced through it with Asodio. She turned to see the other two attacking the Shadow Walker. Caylin had to give the woman credit — she was taking two on as if it was nothing but second nature for her.

Lyssa wound her lasso up and flung it through the air. It wrapped around one of the shadows, and it screeched. She pulled it tight, and the shadow exploded right on the spot. The other one charged at her, but the Shadow Walker flicked her wrist and disappeared on the spot. She reappeared right behind him and conjured an energy bolt that she plunged into the middle of its body. The shadow wretched as if in pain before it shattered into pieces.

Lyssa looked at Caylin. "I liked it so much better when they floated. Human forms are just downright creepy."

Caylin blinked at her. This Shadow Walker was nothing to

bat an eye at. She now realized that if Lyssa had wanted to take her out earlier, she could have. The woman had just been letting her vent her aggression on her. Would Caylin had been able to control her temper nearly as well? As much as she wanted to ask her, Caylin knew it was not the time. Four more shadows were moving toward them. "These guys don't give up."

"It's part of their DNA, I think. If they have DNA." Lyssa shot a firebolt at one of the shadows, who seemed to absorb it and grow larger.

"That's not good." Caylin gripped Asodio.

"No, it's not. I haven't seen one of them do that before. It's like they're evolving. As much as I'd like to continue, I think it's time to get back to the Watch Tower. If you're ready?"

Caylin gave her the evil eye. "And if I don't go with you?"

"You're on your own," Lyssa answered with a slight smirk on her face.

Caylin did not like the haughty air this Shadow Walker had, but what she liked even less was the approaching shadows that seemed hell-bent on taking them on. It was like they had some extra power source pushing them forward. Was it true? Were they searching for her? And why? Caylin knew the only way she would find the answers to these questions was to go with Lyssa. That knowledge really chapped her ass, too.

Caylin knew that she was not going to take on this many shadows at once. In a way, this was what Remie had been trying to tell her. She hadn't wanted to listen to him because she was furious with him. "I'm damned if I do, damned if I don't."

"Perhaps."

"I'm keeping my sword." Caylin gripped it so tightly it flashed red.

"Fine with me." Lyssa offered her hand to her, and Caylin took it. "You might want to close your eyes. Teleporting is not a pleasant experience in the beginning."

"Now, you tell me." Caylin took a deep breath and closed her eyes. "Okay. I'm ready."

Just like that, she was whipping through the air again. At least this time, she wasn't getting dizzy from the changing scenery around her. She just kept her eyes shut, praying they would make it to their destination before the temptation to open her eyes took over.

Chapter 8

This time when Caylin landed, she was on her own two feet. She stepped away from Lyssa and smoothed her jacket around her. Reaching behind her, she found Asodio right where she had placed it before they left. The Shadow Walker had been true to her word. Caylin was still itching to fight but knew that Lyssa was not the one she wanted to take her anger out on. Two men sprang to mind — the one who should have been her friend and the one who thought he could manhandle her. Neither one would be expecting her retribution when it came.

She took a brief moment to check out her surroundings. They were in what looked like a swanky hotel. The colors were earthy tones with some brighter blues thrown in for accents. The tile floor was a tan marble with golden flecks that seemed to sparkle in the overhead lighting. There were a few seaside paintings around the lobby. The furniture was bright turquoise, which contrasted against the rest of the area's bland nature. Nothing seemed out of place or extraordinary. For all Caylin knew, they were just in another hotel somewhere halfway across the country.

"Where are we?"

"The Watch Tower — Sector Fifteen to be exact." It was if

Lyssa expected her questions.

"Looks like a hotel to me. What's to keep them from coming after us here?" Caylin didn't feel their energy, but sometimes they came out of nowhere, with no warning.

"Look out the window." Lyssa waved her hand to the windows that were nearby.

For once, Caylin complied. Walking over to the windows, she looked out and was not prepared for what she saw. "Are those stars?"

"Yes," Lyssa answered.

"How in the world? Where in the world? Are we even on Earth anymore?" A lot of questions surfaced at once.

"Yes, no. We are everywhere and nowhere." Lyssa walked closer to her. "I have a story to tell you if you have the patience to listen."

"Patience is not one of my strengths," Caylin warned her.

"Then maybe it's time you learned," Lyssa smirked and nodded for her to join her on the couch. "Please, join me."

Caylin reluctantly moved over to the chair across from the couch and sat down on it. While Lyssa had gestured to the couch, she did not feel all that comfortable mixing her energy with anyone else's at the moment. It was far better for her to sit here away from the rest of the world. That way, she could start the process of shutting down. She would listen to what the woman said, but that did not mean she had to care about the message she relayed. Caylin let her stone wall rise up inside her, not knowing what might happen next.

"I was young, in college, when they first found me—the shadows. Although I feel they must have been there most of my life, controlling and manipulating those around me. But that is another story entirely. When I finally liberated myself from my circumstances, I found myself in a world I never imagined, with abilities that did not make sense—"

"I never questioned my abilities. They've been here forever," Caylin interrupted her, almost defensively.

"You are fortunate then to remember what the universe had planned for you. I had to discover it one step at a time. As I delved into the world of Wicca, I learned about the magic in the world around me, and that I had powers within me that had been dormant. I foolishly used those to vanquish a few shadows. In doing so, I was put on the Revenant's radar, as well as the Watch Tower's."

"What is a revenant?"

"I'll get to that. First, I need you to understand that I know what it is like to leave the world behind and put your trust in strangers who proclaim they are trying to protect you. You're probably feeling pretty used right now." Lyssa smiled softly.

Her words hit home. She was right; Caylin was feeling like everyone in the entire world was out to manipulate her for their own personal gain, whether that benefitted the rest of the world or not. No one seemed to care about what she needed, not that she was trusting enough to let them see her weakness.

"I was whisked away to the Watch Tower and recruited to be a Guardian in Sector Four. I had an inane ability to locate the shadows and was the first person that figured out how to mask my aura so I could walk amongst the shadows. I also learned one of their weaknesses."

"Which is?"

"Love."

"Excuse me?" Caylin fought the urge to laugh. She had to be kidding. Love?

"I know, it seems like a far fetched notion that something that can make you feel so weak could also be powerful. We discovered that the shadows were being powered by the souls they devoured in the Land of the Shadows."

"Land of the Shadows?" Caylin bit her bottom lip. "What does it look like?"

"When darkness falls, the shadows rise from the ground, but the world beneath our feet isn't made of fire and brimstone, as many zealots predicted. It takes many forms, as it is many extensive dimensions."

"So, the shadows come to our world from their own portals??"

"Yes, invisible to the normal human eye. We've found them by locating powerful vortexes around the world. That's been part of what I've done since I first came here. We've located close to three hundred portals so far, each one leading to a different part of their dimension."

Caylin looked away from her. Could she believe what Lyssa was telling her? It was absolutely crazy, the more she let it register. A land beneath their feet? But then again, she was currently hovering in space somewhere, and she knew the shadows were real entities. She'd been fighting them for years now. Why did she suddenly have all the attention on her?

"My curiosity took me too far in, alerting them to my presence. The Revenant almost got his claws in me too. I still feel him inside me." Lyssa held her hand up to the back of her head. "Mine was caused by a physical injury; yours is more complicated."

"What do you mean?"

"He is drawn to the darkness inside you. You take pleasure in your own destruction."

"I may be dark and twisted, but I am not in self-destruct mode." Caylin crossed her legs and arms before glaring at Lyssa.

"Aren't you, though? You would rather destroy than trust."

"I have no reason to trust any of you."

"But you trusted Remie," Lyssa interjected.

"And look where that got me." Caylin rolled her eyes.

"You didn't have to come here."

"Like I really had a choice," Caylin deflected. She didn't want to admit that she was intrigued by any of what Lyssa had told her. So what, she was the Shadow Walker. Walking among shadows was nothing. That was where Caylin spent her life. The darkness was a salve to her wounds, wounds that were buried so far deep inside that they would never be repaired.

"You could have stayed and fought. You might even have been successful," Lyssa challenged.

"I may be a hothead, but I am not an idiot, Lyssa. I know my limits," Caylin argued.

"Good. You're going to need to know your limits. Even the Stalker needs to be able to regulate herself."

"Stalker...you keep using that word."

"Because you can track them."

"What? I don't track them. Not really. They usually just come to me." Caylin never went looking for them, not really. Did she have an idea where she could find them? Yes, because they were creatures of habit. The ghostly ruins of the city filled with dark decay was a breeding ground for their kind. The streets were filled with people in the throes of despair. When Caylin walked them, she felt the depravity around her. The drugs, the violence, the abuse. The back alleys were filled with enough darkness to fuel even the hungriest shadow.

"You just need the right tools. It's in you. I can feel it, and I've seen it."

"Let me guess, you rubbed a crystal ball?" Caylin rolled her eyes and snorted.

"You have them too. The dreams."

Caylin uncrossed her legs and put her elbows on her knees. "So what, I have dreams."

"Did he mark you?" Lyssa asked her.

"Mark me? I don't think so."

"Really?" Lyssa stood up and walked over to the chair. She waved her hands over Caylin's body.

"What are you doing?" Caylin felt the hair start to rise on her back as Lyssa probed her aura.

When she stopped over her mouth, Lyssa jerked her hands away. "There. Tell me what happened in your last dream."

"I followed the shadows to what looked like a meeting ground. There was a large black prism in the middle of a large park. They were all gathered around it."

"And then what happened? Any piece of information could be helpful."

"When Griffin blocked the dreams out, there was a voice that still called to me. He was like the shadows, but he was a solid figure. He touched me and told me he wanted me to be his. Then he kissed me." Caylin shivered. "It was like a million screams erupted around me at once. This thing, it collects souls."

"Yes, it does. It feeds on them. And we want to take him down, or at the very least, stop him from getting his reaches into our world. Our first goal is to destroy as many portals as possible. We believe you might be a key to tracking him."

"You want me to track that thing?"

"Not until you are ready. There is much training to do. But first, you should get some rest."

"Rest?" Caylin imagined sleeping would be easier for the rest of them to do. Right now, Caylin was nowhere near ready to go to sleep, especially if that thing had attached itself to her.

"You are safe here. Sector Fifteen has created a safe space

for you to sleep. If you want a dreamless sleep, we do have a few tonics for that," suggested Lyssa.

Caylin wasn't sure if she should believe her. Everything the Shadow Walker had told her was so farfetched. Not that Caylin was grounded in reality. Virtually everything around her was like something out of some crazy person's imagination. Who knows, maybe Caylin was already asleep or a figment of someone else's imagination. The product of bipolar disorder? As much as she wanted to sit here and debate this, what she wanted more than anything was some peace and quiet to collect her thoughts. "Quick question."

"Yes."

"What happens if I leave through the door right there?" Caylin nodded to the exit.

"You're welcome to try, although no one ever has," Lyssa answered her with a serious expression on her face. "Give us a chance, Caylin. We may not look like much, but we are a family here. The Guardians take care of each other."

"I don't need a family," Caylin argued.

"Well, seeing as how you don't actually know how to portal out of here yet, you are at our good graces." Lyssa seemed to be losing patience with her. "Your room is upstairs on the fourth floor—room 406. Go get some rest. Give yourself time to think."

"And if I leave?"

"The world will have lost one of its greatest champions." Lyssa rose from the couch and snapped her fingers, disappearing from sight.

Caylin snapped her fingers and grumbled when nothing happened. "Show off. Guess I'll stick around for a little while."

"Good choice," a voice interrupted from behind her.

"You!" accused Caylin. She was still very upset with him.

"They'll take good care of you here, Caylin."

"I can take care of myself, Remie." She wanted to throttle him.

"Yes, but they can help you grow more than I ever could. I'm not the best role model," he grinned.

"No, a role model you aren't. Are you staying?" Caylin asked him.

"No, unfortunately, my job is fulfilled. I need to return to the Ghost District."

"Protect them…," she whispered. She thought about all the lost souls of the women who depended on the dark angel to protect them. If she was not able to be there, someone would have to be.

"As if they were my own," he promised.

"Will I see you again?" she asked him.

"Here and there." He nodded to her and raised his hand to snap his fingers, but Caylin stopped him before he could.

"Remie, wait!" Caylin jumped up from the chair and raced over to him. She flung her arms around his shoulders and kissed him like a woman might kiss her long lost love. When she felt nothing, her shoulders were deflated.

"Don't worry, love. I always knew you were destined to be with someone else. Who knows, maybe you'll even find him here." He winked at her before kissing her on the cheek. He stepped back from her and snapped his fingers.

Caylin looked down at the floor and a few tears formed in her eyes. She had the distinct feeling that she would never see him again. He had been the only man who had taken the time to understand her without judging her. She resigned herself to see where this road would take her, if only for the moment.

Chapter 9

Caylin stood outside room 406 with a slight trepidation. Not quite sure if she should trust the people here at the Watch Tower, she was almost afraid to open the door. What if it was some kind of dungeon? Not that it would have been much different from the world of the Ghost District. Caylin had been thankful for her place with Remie. It was far better than the cold streets, but it had been lackluster and hardly what she would have wanted for herself years ago.

Years ago...there had been an innocent girl in there somewhere, hadn't there? Caylin found it hard to imagine anyone but the woman she was currently. She barely remembered that part of herself. As long as she could remember, Caylin could feel the darkness surrounding her, even amidst the rainbow and unicorn dreams that had budded deep inside her as a child. Over the years, those magical things were replaced with the things that went bump in the night.

Twisting the doorknob, Caylin took a deep breath. "Here goes nothing." When she entered the room, Caylin was actually surprised. "Okay, so not a dungeon."

That was only a small relief because Caylin knew better than to trust the charity of others. When she had first left home, one of the pimps on the street had offered her a place to stay. This was after she had spent a few months on the streets trying to survive without any comforts whatsoever. At the time, Caylin had not known that Gregory wasn't offering her a place out of the goodness of his heart. She shivered, just remembering the year of her life spent in that hellhole. Sure, it had looked like a well- established place, but the depravity of the depths below was enough to give her nightmares even now. Heaven help him if Caylin ever got her hands on that cretin.

Caylin took in the room around her. It was like a hotel suite, with separate living and sleeping quarters. The walls were blank, white with nothing to make them stand out. The furniture was all shades of brown. "Blah."

"Not to your liking?" a voice called over her shoulder. Griffin was standing in the doorway, watching her every move. Did he think she was going to steal something?

"What are you doing here?" Caylin realized at once that she had forgotten to close the door. "Don't you have any manners?"

"Forgive me. I just wanted to make sure you were settled."

"I may be here, but I haven't settled on anything." Her nose twitched slightly, a precursor to the irritation that was growing inside since the minute he stepped into the room. She had no idea why he made her feel this way.

"I see. Do you have everything you need?"

What did he care? "I've barely looked around."

"Right. Well, let me give you the tour," he offered. He gestured to the small room to the right. "This is your kitchenette, which we try to keep stocked each day. You are welcome to join us in the dining room downstairs."

"Doubtful." Caylin didn't think she would be trying to make nice with any of them any time soon. She would be civil, but outside of that, everything else was off the table.

"If there is something you need, just ask, and we shall provide."

Caylin wondered what strings would be attached to it. Everything had a price in the real world.

"No strings, Caylin," Griffin said gruffly.

Damn it. She had meant to keep her thoughts on lockdown. "Didn't your mother tell you it's not polite to read people's minds?"

"She might have if I ever met her," he answered curtly.

"Is this where you are looking for sympathy?" Caylin rolled her eyes.

"The world only offers sympathy to those who don't deserve it."

That was something they could both agree on. Money, power, status, those were all things that solicited any kind of human empathy. For those who were not born with any of those things the rest of the world saw them as expendable. The streets were filled with lost souls who had no place to rest their weary heads. No one gave them a second glance, really.

"As you can see, this is your living area, couch, table, and television if you care to watch something."

"You get cable here?" Caylin asked curiously. She couldn't remember the last time she'd watched anything on cable. The Ghost District didn't really have many cable providers willing to walk anywhere near those streets.

"If you wish." Griffin picked up the remote from the coffee table. "Just push the button here and ask for the kind of show you want. Kickboxing."

The television pulled up the top shows related to the topic he had picked. Caylin tried not to be visibly impressed. Technology had sure come a long way for those that could afford it. She nodded. "A little blood sport never hurt anyone."

"My thoughts precisely."

So, he liked violence. Or was it the action that thrilled him? Not that she could tell. His thoughts were definitely on lockdown. The way he looked at her told her that he knew she was trying to probe him. "The bedroom is right here. Like a master bedroom and bath, really."

"I see." Caylin looked around her and saw a large four poster bed with a simple white bedspread. "Not much color, is it?"

"You are welcome to change the décor. We like to keep it neutral for those who are new to Sector Fifteen."

"How many are there in Sector Fifteen?"

"Five Guardians—six if you make this your home too."

Caylin checked out the bathroom and her heart almost did flipflops. The garden tub was large enough for her to take a bubble bath in. The bathroom at her apartment barely worked, so she was lucky to do a quick wipe down. Sometimes she would steal a quick shower at one of the gas stations that was a truck stop. This place was more luxury than she'd seen most of her life. That in itself almost convinced her to stay, but she wasn't making any guarantees.

"Well, that concludes the tour, right?" Caylin turned to face him. When his eyes met hers, she felt some message was hidden deep inside them. She was too tired to try to translate it.

"Yes. Unless you would like to take a tour of Sector Fifteen."

"Maybe later. Right now, I have other things to do." Like, take a long soak in that tub.

"Just use the buzzer in the kitchen if you need any of us." Griffin pointed to the black console on the wall. He waved his hand and disappeared from sight, almost as if he had evaporated.

"Show off." Caylin shook her head.

She walked to the tub and turned the water on as hot as she could. Even if she burnt her skin, it would be worth it. Looking around at the toiletries, she found bubble bath and opened the lid to smell it. Lavender. Caylin poured in half the bottle and smiled as the bubbles started to rise. Before long, the tub was filled. She stepped into it and sunk into the bubbles.

"Ahh!" For the better part of an hour, Caylin soaked in the tub, only getting out when her fingers and toes were wrinkled past recognition. The towel was plush and warm against her skin. Looking down at the pile of clothes, she realized she didn't have any of her own things to wear. Not that she wanted to put them on after cleaning off all the excess grime.

She walked over to the closet in her bedroom and opened it. "What the...?"

The entire closet was filled with clothes, all of which were in different shades of black, white, and red. Caylin smirked. Apparently, they had been watching her for some time if they had her taste down this perfectly. Opening a drawer at the side of the dresser, she found undergarments and sleepwear. She chose a pair of black pajama shorts and a white tank top.

"Well, it would appear they are off to a good start, but it will take a lot more than personal amenities to keep me here." Caylin was too used to being independent. Even though Remie had been around, he had not been overly attentive to her. Caylin wasn't sure what they expected from her. Time would only tell.

Sliding under the covers, Caylin closed her eyes and took a deep breath. The bed was almost too soft, not what she was used to at all. Fortunately, her body was too exhausted to fight the sleep that was just beneath the surface. Before long, she was asleep.

When she entered her dream state, Caylin was in the middle of a white room. The air around her was thick, and she saw the smoke rising from under the cracks of the door across from her. She started to choke, and her eyes started to blur. If she stayed in this room, she was a sitting duck. There was only one way out. Opening the door, she held up her hands as a blast of dark flames erupted around her. Caylin looked around her fingers and saw that the flames were rebounding off a shield that had been cast around her.

"Hmm…interesting." She looked around her dream world to see if anyone was casting the shield. "Must be a reflex." Caylin looked around her and found herself walking down the path she always walked. "Not again." Why did she always come back to the same place? She saw the fork in the road and let out an irritated sigh. "Seriously?"

So, the dark path or the one covered in trash? Last time the dark path had led her to the meeting grounds. It called to her even louder than before, but Caylin had learned her lesson last time. Why repeat it? If this Revenant was looking for her, she was not going to make it easy on him, no matter what it took. Even if it meant traveling the path that was covered in things she did not want to touch.

Caylin put one foot in front of the other, holding her nose as she walked over the debris covering the ground. Her feet were soon covered in muck, as the solid ground changed into something murky. Had a sewer erupted around here? She gagged when the putrid aroma festered around her.

"Walk in darkness or be covered in shit. Why does that seem like a metaphor for my life?" Caylin shook her head and snarled. "Why would anyone want to go through all this?"

"Sometimes, you have to get through the crap to find something better," a male voice whispered.

She almost recognized it, but it was so faint it was like an echo of someone she should have known. Regardless, she shrugged it off. She had been going through crap for most of her life and had yet to find anything better than the scraps the world threw at her. "Better! Ha! There isn't anything left."

"Hope, Caylin. There is *always* hope." The voice was stronger this time, but it wasn't coming from anywhere around her.

This made her realize that what Lyssa had said was true. Her dream was being protected by someone, and while that would seem like a wonderful thing to most people, it was an intrusion for Caylin. She didn't like anyone meddling in her own business. "Hope is a lie. Leave me alone."

"As you wish." The voice may have spoken those three words, but Caylin knew that whoever it was, did not plan on leaving her anytime soon. She could still feel his energy hovering over her. The closer it came, the easier it was to recognize. Griffin. Why was he wasting his time delving into her dreams? He did not belong there. That didn't seem to stop him, though.

"You're not fooling anyone, Griffin. Show yourself." Caylin crossed her arms and waited for him to appear.

A white orb started to float in the air. It ebbed and flowed as it grew into a human shape. When he was finally materialized, he nodded his head to her. "Caylin."

"What are you doing here?"

He gave her a cheeky smile. "You asked me to come."

"I did not…." She stopped herself. "Why were you here in the first place?"

"To make sure you are safe," he answered matter-of-factly.

"Why does that matter? Don't want to lose me before you all can use me?"

"No one wants to *use* you, Caylin. We want to help you."

"Help me? Ha, that's rich. No one helps someone else

without an ulterior motive."

He stepped closer and put his hands on her forearms. He rubbed them gently and looked into her eyes. "Not everyone is out to get you, Caylin."

"Aren't you, though?" she whispered. Caylin did not understand why he made her feel so weak. She had spent half of her lifetime building up the strong exterior to fight off any emotional attachment to any living thing.

"I...." He looked as if he wanted to kiss her.

"Don't." Caylin didn't want to feel his touch. There was something about it that was dangerous, and not because she was afraid he would physically hurt her. In fact, the more she thought about it, it was as if he wanted something from her that she might not be capable of giving. Having never accessed that part of herself before, it made her extremely uncomfortable. Not like when Remie touched her. He was like an older brother, even though he had hinted that he could want something more if she were ever interested in pursuing it.

Even though she knew Griffin was attracted to her, there was something else buried deep inside. Caylin was well experienced with male desire, having seen more of it than she cared to remember for one life. He wanted more from her as if he wanted to possess pieces of her that she refused to hand out to anyone and that knowledge at that moment was far more dangerous than any other earthly desire. Jerking her arms away from him, she started to walk again.

"I have a job to do." Caylin didn't even bother to see if he followed her. The muck around her was more tolerable than the way he was making her feel.

"Then do it. Stop fighting it." Griffin's eyes were cold when she next looked at him.

"I'm already doing it!" she shouted at him. "I've been out

on the streets every night taking them out. Where the fuck have you been?"

He ignored her question. "You're only using a portion of your potential."

"Oh, I beg to differ. I've given blood, sweat, and tears. I've given everything."

"If you weren't so afraid of actually connecting to other people, you could learn to do so much more."

"I'm not afraid of attachments. I find them useless and manipulating."

"You haven't met the right people yet." His voice was soft and almost sad.

"I've met all kinds, Griffin, and I've seen the aftermath."

"If you care about our world the way you say you do, then why wouldn't you want to do *more* than you are? What are you afraid of?"

Caylin's nose wrinkled in anger, and her lips wobbled dangerously. "Fuck you! I'm not afraid of anything."

"Right. Liar." He looked at her knowingly before he waved his hands in the air and disappeared.

"Ugh! Men! Why do they think they are God's gift to women?" Caylin stomped her foot, and sewage splashed up in her face. "Damn it."

Closing her eyes, she willed herself away from this world. She went back to the white room, where she closed her eyes and fell into a deeper sleep. She did her best to shut his face out of her mind, but every time she tried, another version of him appeared.

Chapter 10

By the time Caylin awoke, she was ready to slam her first into Griffin's face. It was as if he taunted her in her sleep. She would have to learn how to block him out when she slept. During dream time was when she was at her weakest, even she knew that. Had he projected himself there, or was her mind playing cruel tricks on her?

Throwing off the covers, she shivered in the cool air around her. She had been safe and warm in her cocoon of sleep. Looking over at the clock, she saw it was nearly lunchtime. How had she slept so long? Caylin could not remember the last time she had slept so long, and even though she was annoyed at Griffin, she had still slept relatively peacefully. When her foot touched the floor, she was surprised to find it was warm and toasty. Either a magical trick or the tiles were heated. Both were possible.

Caylin walked over to the closet and picked out a new outfit for the day. Tight black jeans paired with a white tank top that she wore under a grey tunic sweater with a scoop line neck. She found a pair of black boots, and the outfit was then complete. Caylin pulled her hair up into a tight ponytail, pulling just a few blonde strands out around her face. It had been a long time since she had felt this fresh and renewed.

She saw makeup in one of the drawers near the vanity and smiled. When was the last time she had actually had makeup to put on that she wasn't using to cover bruises on her face? Those days were long gone. She wore her wounds like a warrior, especially when she was able to knock some sense into a man who brutalized one of her friends. At this moment, though, it was like an indulgence. Caylin pulled some of it out and started to do up her face to look natural, not like a prostitute looking to attract her next John. Caylin actually appreciated the smoky look that brought out the different shades of her brown eyes when she was done.

Caylin's stomach started to rumble angrily. "Fine. I'll eat."

After making herself a sandwich and a small salad, Caylin was finally ready to face the day, even if it meant seeing Griffin's face. It was a nice face, handsome even. In another time and place, he might even be the kind of man she would be interested in. She could not afford the distraction, though. She closed her eyes and called up the face that had haunted her all night. Even now, it teased her, and Caylin could not figure out why it bothered her as much as it did. Why was she letting him get to her?

"Ugh. It's going to be a long day." Especially if she had to spend her time with him. Maybe she could ask for a different sector—that could solve that problem. As strange as it was to think about, deep down, she knew she didn't want to do that. Maybe she liked the challenge too much? Was there a part of her that was attracted to him?

"Like hell." She bit her bottom lip and clenched her fists. Damn it. Maybe she was. She couldn't remember being attracted to anyone in her life. More than anything, she wanted to lash out at him every time she saw him. Was anger attraction?

Caylin closed her eyes and reminded herself she was in a

place where anyone around her could delve into her thoughts. She did not want anyone reading her mind. Concentrating hard, she pushed a barrier up to keep any intruders out. No one should have the right to steal someone's private thoughts. When she was sure no one would be able to pilfer her brain, she headed downstairs.

The elevator seemed to take forever as it made its way downstairs to the lobby. If Caylin knew how to teleport like the rest of the Guardians, she would just whisk herself down to the meeting rooms, wherever those happened to be. She strolled across the lobby, her heels making clacking sounds as she crossed over the tiles that were so much louder than the usual silence that buffered around her. Caylin was half-tempted to tip-toe just to keep the sound from ricocheting.

There were no signs marking directions like most hotels had. She remembered Griffin telling her about a dining hall. If she just walked down the hall here, maybe she would find some of the common areas. As she walked, she saw a laundry area. Too bad. She half-hoped the laundry would do itself. It was definitely not one of her favorite things to do. Of course, she would most of the time just wash them in her sink and hang them around the apartment to dry, whatever it took to save money.

As she walked further, the hall twisted and turned. There were other rooms, only a few of them marked with numbers as if they were the only ones occupied. She came to room 108 and felt a strange pull to it. For some reason, she stood outside it and contemplated knocking on it. As if the occupant heard her outside, the door opened.

"Caylin…." Griffin was visibly surprised by her appearance at his door. "Do you need something?"

"Um…sorry. I was…." Caylin was surprised to find herself

standing outside his door too. How in the world had she known? Why were her instincts deserting her today? "I was just exploring. And for some reason...."

"I see. Well, I'm just about to meet with the others. You are more than welcome to join us."

"Oh...yes. I think that would be appropriate." Appropriate? What the hell was wrong with her? Caylin suddenly felt like she had lost the edge she kept so close to the surface. She did not want to feel weak around anyone, but here she was almost a puddle at his feet, so completely at odds with herself.

"Good. They're pretty curious about you." He smiled softly at her, and she realized his features were actually even more attractive with a relaxed face. For some, that would be a good thing, but for Caylin, it was horrible. She didn't want him to look attractive, especially considering how mixed up and confused she was inside.

"That doesn't mean I'm staying," she threw in. Caylin suddenly felt like she was in defensive mode.

"Of course not." He grinned as if he knew something she didn't.

She narrowed one of her eyes on him. "Why are *you* in such a good mood?"

"It's not every day I open my door to a beautiful woman standing outside it." He winked at her, and Caylin was nearly destroyed.

"Don't get used to it," she almost snarled at him.

"What's the matter? Didn't you get any sleep?" he asked her with concern.

"You should know." She held her head up and refused to meet his eyes.

"I was here. All night. Didn't leave my room once."

"But you were there," accused Caylin.

"I was? Huh...fancy that." His eyes teased her.

Caylin shook her head and let out a sigh. "You are a piece of work."

"I'll take it," he said as he closed the door behind him.

"Take what?" Caylin asked him in confusion.

"The compliment." He gestured for her to follow him. "This way, my dear."

My dear? Who did he think she was, Scarlett O'Hara? She wasn't anyone's dear. She was about to tell him that when she saw him grinning at her. "Why do you always do that?"

"What?" he asked her innocently.

"Taunt me?"

"Because I like the way your eyes flash when you're angry. And because you seem more comfortable with that emotion."

Those two things aggravated her, yet made sense at the same time. Anger was the only emotion that had been her truest friend over the years. Anger helped her push herself to the limits, to evolve into someone who could take care of herself and keep others from taking advantage of her. She refused to comment on that, though. Instead, she followed him because she was afraid his hand would touch hers if they walked too close together. Sparks would likely erupt if he tried to touch her at all.

He stopped outside a room with a red door. "This is the Library. On the other side of the hall, down there is the dining hall, which is connected to the kitchen."

"Wow, all this place is missing is a pool," remarked Caylin.

"Oh, we have that too. If you head back to the lobby and take the hallway on the left instead, it will lead you down to the pool and recreational center."

"So, you literally live in a hotel?"

"Yes. Not every sector is like this one. Some of them are in the slums. Some are houses. One is built into an underground cavern."

"Really?" Caylin could not imagine living under the earth. She would miss the feel of the air on her face. Although, if they were in the middle of another dimension, surrounded by space and time, she would have to return to the real world to get real air.

"Yep. I've been there before. Much more spacious than you'd think." He winked at her.

Caylin fought the urge to roll her eyes. Didn't he know not to try to flirt with her?

Griffin opened the door for them. "After you."

Caylin stepped through the threshold and was surprised that the room did, in fact, look like a library, a place she had snuck into over the years to continue her own education during the waking hours. Sometimes she'd stolen a book here and there, which she always returned in its proper condition. "That's a lot of books."

"It's adequate. We have an even bigger library that all Guardians have access to. Its data is extensive. All information from the beginning of time is stored within its pages."

"I see."

Caylin continued to look over the first room, as the library was split into sections. The walls around her were lined with books from floor to ceiling. A long mahogany table stretched the length of the wall and had eight matching chairs with delicately carved backs. The light overhead seemed to come from the skylight, which she found odd considering the building was probably set in the middle of nothingness. There were also two overstuffed armchairs with footstools in two corners of the room.

As they continued to walk to the next area, Caylin was

impressed. "Is that a globe?"

"It is." Griffin nodded for her to follow him. "Let me show you."

They walked closer to the table, and she was surprised to see it was actually turning. It gave the illusion of the earth spinning on its axis. She looked under the table and saw nothing protruding as if the table swallowed the globe on its rotation. Caylin knew it was the magic of the Watch Tower, the same magic that ran through her veins.

The minute she walked into this room, Caylin had known she belonged here. It was an odd sensation as if this place had been calling to her all along even though she had not known of its existence. "Can I touch it?"

"Sure."

Caylin touched the globe, and it immediately zoomed in on the area, as if it had global positioning. The more she touched that area, the further in the picture zoomed. When she found the Ghost District, Caylin saw Remie sitting outside on their stoop. She was relieved to see he was okay.

"Do you miss him?"

Caylin didn't know what Griffin was really asking her. Those four words seemed to ask so much more than whether she missed someone. "Remie has been my friend for years. He saved me when I was unable to help myself."

"He was doing a job," Griffin said curtly.

"He did it well, then." Caylin was slightly miffed that he wanted to paint Remie in any kind of light. Remie had never pretended to be anyone's savior. Caylin knew he wasn't perfect, but she liked to think that whether or not he had been sent to find her, he would have helped her regardless. No one told him to protect any of the other women on the streets. That she was sure of. So did it matter to her that some magical organization fostered his way into her life? No. It did not. Although, it was almost entertaining the way Griffin was trying to buffer Remie's light. He was jealous that she was sure of.

Caylin released the image on the globe just as the rest of the Guardians entered the room. They walked over to the table and took their spots around the globe. Caylin wasn't sure what the next step was. It seemed to be some kind of formal meeting, or was it merely a part of their daily ritual? They barely even made eye contact with her as they sat.

Caylin watched them close their eyes and enter what looked like a trancelike state. Their arms were open, palms facing upward on the table. That was when she saw the tattoos on their forearms. Each one of them had a black Roman numeral fifteen. As they breathed in and out, the tattoos seemed to live and breathe. The ink shifted and sparkled as it moved in its lines. When they opened their arms, the ink settled back in place.

"Good morning, Stalker," one of the females greeted her.

"I have a name," Caylin said tersely.

"Of course—Caylin, right? I'm Lia." Lia was probably in her mid-twenties. She had purple hair that she had pulled back into a low ponytail on the back of her head. Her eyes were a sparkling blue that gave the hint of how easily she could get up to mischief.

"I'm Campbell." Campbell appeared to be the oldest. His dark bald head seemed to shimmer under the lights above. He shifted the silver metal-framed glasses on his nose. "I'm the leader of Sector Fifteen."

Caylin nodded to him. "Tough job?"

"Sometimes." He grinned slightly and nodded to Griffin. "This one keeps me on my toes more than I'd care to admit."

"I do not." Griffin seemed to clench his teeth under the

negative image his leader was painting."

Caylin was enjoying his discomfort. "I can see that."

"I'm Devon. I'm the youngest one here." Devon was dark skinned with amber eyes. Her long hair was pulled back in long dreadlocks of blonde, black, and brown strands. "Don't let my age fool you, though."

"Never." Caylin smiled at her and gave her an appreciative nod. She must be in her early twenties, and probably just as misunderstood as Caylin had been most of her life. Caylin sensed a kindred spirit in Devon.

"Bryce." He gave her a nod when she turned her eyes on him. Bryce looked like a man of few words. His black hair was trimmed close to his head around his ears, but the top was longer and combed over, making him look like a well-manicured rock star. His green eyes were the kind any woman could get lost in.

"And you know me already." Griffin was clearly not happy with her perusal of Bryce.

Was he jealous? The thought thrilled her slightly. That was something that could give her the upper hand when he was annoying the hell out of her.

"So, how do I sign up?"

"You've already decided?" Griffin seemed surprised.

"What do I have to lose?" Everything she wanted to add, but Caylin could not be afraid of moving forward just because her feelings were affected by Griffin's proximity. She could learn to push past that.

"Hold your hand out," Campbell directed her. He snapped his fingers, and a wand appeared.

As Caylin held her arm out, he swished the wand over it and a dark ink filtered through the air. When it touched her arm, she was surprised that it did not hurt. Instead, as it shifted into her skin, it tickled her. Wrinkling her nose as the ink started to form the tattoo, she glanced at Griffin, who was watching her intently. When the ink finally slid into place, she looked around the room. "All right. So what's next?"

"Training, and lots of it," suggested Lia. "Especially considering what we're going up against."

"I can hold my own," Caylin tried to defend herself.

"No one is saying you are not already capable of doing so, but the shadows you have been dealing with, they are changing," Devon interrupted.

"Your combat skills are not what we're worried about." Campbell held up his hand as if to wave her concerns away.

"Then what is it?"

"Detection," Lia answered. "You have no way of masking your energy."

"I do fine." Caylin felt her anger rising to the surface.

"We felt you from down the hallway," Bryce interjected.

"But you knew I was here," Caylin countered.

"And so do the shadows," Griffin added. "They know you are with us. They have your scent down to a T."

Caylin pulled her shirt out and sniffed. "Do I smell that bad?"

Lia chuckled slightly. "No, but your energy has a certain mark to it. We can help you lower your resonance a little."

"Bring it."

"We'll get started in a few hours. For now, you should explore the library." Griffin nodded to the room they had just left.

"Why do I feel like I'm being dismissed just so you can talk about me?" Caylin crossed her arms over her chest.

"Because you are." Griffin's top lip turned up at the corners, twitching slightly before returning back to his stone cold face.

"What dunderhead here means is that we have to come up

with a plan of how to help you." Lia looked like she was ready to throw something at him.

The familiarity between them made Caylin wonder if there was something between them. Not that it was Caylin's business. It smarted regardless, not that she would admit it to anyone else. "Fine. Any suggestions for reading material?"

"There are a couple of page turners on how the Watch Tower came to be," suggested Campbell.

Caylin tried not to snort. Page turner? A history book? Not likely. Give her an action or adventure any day, but non-fiction simply wasn't in her wheelhouse. She pushed away from the table and turned her back on the others. How she wished she could be a fly on the wall when they talked about her. Had she even made a good impression? It had been almost a lifetime since she had actually cared what others thought of her. Being independent, she couldn't lean on any crutches like that. The only opinion she had been able to count on was her own, and occasionally Remie's. She resigned herself to a boring afternoon, reading something that her brain was not likely to retain under these circumstances.

Chapter 11

When Campbell came to get her a few hours later, Caylin was in the middle of a book that had detailed information about the ways the Watch Tower had been watching over the world for the last few centuries. The history was much more expansive than she'd first thought. She was so lost in the pages, she didn't know he was there. When he cleared his throat, her head popped up.

"Oh, sorry, Campbell. Did you all decide?"

"What?"

"What you're going to do with me." Caylin closed the book and set it on the table before her.

"First, we're going to try to remove some of your negative energy." He pursed his lips thoughtfully. "Perhaps I should have worded that differently."

Caylin enjoyed his discomfort. "I think I know what you meant. Lyssa mentioned that I had been marked by the Revenant."

"Yes, and while that might allow us to track him, too much of that leftover energy could be dangerous for you and…."

"Anyone else around me?" she suggested. Caylin understood they were worried about her bringing the wrong kind of energy here. For far too long, her whole world had been covered in it. Maybe it was time to release some of it and learn to approach life differently. As long as she could still take care of herself like the badass she had become over the past few years, would it really be so bad?

"Precisely. Being part of a family means you have to watch out for each other."

Family? Caylin wasn't looking for a family. In her experience, family was the one thing that had left her shattered and disillusioned in this world. Blood was just that, blood. It did not really tie anything together. It just ebbed and flowed like a crimson poison filled with deception and lies. She would not think of them as her family. If she did, Caylin would not even bother trying to protect them. Family had never protected her.

Besides, there was no way that Griffin looked at her like family. His eyes clearly projected a desire that wouldn't be legal in any state. She recognized the signs. Caylin had been trained by men who were never interested in anything but their own personal pleasures. Caylin blinked and tried to clear those images from her mind. Sometimes she wished she could find someone to erase those memories completely. They only made her feel bitter and diseased.

"Well, if you'll come with me, I think I can help you with that." Campbell gestured for her to follow him.

Half-tempted to stay put, Caylin reminded herself that these people were not here to hurt her. Annoy her, probably — anger her...more than likely. Most people did both of those things. She did not feel like they would do anything to hurt her, but even so, her guard was up.

"Lead the way, oh fearless leader." Her voice was filled with sarcasm, but he didn't seem to notice. Caylin followed after him and wondered where he was taking her. Griffin had only mentioned the dining hall and library, really. What else was there? Considering he was leading her down the hall away from the lobby, she figured it also wasn't the swimming pools, since they were on the opposite side of the hotel. If she could call it a hotel.

Thankfully, he did not lead her far. They stopped outside a large mahogany door that had several different gemstones embedded in the wood. Caylin could not resist touching it. When she put her hand on one of the stones, she felt a bright energy jolt against her fingertips. "I don't think it likes me."

"It can sense the mark of darkness. Not to worry, it can also sense the light."

Caylin felt like laughing. Light? She had not been filled with that in years. Caylin barely even ventured out in daylight. The dark was the only season she knew. Always cold, bitter, and dangerous, Caylin could count on its consistency. "I'll take your word for it."

"After you...." Campbell opened the door and swooped his arms as if to usher her inside.

Even though she considered herself strong, fierce, and determined, Caylin second-guessed every part of herself at this moment in time. To fear entering a room, that should be laughable, but Caylin could not find any humor in this situation. It was like facing your maker at the end of a really long life filled with every sin imaginable, and Caylin had definitely sinned.

"Trust me, Caylin." Campbell seemed to sense her reluctance.

Caylin looked at him and saw the compassion on his face, and while she was tempted to push against it, to deflect any kind of sentimentality, she latched onto it and let it fuel her courage. She took one step over the threshold and felt a blast of air push past her. A blinding light illuminated around her, and she held her hands up to protect her eyes. "Are you sure about this?"

"Keep walking," Campbell instructed.

She did as he instructed. Looking down at the floor seemed much easier. One step after another, until she had made it to the middle of the room, where she saw a large rectangular pedestal.

"You're not going to sacrifice me, are you?"

Campbell chuckled. "Good heavens, no. We're just going to siphon off some of the darkness from your energy field, but not all of it. The altar is a good place to rejuvenate and remove energy that does not belong."

"Why not all of it?" Caylin asked him.

"Because the darkness is part of you, Stalker."

"If it's part of me, then why are you removing any of it?" Caylin crossed her arms and waited to see if he could actually come up with a good explanation.

"We are not removing your darkness, only his taint upon it." Campbell gestured to the altar. "If you would."

Caylin moved hesitantly to the altar and sat down on it. Why would they want her darkness? Their light far outweighed any of the darkness in the world. It was one of the reasons she was drawn to them and repelled at the same time. Her taint made her feel unworthy to be around them, yet here she was agreeing to fight alongside them, even though deep down inside, she did not feel worthy of being in the same room with them.

"Lay back, please," Campbell instructed her.

"What are you going to do?" Caylin had every right to know what he was going to do to remove the Revenant's touch. Was he going to draw blood? Bleed her like ancient rites of days gone past?

"I'm going to use these to draw the energy out. The altar will absorb it and help restore you to a regular capacity." Campbell held large prisms fashioned of smoky quartz and hematite.

"Okay." That seemed safe enough. Caylin lay back and waited to see what he was going to do with the stones. When he placed them at different places around her, she breathed a sigh of relief. Her relief was short-lived, as the stones started to hum, and the altar shook around her.

"Relax, Caylin. Let them do their work."

Easy for him to say. Caylin lay there, barely breathing as tiny threads of light started to creak like decrepit vines that twisted and turned angrily around her. A net of energy was woven around her so tightly she thought it would cut lines into her skin. She struggled against them, ready to rip them off, to leap from the table and fight her way through the misty fog that was starting to float around her. Panic ripped through her as sharp thorns formed from the net, biting against her flesh.

"Get these fucking things off me!" shouted Caylin as trickles of blood oozed down her arms.

"Relax, Caylin."

"Fuck you!" Caylin screamed at him. A lash of pain struck her against her back as the altar sent a burst of something into her flesh.

Relax, Caylin. Don't fight it, she heard a voice whisper into her mind. Don't fight it? She was supposed to let it rip her to pieces right there on the altar and not have anything to say about it?

Breathe, Caylin.

She was breathing. Not only that, she knew that voice. *I am breathing, Griffin.*

Close your eyes.

Fuck you. She did not want him telling her what to do. Who the hell did he think he was? She was so angry at him; she did not notice the net pulling tighter against her. Damn it, that hurt.

Caylin, focus. Close your eyes.

The pain searing against her was excruciating. How was she going to get through this? Why should she? What had these people actually done for her? She barely knew them, and they were torturing her one piece at a time. Caylin felt her fight or flight mechanism breakthrough, and she violently shook on the altar as the vines squeezed her to the point of oblivion. Her breathing was shallow and painful as the attack continued. She was desperate to break free from its hold, but she was completely helpless. *I can't do this.*

You can do this, Caylin. I'm here.

Caylin closed her eyes and wished he was there with her. Conjuring his face in her mind, she took a deep breath and tried to focus on the soft scruff that was creeping up on his face. His brown eyes had a softness about them. Griffin flickered in front of her, and she was desperate to hold on to the image, but it faded, and the pain ripped through her again. This time, she almost lost consciousness completely.

Caylin wanted to beg for help, but she wasn't sure it would come. Had she made the wrong allegiance? Would they break her before she even had a chance to rid the world of the Revenant? Another blast of energy shot into her body, and she felt something pooling out of her wounds. Her eyes opened, and she did not see the blood she expected to see. Instead, a black oozing substance was filtering from her skin. It floated in the air and tried to escape. The rock below her shot out bright white light that decimated the oily substance on sight.

Closing her eyes, Caylin now understood that she was not what was under attack, but that dark oozing energy that was hidden deep beneath her. Even though the thorns continued to attack her, she held her body still and closed her eyes.

Focus, Caylin.

Stay with me, Griffin. She felt weak and desperate for his presence, even though she had no idea why.

I'm here, Caylin.

And she felt like he was. Taking a deep breath, she summoned his image to her mind again, but this time it was altered. She saw a Griffin from another time, one that did not quite make sense. His hair was much longer, his face older. There was a scar barely hidden by his beard. He brought her hand to his mouth and kissed it.

Caylin zoomed out on the image and saw that she, too, was different. Her hair was done up in small braids that were gathered around her head like a crown. She was wearing a long white dress with an embroidered overskirt with crest-like markings. Caylin heard him whisper wife and saw the way she blushed at his whisperings. A crowd of people surrounded them, all laughing and reveling as they celebrated the wedding of their lord and new lady. A joyful time filled with love and happiness. She felt it emanate inside of her, as it guided her to a new consciousness.

The pain was gone as she focused on the happiness of a memory that did not quite feel like her own. But Caylin knew better. She had seen past lives before, several of them, in fact. She had never seen this particular one, but as she lay there, she realized for the first time that this was not the first life she had seen Griffin. There had always been another person in her past life, a man, but her connection to him had been unclear until this moment. This knowledge didn't change who she was at this moment, but it did explain why Griffin got under her nerves as much as he did.

As the last attack on her erupted, Caylin started to lose consciousness as a loud scream erupted from her mouth.

Collapsing against the altar, she heard Griffin's voice. This time it wasn't in her head.

"What the fuck did you do, Campbell?"

"We all agreed on this course," the man answered him. "It was for the best."

"Like hell. There were other ways. You weren't supposed to go this far. If she doesn't wake up, I will be reporting you to the council."

"She will wake up. You're awfully attached to her, Griffin," Campbell pointed out.

"I can't explain it, and I won't. Not to you. If you hurt her—"

"Relax, Griffin. See the lights swarming around her? She's at rest. The altar has done its job."

"If you—"

"You need to distance yourself, Griffin. She is a means to an end. Remember that."

"What the fuck are you talking about?" His voice was almost a growl.

"We are all expendable." Campbell started to gather the stones from the altar.

"Like hell, we are." A loud crash erupted as he slammed the door behind him.

Chapter 12

When Caylin opened her eyes, she was surprised to find that she was back in her room. Her head was pounding furiously, and her mouth was incredibly dry. If she didn't know better, she would have thought she had a hangover. Caylin stretched out and winced as her sore muscles protested. Closing her eyes, she tried to remember what had happened earlier. The last thing she remembered was lying on the altar with the vicious vines sucking the life from her body. The more she moved, the worse the pain was. "Ow."

"Careful," Griffin cautioned her. "You've been through a lot."

"No thanks to any of you."

"I could kill him." Griffin gritted his teeth, and a wave of slow anger filled his face.

"It was necessary." Caylin did not know why she was taking up for Campbell. What that man had put her through had been more painful than anything she had endured in her lifetime, and this coming from a woman with a fairly high pain tolerance. As she took stock of herself, Caylin realized there was something missing. She couldn't quite put her hand on it, but it was as if she felt lighter, which was hard to come to terms with considering the pain her body was still in.

"He let it go far too long." Griffin moved his chair closer and reached for her hand.

Caylin pulled her hand back instinctively. Her mind was still coming to terms with the fact that the universe seemed to be constantly throwing them together, something that he probably had no memory of.

"I'm trying to help." Griffin reached for her hand again, and this time she let him take it.

A slow, calming light rose from his fingers and seeped into her skin. The energy was like a gentle sensation that overlapped the pain ebbing through her veins. The pulsing energy soon enveloped all of her, creating a peaceful cocoon of light that made her feel almost ready to fall back asleep. Caylin yawned and closed her eyes.

Probably a big mistake, for the minute she did, the life she was trying to ignore popped right back into her head. With him so close to her, the images were almost crystal clear. Tender and loving, he had been her one true love, as she had been his. Their life had been filled with happiness, but even from here, Caylin could sense there was an underlying darkness that had toppled them.

Griffin removed his hands with a loud intake of breath. "I think that's enough."

Caylin's eyes flew open. Had he seen that too? Her eyes probed his, but there was a wall now in between them. Not that it mattered. They were two different people in this time and space. There was no destiny throwing them together, only circumstance. Besides, all the times before had been a disaster in the end. At least, that was the feeling she was left with. She pushed the pictures to the back of her mind and decided to keep them on lockdown.

She stretched her limbs, and when she discovered the pain was gone, her eyes flew to his. "Thank you."

"You're welcome. I'm not promising you won't feel pain later, but this should hold for a little while."

"It will do, Griffin."

"I've reported Campbell to the council." Griffin stood up and walked away from the bed.

"He thought he was doing the right thing," Caylin rationalized. She knew it was the truth. The pain wasn't caused by what Campbell had done to her in that moment. It was the lifetime of pain being ripped from her body as the magic of the altar had stripped away some of the darkness. Caylin was the first to admit that the darkness inside her had long been festering. It was like a putrid wound that never healed. Perhaps that was what made her the chosen one, the Stalker who would be able to walk in his world to bring him down once and for all.

"Even so, there are limits. Harm none," he gritted out.

"Griffin, I'm fine." She sat up on the edge of the bed, and a small wave of dizziness took over her. Closing her eyes, she tried to keep the room from spinning. "How long have I been out?"

"Three days." Griffin turned to face her, catching her before she fell to the floor.

"Thanks." Caylin did not like feeling so weak. She wanted to push him away, to tell him she was fine and didn't need his help. Caylin didn't *need* anyone or anything. That's the lie she had always told herself, but here she was weak as a newborn kitten and totally reliant on the man standing before her.

"Back to bed," he ordered with a soft gruffness that was reflected in his eyes and his voice.

"Oh?" she teased him, but only ended conjuring a fantasy in her own head — him on top of her, his flesh against hers. His eyes rock hard as desire shook him. Caylin blinked and looked away from him.

"Are you hungry?"

Hungry? She was suddenly starving, but food was not on the menu. This feeling was foreign to her. Her cheeks were flushed, and her skin felt heightened when he ran his hand over her face.

"You all right, Caylin?" His words were worried, but his eyes informed her that he clearly understood her.

"Yes…I think so." She settled back against the pillows and tried to latch on to anything that would deflect. "I could eat."

"Good. I'll have Lia bring you some food." He moved to step away, and she latched onto his arm.

"You're leaving me?" She didn't know what had brought on her need for his presence, but it was there nevertheless.

"I'll check on you later," he promised her.

Caylin had the distinct impression he was running from her. Part of her understood that, for she wanted to run from him too. She didn't like the emotions swirling through her right now. Closing her eyes, she tried to push them as far away from her mind as possible No matter how quiet she got her mind, the noise of his presence seemed to drown out every inch of her existence.

"Someone call for food?"

Her eyes flew open, and Caylin saw Lia's smiling face. "Yes, thank you."

"Don't get up. I'll set you up right here." Lia waved her hand, and a wooden bed tray appeared on the bed. Her purple hair was down today, showing that it was just past her shoulders.

Caylin slid the tray closer to her so Lia could put the food on it. "Thank you."

"You're welcome. How are you feeling today?"

"Sore," Caylin answered as she took her first bite of food.

"Campbell should have been careful. The Altar of Azure is unpredictable."

"Did it work?" she asked Lia.

"We believe so. We think it may have erased enough of the Revenant's hold over you."

"That being is pure evil." Caylin shivered despite herself. "When do we take him down?"

"After you've had more training," Lia answered.

"Bring it." Caylin was ready to get started.

"As soon as you are recovered. It might take a little longer." Lia nodded to the bruises and cuts on her arms.

"Oh, that's nothing I can't handle." Caylin waved off her concerns. She'd had worse wounds to recover from before. This was just a paper cut compared to them.

"Fine. When you can prove yourself capable of walking, then I'll take you downstairs for training," agreed Lia.

Caylin slid the tray aside and sat up on the edge of her bed. She pushed up to her feet and walked across the room, ignoring the small bursts of pain that rippled through her body. She didn't have any time to waste. The Revenant would not put his plans on pause just because she was having a rough day. More than likely, he was already setting other plans into motion. "I'm walking."

Lia shook her head and fought the smile that was trying to inch across her face. There was respect in her eyes. "Very well, Stalker."

"Caylin," she corrected her.

"Caylin." Lia walked over to her and grabbed her arm. "Walking or not, I think we'll teleport downstairs."

Caylin was silently thankful for that. Her energy would

not last forever, but Caylin would work through it. Closing her eyes, she felt the whoosh of air around her as they ported. When she opened them, she found they were inside a white room, one that she recognized. This was the same place Griffin had taken her to in her dreams. She was surprised to find the others there waiting for her, except Campbell.

"How did you know?"

"Lia sent us a message," Devon grinned at her.

"Where's —?"

"Campbell decided it would be best to step back from your training," Bryce answered.

Caylin shook her head. She knew that some of them were upset with Campbell. "He didn't do anything wrong."

"That remains to be seen," muttered Griffin.

Caylin let out a disgusted sigh. "I'm fine. Look."

She turned around with a flourish and turned back. "I'm in one piece."

"So it seems," Bryce grinned at her. "What a piece, too."

"Shut it, Bryce." Griffin glared at him.

Caylin fought the urge to giggle like a schoolgirl. The two of them had some beef between them. Or was that just raw jealousy? Either way, they both kind of looked ridiculous right now. "So, what's it to be?"

"Learning to hide your energy," Lia answered first. "Just draw it inside as much as you can. Close your eyes and focus on shielding yourself."

Caylin wasn't entirely sure that could work. "Are you sure?"

"We'll prove it. Close your eyes. We'll do a Marco Polo of sorts. Use your energy to find us."

Caylin closed her eyes as directed and started to move around the room, trying to find the others. At first, she felt them, but before long, she started to wonder if they had left the room completely. She moved forward one more step, and when she opened her eyes, she found Griffin standing right before her, his body just a few inches away from hers. She would have sworn she would have known his energy anywhere, but even now, she didn't feel it, and he was standing right in front of her with an annoying smirk etched across his face. "Well, clearly, it works. So what do I do?"

"Surround yourself with a shield that masks itself with the air around it," Lia answered matter-of-factly, which annoyed the hell out of Caylin, who had never cast a shield like that in her life.

"We're being summoned," Bryce interrupted. He rubbed his arm as to indicate a communication.

"I think I can take it from here," Griffin suggested, and some kind of telepathic message seemed to float between them.

"If you say so." Bryce winked at Caylin before waving his hands to disappear.

When the others left, Caylin was left in the white room with the one person she really wanted to run from at this moment. Being alone with him was dangerous. She wasn't in physical danger, she knew that. But the mixed-up emotions inside her were far more deadly. She refused to look at him.

"Caylin." His voice reached across the divide inside her mind, and she could not deny it.

"Yes?" she whispered.

"You have to focus." He grinned at her.

"Easy for you to say, you already know how to do this," she pointed out.

"We all started somewhere. Just relax. Sit." He sat on the floor and waited for her to join him, which she did tentatively. He reached for her hands.

"What are you doing?" she asked him. Every inch of her wanted to retract her hands from his.

"Showing how to mask your energy."

Like hell, she wanted to rebut. If anything, her energy was zipping all around inside of her. His nearness was dangerous right now, something she could not fight no matter how hard she wanted to. Caylin tried to rein in her emotions. As his energy seeped into her hands, she started to feel the calm, gentle flow run through her. Her energy, his energy, they melded together until there was only one resonance around them. She closed her eyes and let herself relax.

Caylin wasn't sure how long they spent there in that moment. It felt like hours, but it could very well have only been a few minutes for all she knew. When she opened her eyes, she saw him looking at her with a soft look on his face. "What?"

"I think that's enough for now."

"Where are you going?" Why was he suddenly racing out of here? "Did I do something wrong?"

"Wrong?" He smirked. "No. Not at all, I just need some air."

"Am I that hideous to you?" she whispered. Caylin didn't know where the words had come from, but they had been lurking beneath the surface for quite some time.

"What?" He looked at her like she'd lost her mind. "You are not hideous."

"Then why are you racing out of here?" she asked him. Caylin prepared herself for all sorts of answers, all but the one she received.

"Because if I stay, I'm going to kiss you." His eyes held a dangerous gleam to them as if he were trying to make part of himself disappear.

"Oh...." Caylin almost felt triumphant. So, he did feel it

too. She moved closer to him and put her hand on his chest. Her mouth was just a few inches from his at this point, and she felt him shiver beneath her touch. "Would that be so horrible?"

Before she knew it, his mouth covered hers. This time, Caylin was ready for it, matching each movement with her own. Confusion rippled her mind as a feeling she didn't quite recognize moved through her. She pushed away from him and tried to catch her breath. Closing her eyes, she wished she were anywhere but here at this moment. The air shifted around her, and she felt the winds shifting around her, as she was pulled through time and space, unsure of what exactly was happening. She heard Griffin call for her, but he was unreachable. She realized she had teleported for the first time on her own, but as she flew through the air, she had no idea where she was heading to.

When her feet touched the ground, she found herself standing on the steps just outside her old apartment in the Ghost District. Remie was sitting on the stoop, watching the dark streets below.

"Remie?" she asked him.

"Caylin...what are you doing here?"

"I'm not quite sure," she whispered. Her hand touched her mouth, and she closed her eyes.

"Running from something?" he teased her.

"No...." Her eyes flew to his, and she realized Remie knew her far too well. "Maybe...but I didn't mean to."

"Why did you run?"

"I...." Caylin looked down at the ground.

"I've never known you to be afraid of anything, Caylin."

"I'm not afraid." She felt like spitting, she was so angry. "I'm not a coward."

"Why are you here?"

"I...." Caylin felt tears fall down her face and touched them in confusion. Was she crying?

"Did he hurt you?" Remie clenched his fists. "I'll kill him."

"What? No! He didn't—"

"Why are you crying?" Remie asked her.

"I wish I knew."

"Caylin?" The voice behind her was tentative. Griffin had followed her.

"Oh, look at the time. I have places to be. Caylin, you're always welcome here." Remie looked over at Griffin, and a hidden message passed between them.

When Remie disappeared, Caylin remained frozen in her spot. She couldn't look at him. It was as if she had turned to stone, unable to speak, to think. Nothing seemed to work right. He stepped closer to her and put his hand on her cheek.

Caylin flinched. "What are you doing?"

"Trying to read you, but you won't let me in." Griffin cursed softly. "Damn it, Caylin. You are the most confusing woman I have ever met."

Her lips turned up slightly. She knew exactly what he meant. Whatever was between them was confusing. It was unknown too, which was the only thing Caylin had ever feared in her lifetime. If she could not control her circumstances, she felt weak and dependent. She did not want to depend on any living soul ever again.

"Don't run from me, Caylin." He stepped closer, and her heart almost stopped in her chest.

"What are you doing, Griffin?"

"One kiss, nothing more, Caylin," he whispered just before his lips touched hers.

Caylin could have pushed him away. Part of her wanted to, but the rest of her was curious. One kiss, two, three, and now this one? Would the next one be the one that could break her addiction for him? Kissing was not something she did, not even during her time on the streets. It was too personal. With his mouth moving over hers, it was clear she had been right to close that part of herself off. Caylin was completely vulnerable to his touch. She trembled against him and put her hand up to push him away.

"Stop." A tear fell down her face, and she wiped it away. "Damn it."

"It's okay, Caylin."

"It's not okay. Nothing about this is okay. I don't want to…."

"You don't want to what?"

"Feel." She looked away from him and tried to steady her breath.

He gathered her into his arms and stroked the back of her head. "You're like a wild animal, Caylin. You're afraid of being tamed."

"I'm not afraid of anything."

"*Liar.*"

"I hate you."

"Liar."

There it was again. And he was right too. She was lying. She didn't hate him, but Caylin wasn't entirely sure what it was she felt about him. Caylin lay her head on his shoulder and wasn't surprised to find them teleporting away from the Ghost District. When they stopped, she found herself standing outside her door at Sector Fifteen.

"I'm a patient man, Caylin." He kissed her on her forehead and stepped away.

"You might wait forever," Caylin challenged him.

He gave her a grin. "I doubt it."

She glared at him and punched him on the shoulder. "Keep dreaming."

"Oh, I will. So long as *you* do too." He winked at her and waved his hand, whisking himself from her presence.

Damn it! He was right. She probably would dream about it. Damn him. Caylin opened her door and slid inside. He was downright irritating. There were so many sides to him that Caylin could not figure him out, and her past lives were not making this any easier. They did not belong in this time and space. Did she really need that reminder? Every life should be another chance to alter the course of her life.

"Fuck destiny," she whispered. Caylin swore she heard a chuckle in her head and realized that she had not put her thoughts on lockdown, something she quickly did.

Caylin spent the rest of the day blocking out the thoughts in her head as she worked on her shield. She'd show them all! It was time to focus so she could get this show on the road. The sooner she was done destroying this Revenant, the sooner she could move on with her life, a life that would be much safer for her if Griffin weren't in it.

Chapter 13

Caylin was eating breakfast in her kitchenette when something strange happened. Her arm burned, and she saw that her tattoo was puffed up slightly. "What the hell?"

Something must be up. Caylin found Asodio in its sheath and quickly attached it to her back. She would need to be ready for anything. Closing her eyes, she tried to remember how she had teleported by herself the day before. Her mind reached out for the place she wanted to move to, and she opened her eyes again. "Here goes nothing."

Caylin waved her arms over her head and found herself zooming through the air. Rather than close her eyes like she normally did, Caylin kept them wide open. She saw a swirl of energy and light as she moved through space. When her feet touched down on the floor, she was pleasantly surprised to find herself in the middle of the library.

"I could get used to that." She walked to the room with the globe and found all the others surrounding the table.

"Caylin," Campbell greeted her. His eyes were apologetic. "I'm sorry that—"

"I'm fine, Campbell. Good as new." She nodded to him and sat down at one of the empty chairs. It was a half-lie. Caylin wasn't good as new. Her head had started pounding furiously last night when she slept. She had the distinct impression the Revenant was trying to break into her dreams. The fact that he was unable to had pissed him off beyond belief. Her body had fought him off all night, shielding her from any of his advances. That was why she had woken up exhausted this morning — that, and the handsome man whose eyes were probing hers.

"Good." Campbell looked slightly relieved.

"So, why is this being weird?" Caylin pointed to her tattoo.

"It's our way of coming together," Lia answered her.

Caylin wondered if she would always know where to head to. Was that something else she would have to learn? "So, why are we here then?"

"We've been summoned to help some of the other Guardians in the Land of the Shadows," Campbell explained. "We were just getting the details."

Caylin nodded. She was ready to head into the fray. She was tired of dreaming about it. Now, she would get her chance to see it through waking eyes.

As if sensing her thoughts, Griffin shook his head. "She's not ready."

Caylin wanted to throw something at him. Who was he to decide that for her? Caylin could hold her own. She was fairly certain she could hold her own in the Land of the Shadows too.

"You're right," agreed Devon. She crossed her arms in front of her. "Who is going to stay behind and train her?"

"I'll do it," offered Bryce. His green eyes indicated he would be willing to teach her many things.

"No." Griffin looked ready to launch himself at Bryce. "I'll stay."

"You've already had your chance to train her. Maybe she needs a different touch?" Clearly, Bryce was enjoying himself.

Caylin was caught between watching the two of them fight over her and the need to defend Griffin, which in itself was a strange feeling. She sat there and feigned boredom as the two stared each other down. What, was she a possession to fight over?

"Do they always do this?" she whispered to Lia, who was closest to them.

"Not typically," Lia smiled ruefully.

"Why don't you let her choose?" Bryce suggested.

"And it's between the two of you?"

"Those two are the only expendable ones on this mission," teased Devon.

"Hey!" Bryce pouted. "I wasn't so expendable last night."

"Shut it, Bryce." Lia narrowed her eyes on him.

What was this? Some complicated love triangle? She could feel sexual tension building around her, and hardly any of it belonged to her. Were they together? Casual couple? Free for alls? Had she teleported into a group of swingers? The very thought sent a disgusting chill up her back.

"So...?" Bryce asked her.

"If I *have* to choose, I suppose I choose Griffin." Caylin plastered a disinterested look on her face.

Griffin wasn't buying it, though. A slow grin curved on his face, and his eyes twinkled ever so slightly. "Well, there you have it. She chose me. Now move along, Bryce."

"To be fair, I would have chosen one of the girls," Caylin pointed out.

"Oh? Really?" Bryce twisted her words to imply that she was sexually attracted to women instead of men.

"You're an idiot!" Lia shook her head and looked over at Caylin apologetically. "You'll have to forgive him. He's a sex crazed lunatic."

"I gathered," Caylin answered dryly. She should have spotted that first thing, actually. She'd been around enough of those to last a lifetime.

"I'm not a lunatic." Bryce held his hands up in defense.

"Notice he did not argue the rest?" Devon rolled her eyes and flicked her dreadlocks behind her shoulder.

"Well, it's been decided. We'll report back with what we find later. Good luck, Griffin," Campbell smirked.

Yeah, good luck. He was going to need it for sure. Caylin was not about to give him an inch of her sanity any longer. She watched as the others teleported from sight, leaving just the two of them in the room.

Caylin refused to meet his eyes. "So…."

"Are you ready?"

"Bring it." Her nose crinkled up slightly, her determination rushing through her. She was not going to allow her attraction to him to distract her today. If she wanted to go on the next assignment, she would have to prove herself capable of defending herself.

"Not here."

Caylin stood up and walked over to him. She put her arm on his. "I'm ready."

He seemed surprised by her trust, but he did not make any comment on it. Instead, he stood up and held onto her arms. Caylin kept her eyes trained on his as they floated through the air. She saw a warmth in them that almost taunted her. She didn't like the way his presence made her feel. Caylin might never get used to it. Maybe that was the whole point of it all.

When they landed just outside the mahogany door, Caylin stepped back slightly. "I'm not sure I want to go back in there."

"The altar's not there now, Caylin." His eyes were deeply sorry. "I won't let them do that to you again."

But he let them the first time. She refused to meet his eyes. Trust was something that wasn't easily earned, but Caylin knew she had to move forward to do what the universe had put her here to do. She turned the knob and pushed the door open without looking back at him.

Caylin was surprised to see the room was no longer recognizable. The white room that had existed before was gone. In its place was a black room, which gave the appearance that they were standing in the middle of a starry sky. Looking down at her feet, she saw the ground was covered in grass. "Where are we?"

"In a safe place," Griffin answered her.

"Are we at the Watch Tower?"

"No." He grinned at her.

"So we're somewhere in the middle of nowhere. Are we on Earth?"

"Perhaps...." He had the look of someone who would never tell.

"I see. Well, what is the lesson?" Caylin did not want to be out under the stars with him. There was an intimacy involved with that which made her shiver uncomfortably.

"Are you cold?" he asked her.

"No." Yes, cold as ice. He would be better to learn that too. Caylin would probably break him in two before she was done with him if he tried to pursue what she assumed he would. A relationship with her, it was dangerous. Nonexistent. She was not fit for any kind of relationship. Not that he was asking her for one.

Griffin was watching her as if he were trying to determine her thoughts. "Ready to get started?"

"Sure."

Griffin launched a fireball at her, which she deflected easily.

"What is the point here?"

"Defend yourself."

Caylin's hand flew up, and a bolt of purple light shot from it like a bolt of electricity. "Whoa...!"

Griffin grinned at her. "That's just the bottom of the barrel, Caylin. Now that his darkness has been erased, your power is what's left."

Caylin dodged another ball and thought about the ways she had attacked in the past. She had always thought herself to be fairly strong, able to handle herself in any situation. As he cast a lasso of light, she watched reflectively and created the same with her own magic. Their two lines of light clashed in the air, sending both of them flying backwards. Caylin landed on her back with a loud oomph.

"Is that all you got, Caylin?" he taunted her.

He thought this was funny? Oh, hell, no. Caylin did a front handspring and catapulted her body through the air. She crouched low when she landed on her feet. "I can give as good as I get," she almost snarled at him.

"Really, because I've only just gotten started."

He sent a shockwave through the air, and she was pushed several feet backwards, her hands and feet marking the grass as she did.

Caylin felt steam rise from her ears. Time to serve it up on a platter. Caylin didn't even think as her hands whipped out in front of her. The ground shook under his feet, but he easily sidestepped the fiery cracks she had sent his way. Another shockwave came her way, but this time Caylin threw up a shield to deflect it. Closing her eyes, she let all the anger inside her form into a tight spring, which came out of in a gust of black winds. The air picked up around her, and her hair stood out, flapping dangerously around her face. Her feet left the ground, and she levitated on the spot. When she released the wind, she landed on her feet as the rush of air pushed Griffin backwards.

He looked up at her appreciatively. "Not bad. But I think you can do better."

Better? Was he fucking kidding her? Caylin growled and pulled Asodio from its sheath. She launched herself at him with a battle cry. Griffin cast a white shield and easily deflected her. That did not slow her down. A rage was building inside her, and she felt dangerously close to imploding. The more he sent at her, the more she charged against him. Caylin refused to give in.

Sheathing Asodio, she held her hands out and summoned a storm cloud that obscured the world around her. The air ripped around, sending shards of debris so close it scratched against her flesh, but Caylin refused to release it. Everything she had inside was building to a deadly close before she felt something wrap itself around her, throwing her off balance. Caylin looked down and struggled against the lasso of light that held her tight.

"Let me go!" she screamed at him.

Griffin yanked the rope, and she was pulled into his arms. "Enough, Caylin."

"I'm not done. Let me go!" She squirmed against the rope, wanting to break free from its binds.

"Never," he whispered just as his mouth dropped to hers. His lips moved angrily over hers, and Caylin could barely hold him off.

Her lips met his, refusing to let him master her. Caylin was the master of her own destiny. It was time he learned that. She held him tight and sent them spiraling through the air.

Caylin broke the kiss first and tried to remember how to breathe. It was then that Griffin realized where they were.

"What are you doing, Caylin?" he whispered hoarsely as

he looked around her bedroom.

"What we both want." She pulled his mouth down to hers again and felt him tense in her arms. What was his problem? He was interested. So was she. They were both consenting adults. What was the hold up?

"We can't do this, Caylin." His eyes looked remorseful.

"Why not? Are there rules?" Caylin surely hoped not. He was the first man she'd ever wanted to sleep with. Maybe he could erase all the men who had come before him.

"You're—"

"If you say broken...." She felt a rage building inside her. Her hair was filled with static electricity.

"But you are." Griffin touched a hand to her face. "And I don't want to make it worse."

Caylin shoved him away. So, he didn't want her at all. He was just using her to further the advances of the Watch Tower. Like any man, he was not to be trusted. Maybe the memories had been planted inside her. That was entirely possible. "Get out."

"No." His voice was hard.

"Get out!" she shouted at him.

He crossed his arms and refused to budge as if taunting her to make him. Caylin seethed. Launching herself at him, she lashed out at him. Her feet and arms sought contact with any physical piece of him, and he just stood there, taking it. When she was almost hurting herself, he wrapped his arms around her, holding her arms close to her sides. His mouth was on hers before she could think, and she relaxed against him.

This time his kiss was gentle, and it soothed the storm of emotions that swarmed inside her. She sighed against him, and he released his hold. Wrapping her arms around his neck, Caylin brought herself as close to him as she could. She had a need to feel his body hard against her own. She broke the kiss and whispered desperately, "Please."

Griffin steadied his breathing and stepped away from her. He turned his back as slow, ragged breaths left his chest. He ran a hand through his hair as if trying to calm the thoughts swirling in his head.

Caylin walked over to him and wrapped her arms around him. She lay her head against his back and tried to bring him back to her. Caylin felt like she had lost him, and she wasn't entirely sure why. She moved away from him, feeling slightly defeated. Maybe she was too tainted. A tear fell down her face. That had to be it. He must know about everything she had been made to do all those years just to survive the hell of the world around her. Caylin had always known she was unworthy, but to feel that way here and now almost broke her to pieces. She sat down on the edge of the bed with her shoulders slumped as the tears fell through the numb cloud that was starting to circle around her. Maybe the void that had been her life would return.

Caylin heard him call her name, but it was from much further away. It wasn't until he knelt before her that she realized he was still there.

"You should go."

"I can't." His hands touched her face and made her look at him.

"Why are you still here?" Caylin wanted to push him away.

"Because I can't make myself go, even though it's the right thing to do."

"Because I'm trash?" she asked him in a hollow voice. Caylin should have known better. The taint of the streets would follow her until the day she died. She had known long ago that happily ever after would not exist for her.

"Don't you ever say that, Caylin." His voice had an angry tone to it.

"If you knew all the things I've done...." Caylin couldn't meet his eyes. Images of her former life swarmed around in her mind.

"It doesn't matter," he tried to assure her.

"But it does. You know, you're the only man I ever wanted to do this with?" Caylin wished she could have stopped the words before they left her mouth.

"Then I'm a fortunate man," he murmured as his lips touched hers. "But I don't want to take advantage of the situation."

"What do you mean?"

"You're in a new place. There's a lot going on in your life. I don't want to add to your confusion."

He was trying to be chivalrous? Caylin's eyebrows furrowed slightly as she considered that maybe he was fighting the same internal demons she was. "I see. Then why are you still here?"

"I...." He looked thoughtful for a moment before his mouth came down to hers again. This time, he had the air of a man who was too far gone to change his mind.

Caylin sighed as he moved his body over hers and eased her back against the bed. When he hovered over her, Caylin knew he was trying to make himself go. She refused to let him give in to it. Reaching out for any tangible piece of him, she drew him under her spell. When his lips met hers, they were gentle. Caylin wrapped her hands in the black T-shirt he was wearing, longing to rip it from his body so she could finally see what was buried beneath. When her fingers slid underneath and touched the heat of his stomach, he flinched against her touch.

She was just about to remove it when she felt her arm start

to tingle. What the hell? Looking down at it, she realized they were being summoned.

Griffin broke their kiss and pushed away from her. Caylin couldn't tell if he was upset or relieved. Either way, it seemed to be a saved by the bell moment.

He held his hand out to her. "Shall we?"

Caylin couldn't even look at him when she took his hand. He wrapped his arms around her and whispered in her ear, "Another time, Caylin."

Somehow, she sensed his relief as they traveled through the air. It was a bitter pill to swallow when the man she was attracted to was actually happier being pulled out of her embrace than into it. She made the resolution to not fall into his arms so easily next time, or pull him into hers, as it were.

Chapter 14

The minute they landed on the ground, she moved away from his embrace. He called her name, but she refused to look at him. Instead, she looked around them for the others. They were in a room, much like the one in their library, but the decorations were different. There was a large screen that had descended from the ceiling. The only other person in the room with them was the Shadow Walker.

"Lyssa," she greeted her.

"Caylin." Lyssa nodded at her. "Griffin."

"How's Hunter doing?" Griffin asked her politely.

"He's on daddy duty right now." Lyssa smiled at him.

"How old is James now?"

"Two, and quite precocious."

"You've got a kid?" Caylin was surprised. How could anyone in the Watch Tower have enough left over to be a parent? Caylin couldn't even imagine having a family, like ever. Not with…well, it was less than likely that she would ever have that kind of emotional attachment with anyone. Life had damaged her too much.

"Yes. Spunky little guy," Lyssa grinned. "We split our time here at the Watch Tower."

"Your...."

"Husband. Yes, Caylin, he's from the Watch Tower too. I met him here." Lyssa seemed to understand her concerns. "Anything is possible."

Caylin cleared her throat uncomfortably. "So, why did you summon us here?"

"We're going to retrieve one of the orbs from the Craven. Feel up to a fight?"

"Always." Caylin rubbed her hands together. This was the perfect time to get her aggression out on someone else. If she weren't careful, she would take them out on Griffin, and that would just lead her back to where she was moments earlier. Sleeping with him would probably be the worst mistake of her life. Caylin couldn't afford the distraction, no matter how much she wanted it.

The fact that he was reluctant should have been a red flag for her anyway. He said it had nothing to do with her, but she knew it had everything to do with her. Caylin looked back at him and saw his eyes on her. How was it that he could stand there so aloof and unaffected? Damn him. Turning back, Caylin resolved herself to the task at hand. "Where are we headed to?"

Lyssa pointed to the globe on the table before her. A red light flashed like an alert of sorts. "This area is crawling with them."

"And why are we seeking out this orb?"

"Remie gave us the last one you found. They use it to communicate?" Lyssa asked her.

"They seem to. What happened to that one?"

"It didn't hold up to our experiments so well. We'll have to try a different tactic." Lyssa looked over at Griffin. "You sitting this one out?"

"Like hell." His voice seemed almost angry at the suggestion.

"I thought as much. Well, has she mastered teleportation?" Lyssa asked him.

"*She* has. And I can speak for myself. Let's get to it." Caylin didn't wait for them to give her the go-ahead. She whisked herself away without second guessing herself. She'd show them teleportation.

When she landed on the ground, Caylin looked around her. She was standing in a dark alley behind a rusty green dumpster. Thankfully, she had not landed inside it. As two other whooshes sounded behind her, she knew that she was in the right spot. Not that she would ever admit to either one of them that she had doubted herself in the least. Caylin was good at appearing confident to the rest of the world. No one else had to know how weak she felt inside.

Caylin felt Asodio humming behind her and unsheathed the athame. "They're not alone."

"They rarely are," whispered Lyssa.

"Time to kick some scum." Griffin conjured his lasso of light and held it in his hand.

"Bring it." Caylin leapt from the alley and found herself facing one of the shadows. It seemed surprised by her appearance, as it faltered in its steps. A loud pitched shriek erupted from it as it signaled the others. Caylin wasn't afraid of a fight. The more, the merrier.

"You're still impetuous, I see," grinned Lyssa.

"You're surprised because…?" Caylin sliced off the arm of the shadow before her. That was not enough to stall its attack as the rest of it towered over her. She wondered how it had gotten so tall in a matter of seconds. No matter. Caylin held Asodio in one hand and released a bolt of purple lightning from the other. The shadow sizzled on the spot and fell into a pile of ashes.

"Impressive," complimented Lyssa.

"I've been practicing." She glanced over at Griffin. "I'm an easy study."

He glowered at her slightly before whipping the next shadow into shape in front of him. "Time to gloat later, ladies."

Caylin avoided a blast of red light as one of the Craven entered the fray. He was nothing to write home about really, being a foot shorter than her. She held up her free hand and signaled for him to come and get her. With Lyssa and Griffin clearly occupied by the oncoming shadows, the Craven was fair game.

The man conjured a large black axe made of some kind of dark metal that reminded her of the hematite rocks that were used to ward off evil. She wondered how they could manipulate these stones' properties for their own devices while keeping the stone intact. Caylin had very little time to contemplate this, for the man lunged at her with the axe, nearly slicing her arm in the process. It was clear she couldn't underestimate her opponent. The next time he lunged at her, Caylin ducked at the last second and swept her leg under his, knocking him on his back. That didn't keep the man down. He flung his body up easily and balanced himself on his feet.

"Screw this." Caylin opened her arms and conjured the electric storm she had practiced on Griffin earlier. The winds picked up around her, and sparks shot from her fingers. When she had gathered enough energy, Caylin sent the winds to the shocked man standing before her. He barely had time to react as he threw up a red shield. While the winds pushed against him, he was shoved backwards a few feet, which startled him enough to lower his shield. Caylin sent several bolts of lightning at him, which electrified every inch of him. The minute his life force left his body, the orb shattered into pieces, and a small black fog spiraled in the air from it.

"We need one alive, Caylin," cautioned Lyssa.

"Right. Sorry." She wasn't, though. Besides, the last time they had taken an orb, they had retrieved it from the Craven before he died. As long as it didn't get destroyed in the process, she was pretty sure the orb would still work.

Shadows continued to rise from the ground as if they were honing in on them. Caylin looked over at Griffin with panic on her face. "Maybe it didn't work. They can still find me."

"It worked, Caylin. They're just calling each other." He pointed out to the shrieking cries that filled the air.

She hoped that's all it was. Caylin wasn't sure she could survive that Altar of Azure again. It had taken almost every inch of her sanity the last time. As another shadow approached her, Caylin barely dodged its attack. Casting a shield at the last second, she enjoyed the sizzling sound as the dark being singed itself against her light. When it backed up, she released the shield and lunged at him with Asodio, slicing him in half.

"Look out, Caylin!" Lyssa shouted.

Caylin pivoted with her athame and shoved it into another shadow behind her. She shook her head at the dark creature that shriveled in front of her. The shadows were just going to keep coming. "We have to keep moving. Let them follow us."

Caylin advanced on the four Craven that had gathered around a few women who were huddled in fear. Fucking bullies! Caylin didn't even stop to think. She raced at them with a fiery purple blast that knocked three of them off balance. The fourth one glared at her and took out a wand. She shook her head. "If you think that's going to help you, you have another think coming."

"Bitch!" He made an arc of red light in the air, and a wave of air went rushing toward her like a typhoon.

Caylin was knocked on her back and winced as her shoulder

fell against something sharp. As she stood up, she realized there was a small metal spike embedded in her shoulder. That didn't stop her, though—it only made her very angry. Her hair rose around her face like tiny strands of snakes as she gave him a stony glare.

"You shouldn't have done that," chuckled Griffin. He stood back, fully aware of what was about to happen next.

"They never learn, do they?" Caylin used Asodio to make a purple circle in front of her. Using her other hand, she created a symbol inside. The circle rotated like a camera lens as it zeroed in on its target. She released the energy pulsing at her fingertips, and the circle shot through the air, attached to her target, and started to electrocute him on the spot. Caylin watched as his body twitched on the ground. She stepped closer to him and ripped his necklace off his body before it could recognize its wearer's demise.

One of the other Craven that was getting up grabbed one of the women from the ground and held her up like a shield. Caylin looked over at Griffin and prayed he understood her message. It happened in a flash. Caylin whisked her hand and teleported to just behind the man. Before he knew it, Asodio had made its mark. Griffin moved forward and moved the woman out of the way before the Craven could retaliate against her. Caylin used that moment to send all her anger through the blade. She smelled the burning flesh and reveled in the howling cries that came from his mouth. That was nothing compared to the pain he received when Caylin yanked the stone from his neck and tossed it on the ground. Stepping back, Caylin watched the flames rise up from the ground and incinerate him on the spot.

The other two Craven evaporated on the spot as if they realized they were outpowered. Caylin looked over at the four women. "Get off the streets."

"Yes, Caylin," one of the redheaded prostitutes mumbled.

"Ruby, I've warned you about this." Caylin shook her head at her.

"Well, I left the Ghost District." Ruby shrugged her shoulders. "I guess it's a shithole everywhere."

"Wait, this is Caylin?" The blonde was sitting there with her mouth open. "She's...."

"Taller than you expected?" offered Caylin with a sarcastic smile.

"You're amazing." The blonde was clearly impressed.

"Ladies, Caylin's right. It's not safe here. You need to clear out," Lyssa added to the conversation. "Stay away from any man wearing a black orb necklace. They're bad news."

"She's right. Live and learn...now get moving before they come back." Caylin saw the four girls were in agreement. Thankfully, they raced away as fast as their feet could carry them.

Caylin turned to find Griffin staring at her. Was that disgust? Of course, it was. He didn't really know the life she had been forced to live. It must have been quite the surprise to find out that an every day hooker knew her better than he did. True colors—they probably showed through now more than ever. Their eyes met, and she glared at him.

"We got what we came for." Caylin waved her hands and returned to the room at Sector Four.

Lyssa was right behind her. "Nicely done, Caylin."

"Oooh, do I get a cookie?" She rolled her eyes as she placed the small black orb on the table.

"Are you okay?" Lyssa asked her empathetically.

"Peachy." She didn't want the Shadow Walker's sympathy.

At that moment, Griffin ported in. His eyes showed a slight concern. "Caylin?"

She ignored him and turned back to Lyssa. "So, what did you want this for this time?"

"Well, we thought you could use it to track them."

"Me?"

Caylin retrieved the orb from the table by the chain. She could feel the hum pulsing from the small glowing rock. As she examined it closer, she saw a small black sphere set inside. A white ring of light glowed around the exterior, its pulse matching the beat of energy she felt.

"What should I do?"

"Well, that we're still working out," Lyssa smirked slightly.

"Right. Well, no time like the present." Caylin grasped the stone in her hand. A burst of blackness shot behind her eyes, and her head fell backward.

"Caylin!" Griffin shouted as he dove closer to catch her before her body crashed to the floor.

Caylin barely heard anything but the loud static shooting between her ears, as the pulsing stone took over inside her. She felt like she was transported to another time and place altogether, even though her body had not left the room. A blurry darkness shimmered before her as a tunnel vision started to take over.

Screaming voices echoed around her, like the souls that were trapped deep inside the Revenant. This was familiar to her. The Land of the Shadows. The Revenant. She saw the dark shadowed creatures standing around him. He sat on his obsidian throne, barking out his orders to his minions.

"Where is she?" the Revenant shouted.

Caylin realized he was talking about her. Even though she sat there tuning in to him, the Revenant had no idea where she was. The relief did not last long, as the darkness inside the orb started to send its icy tendrils into her body. Caylin's throat closed up on her, and she struggled to breathe. Her hands wanted to grasp at the invisible power that seemed to be choking the life out of her, but to do so would mean dropping the orb. Before she knew it, her body fell backward, and two arms caught her before she crashed to the floor. Losing all consciousness, she spiraled into an abyss haunted with shadows and light, each battling for control over her body.

Chapter 15

As Caylin fought her way out of the darkness, she felt herself cradled against a warm body. She snuggled deeper against it, and a feeling of peace filled every inch of her body. Half-asleep, she never questioned the energy that ebbed and flowed between them.

"Caylin?" the voice called to her.

"Hmm?" she murmured against it.

"You need to wake up."

"But why? I'm so comfy here," she complained.

The body shook beneath her as a low chuckle rumbled deep in its chest. "Caylin, wake up."

A hand stroked her face, and she sighed against it. "Do I have to? Can't I just stay here?"

"You could, but my leg is about to fall asleep."

Her eyes opened as the haze continued to filter around her. She was surrounded by a ball of white glowing light as she lay against Griffin's chest. Slow recognition crossed through her mind, and the gentle fog that circled through her almost evaporated. Caylin blinked and sat straight up before pushing off him.

"Wait." He tried to stop her, but Caylin refused to listen to him.

Unfortunately, her legs were not as confident as she was on her escape. She stumbled and fell on her knees. Caylin slammed her fist on the ground. Why did he have to see her weakness? "Damn it."

"Caylin...." He was on the ground next to her.

"Don't do that." Caylin tried to keep the anger boiling inside her, but every part of her was paved in a confusion that she could not erase.

"What?"

"Be nice to me." She couldn't bear it right now. With all the darkness in the world, there was no place for this. They had too much to do. She could not afford to let him into her life. Not like this. This was dangerous.

His hand smoothed her hair out of her face. "Why not?"

"You only make it harder to hate you," she whispered. Caylin tried to hold onto something that would make it easier for her to find the anger inside her, but this time it seemed nonexistent. She felt defeated.

"Why do you want to hate me?" His voice was filled with a gruff emotion.

"Because the other end of it scares the shit out of me."

A tear fell down her face as Caylin realized her past lives were catching up to her. She had feelings for him, whether she cared to admit it or not, but she was not the naïve young girl he had known so many lifetimes before. The world had hardened her this time, with a shell that was so brittle and jagged he would be lucky to break through it.

Griffin's mouth kissed away the tears streaming down her face, and she fought the urge to flinch. When he rained small kisses across her face, she wanted to run. She didn't want gentle and sweet—that tenderness simply did not exist for her. Caylin tried to make herself pull away, but her body just would not comply. Instead, she seemed to pull him closer to her. Wrapping her arms around his neck, her fingers played with some of the hair on his neck. As his tongue delved into her mouth, Caylin pulled him in closer.

She waited for the wall to come up, the one that blocked out any intimate moments. It had kept her protected against the many numerous men who had broken and beaten her over the years, but this time it failed her. Caylin was transfixed in the moment, one that she knew would last forever in her mind.

Griffin broke the kiss and put his forehead against hers. "No more self-destructing, Caylin."

"I can't seem to help myself," Caylin whispered.

"Then let me help you." Griffin stroked her face with his hand, and she was entranced by him.

When his mouth touched hers, Caylin felt the bright light surrounding her start to filter into her like a peaceful lullaby. He soothed her soul in ways she never thought existed with just one kiss. When he seemed to withdraw from her, Caylin pulled him closer. "Please...."

Griffin was caught between the edge of reason and her plea for more. "Caylin...."

Caylin stood up from his lap, even though it meant leaving the safety of his arms. She realized they were in her apartment, which was strange to her because it had never felt this clear and inviting. Maybe that was what his energy brought to her space. She kicked her shoes off and followed it with her socks.

"What are you doing, Caylin?" His eyes followed her every movement.

"Getting comfortable." But she wasn't. The more she removed, the more vulnerable she felt. Her body image wasn't spectacular—it was marred with nightmares that she could never erase. As she lifted her shirt over her head, she heard his intake of breath. Caylin now stood there as exposed as if she were completely naked, as the only thing left was her undergarments.

"Caylin...." His voice was tight as if he were trying to maintain some sense of control.

When he made no move to approach her, she crossed her arms over her body and felt like an awkward virgin standing for his approval. She could not read the emotions on his face. Turning away from him, she closed her eyes and tried to shut out the voices that raced through her head. Tainted, marked, dirty, unworthy. In this moment, the anger that fueled her was non-existent. Her defenses were down, and she felt her heart quivering as it waited to be put out of its misery once and for all. If not Griffin, then no one. Clearly, she had made a mistake. Her shoulders slumped, and she fought the misery that was building inside of her.

It disappeared the moment she felt his arms wrap around her stomach. He pulled her against him, and his mouth rained kisses down her shoulders. When he swept the hair away from her neck and kissed along the inside of her neck, Caylin felt a spark light inside her. She flinched slightly as his hands massaged against her stomach. Never had any man made her body react so easily to his touch.

"So beautiful," he whispered near her ear.

"You don't find me hideous?"

Her whisper made him tighten his hold on her stomach. "Hideous? You're perfection."

Caylin spun around in his arms and sought his eyes. She needed to see the truth in his eyes. As she gazed inside them, it was as if she were the only woman in his universe. Caylin recognized that look—it resonated deep inside her. She was also terrified of it. "I'm scarred."

Caylin referred to the scars on her abdomen and her back. The rough torture of the streets had taken its toll on her flesh many times over. She sucked in her breath when Griffin knelt before her and kissed every single inch of the scars lining her abdomen. Wrapping her fingers in his hair, she felt tears fall down her face. For once, she let them fall. In this moment, she felt beautiful, reformed, worthy.

When he rose again, he kissed her tears away as his hands unlatched the bra clasps. He slid the bra straps from her shoulders, and Caylin sucked in her breath when his finger swept over her nipple. One touch, and she was ready to crumble in his arms. His mouth met hers, and Caylin pushed his shirt up with her hands. She felt the warmth of his stomach as the muscles bunched up under her touch. He lifted his arms, allowing her to remove his shirt. Their kiss broke only for a few seconds before his mouth was on hers again.

Griffin growled slightly when her hands slid beneath his pants. She felt him jerk away from her when her finger grazed over the top of his erection. He was definitely more than ready for this. That knowledge excited her. He pushed her hands away and undid the buttons of his jeans. After he slid them down, he pulled her hard against him. Caylin realized then that he had discarded his briefs as well.

Caylin wrapped her hands around him and planted them firmly on his ass as she brought him closer to her. She whimpered when his mouth moved from hers and started to make a path down her neck. Her nipples tightened against his chest, and she reveled in the way they felt against his skin. He seemed to enjoy it too, for his hands slid under her panties and squeezed her cheeks hard in his palms. Caylin felt a warmth pool inside her and was confused by the moisture that seemed to drip from her. She'd never had that reaction to a man before.

Griffin pushed the band of her panties down, and they slid to the floor at her feet. Now completely naked before each other, Caylin shivered in anticipation. His mouth traveled down the valley of her breasts, and Caylin moaned softly. His lips set her on fire everywhere they touched. When she thought she could tolerate no more, she gasped when he pulled her nipple into his mouth, while his thumb made small circles around the other one. Her legs felt weak and unsteady.

As if sensing her dilemma, Griffin scooped her up in his arms and carried her over to the bed. He lay her gently on the bed and stood back to admire her. "I've dreamed of this moment."

"Oh?" Caylin's eyebrow rose curiously. "What happened next?"

"Well, first...."

His hands spread her legs open, and Caylin was caught off guard. Was that all there was? He would mount her, and it would be over? She was surprised when his lips ran kisses along the inside of her thighs, alternating with small nibbles that made her legs trembled with each one.

"Oh!" she exclaimed when his mouth started to work its magic on her clit. She had clearly not seen that coming. As his tongue slid beneath her folds, she almost lost control completely. Soft like silk, hot and sweet, he worked her over until she was nearly thrashing on the bed before him. Caylin had never felt so crazy for anyone before in her life. The gentle hum that had been singing through her body earlier was replaced with a raw need for him to possess every inch of her body.

He released her and moved up the length of her body with the same teasing movements that were sending her over the edge and back. His mouth took her breast into it again, as his fingers started to fuel her wild desire for him as they stroked her clit. She came hard and fast against him, and a blazing fire burned through her.

"Griffin!"

He bit her nipple, and she whimpered. "So hot, Caylin."

"God, yes!" Caylin felt herself erupt again as he continued to move her to another finish line.

Griffin moved away from her and stood up to retrieve protection. She watched him roll the condom down the length of his cock, and a new thrill filled her body as she thought about how it would feel to be possessed by every inch of him. Caylin wanted that more than anything else.

He turned to see her staring at him, and desire flashed on his face. Caylin sucked in her breath as he walked to the bed with the stealth of a tiger. When his body sunk onto the bed over hers, she opened her legs and prayed he put her out of her misery. Every inch of her was thirsty for him.

"You're sure?" Griffin asked just as he was poised to penetrate her core.

"If you stop now, I might have to kill you," she threatened him.

He chuckled at her words, but when she wrapped her legs around him and forced him inside her, his laughter stopped. Instead, he grunted slightly as she quivered around him. "You're an angel."

"I'm no angel, Griffin."

"Anything that feels this good is divine."

He pushed into her gently, and Caylin dug her nails into his back. His thrusts were slow at first, but the more he moved, the more something beautiful built inside her. When he picked up the pace, she wrapped her legs around him and held on for the ride as she crashed over the next wave of oblivion. Her finish seemed to spur him on, and soon he was pummeling into her like a man obsessed with her possession. When he thrust into her one last time, Caylin trembled around him.

When he tried to pull away, she held him closer. Caylin just wanted to stay wrapped in the moment with him. She never wanted it to end. Reality would creep in on them all too soon. She was not prepared for its cold breath. Not yet.

Griffin pulled out of her and kissed her on the forehead. He left the bed briefly to her disappointment. When he returned, she was relieved. Pulling her into his arms, Griffin ran a hand up and down her spine. She snuggled against him and murmured softly. The two of them lay there in the silence until both of them fell asleep.

Chapter 16

When Caylin woke up, she found herself alone in her bed, which made her wonder if the events from the night before had even happened. Leave it to her to conjure a mirage in her head. Not that Caylin had many sexual fantasies. If that was what it was, she planned on having more in the future, for her body was still feeling sensual and content.

As she stretched under the covers, it was clear that she was naked beneath them. Maybe it wasn't a dream then, but that still did not explain why Griffin was nowhere to be seen. Caylin pushed the covers aside and looked over at the clock. It was already mid-morning. She should have been up long before now. Walking over to the closet, she chose her clothes for the day and set them out. After taking a quick shower and getting ready for the morning, it was already close to lunchtime.

"Damn it." Caylin had slept in more here at Sector Fifteen than she had at any other time in her life. Would they start thinking she was lazy if it continued? Should she care what they thought? She never really sought anyone's approval, but this place was different. Caylin felt like she needed to prove herself, especially after last night's debacle.

Caylin let out a defeated sigh. Maybe she had been a little

reckless in touching the orb the way she had, but she had learned some important information. The Revenant could not sense her, even when she was searching for him. This they could use to their advantage. Hopefully, the others would not be too upset at her for being so strong-willed. There was only one way to find out.

Whisking her hand in front of her, she sent herself down to the gathering room. The other five were having a serious debate about something. They barely even noticed she had appeared. Caylin pulled a chair out and waited to see if anyone would acknowledge her.

Griffin was the first. His eyes met hers, and she shivered slightly as she remembered looking into them the night before when ecstasy had blanketed her entire existence. A small blush covered her cheeks as a knowing smile seemed to curve across his face.

He cleared his throat. "We have company."

"What? Oh." Campbell nodded at her. "Caylin. Recovering fine?"

"Yes." Caylin didn't know what else to say.

"You gave us quite a scare yesterday," Lia reprimanded her.

"I'm fine. No worse for the wear."

She shook off the concern. Griffin's eyes were probing hers, but she looked away. If he wanted to know how she was, he should have stuck around. Waking up to him gone, that had stung. Had they even slept in the same bed? Or had he snuck out of the room as soon as he could do so without catching her attention?

"What happened when you touched the orb?" Devon asked curiously.

"I heard his voice. He was sending them out to find me,

but...." Caylin paused. "He couldn't find me."

"Even with you touching the orb?" Campbell asked her.

"Seems that way."

"Still, you took a horrible risk," cautioned Lia. "I've seen what those things can do. What if you had incinerated like the Craven?"

"I didn't." Caylin refused to think about what could have happened. If she had a destiny to end the Revenant, then some silly ass stone was not going to take her out. That would be far too easy.

"Regardless, you will take more care in the future." Griffin's voice had a definitive sound to it.

Caylin fought the urge to argue with him but resisted. She knew he was right. More precaution would have to be taken in the future; otherwise, Caylin would pass out any time she touched it. How helpful would that be? She needed to be able to partially shield herself from the darkness. After spending some time with Griffin last night, she knew exactly how to do it. The soft, gentle bubble that had surrounded her would be enough to keep her safe from the icy blast from the black orb. She was sure of it. All she had to do was figure out how to manufacture that without Griffin's presence.

"I want to try again," Caylin interjected.

"I'm not sure that's a good idea," cautioned Lia.

"Why not? I'm fine."

"According to Lyssa, you weren't so fine when you left the fight," Lia pointed out.

"I was impulsive. I'll do better. I know what to do." Caylin didn't want to explain how she knew—that would put too much attention on whatever was happening between her and Griffin. They had slept together. That didn't mean they were a couple. For all she knew, Griffin already had someone else in his life. Why hadn't she thought to ask that? Lyssa had Hunter. They were married. Was Griffin? Was that why he had pushed her away before? Caylin realized there was a lot they needed to talk about, but right now was not the time.

"What's your plan?" Campbell asked her.

"I can't really explain it; you just have to trust me. Where is the orb?" Caylin asked them.

Campbell snapped his fingers, and the orb appeared in the space before her.

"Perfect."

"Wait, Caylin—" Griffin tried to stop her.

"Trust me." She wanted more than his trust. Caylin wanted every piece of him, married or not, but now was not the time to cloud her mind with such things. Closing her eyes, Caylin cast a white shield of light, filling it with all the hope and love she had felt rotating around her the night before. She remembered what Lyssa had told her before; love was one of the only powers strong enough to take down the shadows. It would work just as well as her shield.

Caylin felt her hair standing out around her as if filled with static electricity. She blocked out the world around her and let the light fill her. The moment she touched her fingers to the orb, her eyes were no longer her own. It was as if she had become the being she was trying to locate. His every word echoed inside her mind. She heard him yelling at his minions.

Are the cows infected?

Yes. One of the Craven answered him. *The industry will be flooded with them before too long.*

Suckers, every last one of them. Throw them a discount of any kind, and they take it, just to turn more profit. The Revenant cackled gleefully. *They've never figured out where the sickness is coming from.*

What should we watch for? the man asked him.

Insanity, of course. Murder, chaos, mayhem. Bloody massacres. The world will be covered in blood.

Do you want us to harvest more stones?

Yes. Grind it up and put it in the grains at the silo. They'll suspect a rise in mind-altering narcotics before they think to check their food sources.

A brilliant plan, Master. The Craven bowed low before him and whisked himself off.

Caylin looked through his eyes and saw the shadows forming from oily puddles near him. As she tried to zero in closer, something pushed back at her. She could sense the evil laughter rising in him. *I feel you, Stalker. I may not see you yet, but I will find you. You will be mine, or you will die.*

At that point, Caylin released the orb and let it float gently to the table. There were a few things that did not make sense to her. Like if he had sensed her, why would he be throwing his plot out there for her to read? It had to be a trap, a way for him to find her. That she could not let happen, but she would still relay the information that had been shared right before her. Caylin sat there, the thoughts rotating through her mind so fast she was having trouble keeping up with them.

"Caylin?" One voice brought her around.

Caylin looked around for him. Her eyes met his. "I'm fine, Griffin."

She wanted to say it was thanks to him that she had been able to withstand the darkness flowing from the dark crystal inside the orb. Closing her eyes, she tried to decide which points of information were the most important. No matter what, she knew the Revenant still planned on poisoning the grain with rocks they were harvesting. That would be the first stage.

"Did you see him?" Campbell asked her.

"I did." Caylin nodded.

"Did he see you?" Griffin asked her.

"Yes and no. He doesn't know where I am, but he can still sense me." Caylin did not like the idea that some horny dark creature was out to get her. What did he plan on doing with her if he found her? Caylin shivered as her mind ran over some of the possibilities.

"Caylin?" Griffin seemed to notice her discomfort.

"It's nothing. What you need to know is that the Craven has been contracted to poison the world with his darkness. They're going to use our food to do it."

"What do you mean?" Lia asked her.

"They're using dark magic to poison the grains that the cows are eating. This, in turn, will poison any consumers."

"Where?" Campbell pointed to the globe that circled before them. "Show us."

"I can't. They never talked about where it would happen." Caylin wished she could be more helpful.

"We can't be everywhere at once," Bryce pointed out.

"And he'll be expecting you. I think it's a trap." Caylin closed her eyes and tried to clear her mind. Was there anything from there that she could hold on to? An important piece to the puzzle?

"So, we can't stop him." Campbell looked thoughtful. "Can we cut them off from the source?"

"Perhaps," Devon answered. "If they are expecting our attacks on the grain silos, they might not be expecting us to head deeper in."

"That's true. We'll have to use the silos as a diversion." Campbell put his chin in his hand and tapped a finger on his mouth as he tried to think up a plan.

"You can't send people to the silos," cautioned Caylin.

"They'll be like sitting ducks. I guarantee the Revenant will make sure they are well protected."

"Every Guardian knows they might someday meet their maker, Caylin. All are ready to give their lives if it means saving their world."

"I know, but there has to be another way. This would be a meaningless loss."

"Relax, Caylin. No one will enter the fray without adequate preparation. I'll meet with the council." Campbell stood up from the table and nodded at the others before he teleported from sight.

"And what do the rest of us do? Wait for the mass hysteria to break out?" Caylin looked at the others. "There has to be something we can do."

"We can try to locate the source, but that will take time to do." Devon was reflective. "Until then, I think you should continue your training. Whatever you're doing, you need to continue to do it. If you can block him out even further, maybe you can watch without being detected next time."

Do more of what she had been doing? Caylin tried to school her thoughts. That would require a lot more time and attention from the man who had brought peace into her life. She wasn't sure that was possible. Last night had been amazing, but in the morning light, her mind was filled with doubt all over again. Maybe the doubts would have circled around her like petty vultures if she hadn't woken alone in her bed.

Caylin stood up and pushed away from the table. "I guess I'll get to it then." Waving her arm in front of her, she whisked herself back to her apartment, not even waiting to see if Griffin had anything to say.

Chapter 17

Caylin looked around her apartment, wondering what she was going to do. The shield she had cast around her was something that was still new to her. Finding her calm was certainly easier to do downstairs. There were very few reminders of the night before to distract her. Here though, in the room where it had all happened, Caylin was distracted.

She walked into the bedroom and saw the tousled sheets. Visions of their body entwined circled in her mind. The gentle hands and lips had carried her to the brink and back. Doubt would not sneak in to cloud the moment if there had been more words between them. The problem was neither one of them was big on talking.

Caylin heard a knock on her door. She walked out of the bedroom and made her way into the other space. When she stood before the door, she knew who it was. Caylin could feel every inch of his energy pooling beneath the door.

She opened the door. "What do you want?"

"Can I come in?" It was as if he knew the troubled feelings swarming through her.

"Suit yourself. Come, go. Whatever." She turned away from him and went to the living area, where she plopped down on the couch. "What do you need?"

"Caylin...." He had the air of someone about to step into a river filled with crocodiles.

"Yes?" She crossed her arms over her chest.

"We need to talk."

"So, talk." She walked over the kitchenette and sat down on one of the bar stools, where she waited to hear what he said.

"Look, this all happened before—"

"Who is she?" Caylin asked in resignation.

"Who?"

"The other woman. There must be one. No wonder you pushed me away so much." She looked down at the floor and shook her head in disgust. "Here, you were trying to be noble, and I basically attacked you." There was a long pause, and it was enough for her to cement that thought in her head. "Don't worry. I won't bother you again."

Caylin stood up from the stool and moved across the room. She didn't make it very far before Griffin pulled her into his arms. His lips seared hers as she struggled against him. At first, she fought him off, wanting to hide from the feelings that were spiraling inside her. When she finally gave in, the kiss slowed to a tantalizing pace that made her heart flutter in her chest.

Griffin broke the kiss and stroked her cheek with his thumb. "There is no one else, Caylin."

"Then—"

"I was afraid if I stayed, I wouldn't be able to keep my hands off you."

Her breath caught, and a blush rose up to her face. "Would that have been so bad?"

"We have a lot to figure out, Caylin." He pushed away from her and turned around. Griffin ran his fingers through his hair, the telltale sign of a man caught at a crossroads.

Caylin sensed his weakened resistance. Stepping closer to him, she wrapped her arms around his stomach and lay her head against his back. Her hands slid under his shirt and strummed along his muscles that rippled deliciously against her touch. When her fingers moved up and rubbed against his nipples, she felt him jerk against her.

"What are you doing, Caylin?" His voice was rather gruff.

"If you have to ask, I must be really out of practice." She pushed his shirt up his back and kissed him along his spine.

"Caylin...."

"Yes?" she answered him, but her fingers were not listening at all.

He put his hand over hers and stopped her movements. When she thought he would pull away, Caylin was surprised to find him turning in her arms. His mouth covered hers with a small growl. He was definitely interested. She wrapped her arms around his neck and reveled in the desire that passed between them. He wanted her, and Caylin felt like shouting it to the rooftops.

Griffin lifted her into the air and slid her back onto the counter behind her. His hands slid under her shirt and ran along her back. Caylin arched into his touch. He broke the kiss and ran a few kisses along her jaw. "We have to talk, Caylin."

"So talk," she whispered. Caylin was perfectly happy to let their bodies speak for them. Caylin slid her shirt over her head, and her eyes met his.

"You think you're that distracting?" he challenged her.

"Not at all. I was just feeling...." She leaned over to his ear and whispered, "Hot."

"Caylin...."

"Fine." She nibbled on his ear and ran kisses down his neck. "Why did you leave?"

He shivered when she sucked on his neck. "I didn't know if you wanted me to stay."

Caylin released his neck and pulled up to look in his eyes. "You wanted to?"

His thumb worked on the outside of her bra, stroking against the small nub that was beginning to grow. "You wouldn't have gotten any sleep."

"Who needs sleep?" Caylin would have been happy to lose a little sleep if it had meant spending the night exploring his body. She had only seen bits and pieces, as he had taken control over the situation. Even now, she wanted to explore every inch of his body.

His lips caught hers, pushing so hard into her that her head fell back in reflex. They traveled down her neck, imprinting themselves on her skin. His thumb continued to run circles against her nipples, taking his time on each one. Caylin felt them strain against the lace and moaned slightly against him. She twined her fingers in his hair and pulled him tight against her. When Griffin released one of her breasts, Caylin shivered in anticipation.

His mouth devoured it, sucking and biting it until he settled over the rosy bud. As he took her into his mouth, she wrapped her legs around him, forcing his body closer to her. He had been tender the night before, but Caylin didn't want that. She wanted to feel wild and free, to let herself explode in his arms. He was the first man to bring her to the brink. She sensed his hesitation as he pulled away from her.

"Caylin…."

"Yes, Griffin?" Her breath came in small puffs as she tried to think over the chaos inside her.

"I'm not sure I can."

"You don't want to?" She ran her nails under his shirt, not

caring that he was putting a wall up.

"Oh, I want to. But I don't want to hurt you."

"Hurt me?" Her brows furrowed in confusion. "Is there something I should know?"

"You've been ill used. I don't want to be like any of the others."

"You're not," she assured him. In her mind, none of those men existed as more than stills in her mind, snapshots of a past that she kept far away from her.

He kissed her mouth hard. "I'm afraid I might lose control, Caylin."

Control? It didn't belong in this time and space. Caylin could not control the emotions racing through her, even if she wanted to. She wanted it more than the air she breathed, more than the life that flowed through her veins. He filled a void inside her that nothing had been able to penetrate before.

When he kissed her, she bit his bottom lip.

Griffin flinched. "See, when you do that…you are playing with fire."

"Burn, baby, burn," she whispered in his ear before she licked it. Her teeth nibbled it, and she brought his hand down to her breast, forcing him to squeeze it.

His hand squeezed her hard, and his mouth moved down to the curve of her neck. She felt the heat of his breath against her skin and shivered in anticipation. When his lips pressed against her, she sighed until he started to suck hard against it. With his hand squeezing her hard and his mouth working its magic on her neck, she moaned aloud. "God, yes."

"Do you like that?" his hot breath whispered against her ear.

"Yes." One word was hardly enough to describe the swirl of emotions inside her. Last night had been lovely, but this, this was infinitely better.

"I want you dripping for me, Caylin." His hands were pulling down the black leggings from her waist. He lifted her up off the counter, just enough to slide both her leggings and her panties down her waist. He tossed them behind him and ran his fingers in her hair. He pulled her head back forcefully and made a hot trail down her neck to her shoulder, where he bit her flesh.

Dripping? She'd be flooding if he continued along this route. Caylin wanted to know what it felt like to be mastered by him. So often, she was in control of everything in her life. Just once, she'd like a man who was confident enough to take everything he wanted. Caylin was more than happy to go along for the ride.

His fingers released the clasp of her bra, and he slid it down her shoulders to toss in the pile behind him. Caylin ran her fingers under his shirt and raked her nails against his skin as she pushed his shirt up and over his skin.

"God, you're exquisite."

His appreciation of her body made her want to cream on the spot. He slid to his knees and forced her legs open. His mouth sucked her clit hard, and Caylin nearly jumped out of her skin. The feeling was a mixture of pain and pleasure, hard for her to decide which one ruled out. Torn between pushing him away and pulling him closer, her fingers took over for her. They entwined with the curls on the top of his head, pulling him closer to her. She was rewarded for her brazenness when he slid a finger deep inside her. Her breath caught in her throat. He was masterful with every stroke of his fingers. When his teeth nibbled on her clit, Caylin nearly lost her mind.

"Oh!" she cried as her body shook against him. He wanted her dripping? She was definitely well on her way. She felt his tongue lap up her juices, and she trembled against him.

He pulled away, and his breath was ragged. "You taste so good, Caylin."

Caylin shivered as his hand reached up to tweak her breasts. She wasn't sure how much she would be able to take before she begged him to take her. All she could think about was him slamming into her hot core. She wanted that so bad she was afraid she would die without it.

As if sensing her need, he rose up and scooped her off the counter. When he made it to the bedroom, he tossed her on the bed. She watched him pull the condom out of his pants before he undressed. Her eyes stared at his cock, so large that she knew he would burst before long if he didn't possess her. She knew the signs. Licking her lips, her eyes met his. The darkness inside them didn't scare her. She knew it. They were the same, each one fighting for control of the wild beasts that hid deep beneath them. He rolled the condom down slowly, and Caylin was ready to come clawing at him—he took far too long.

"Roll over," he ordered her.

"What?" Surely he didn't mean to….

"Trust me, Caylin. You'll like it."

Caylin was caught between complying and refusing, but she was too curious to not follow his order. She rolled over on her stomach and waited to see what would happen next.

"Get on your knees."

God, she loved the way he commanded her. She rose to her knees with her hands pushed up in front of her. When his hand slid down her back, she trembled and arched against it. Griffin spread her legs wide and positioned himself outside her dripping core. Caylin was relieved to know he wasn't planning on sticking it somewhere else but had little time to think about that as he shoved himself deep inside her.

His hands squeezed her ass as he drove in and out of her. She felt his nails press into her flesh, and she shivered against him. He stopped moving and leaned over to kiss her back as he yanked her head back with her hair. "You feel so good, Caylin."

She barely had time to consider his words before he started to move fast and hard against her. One of his hands slipped around her belly and pulled her tight against him. It traveled up her stomach and pinched her nipple. "Oh!"

"That's right, Caylin. Cream for me. God, yes." His thrusts came faster and harder.

Caylin had trouble keeping any thought inside her head. They all seemed to float on the wind as his body mastered hers. Surely he couldn't keep this up forever, not that she was complaining. Her body quivered around him as the rising flames continued to roar to a feverous pitch. When the next wave came, it nearly knocked her off balance as she shook hard against him. He rammed into her a few more times as he reached around to grab her chest. She felt his hands squeezing hard against her as he rode out his own orgasm.

She almost felt empty when he pulled out of her. Collapsing on the mattress beneath her, Caylin tried to still her racing heart. Lost in the haze of desire, she did not turn over right away. Griffin's arms reached for her, but she felt herself retreating slightly.

"Caylin." His voice was gruff. "Look at me."

Caylin turned around and looked up at him through the fog. "Griffin?"

"Yes, Caylin?" He looked worried.

"Can we do that again?" She grinned up at him.

He swore under his breath and scooped her up in his arms. "I was worried I had gone too far."

"That was fucking fantastic...or fantastic fucking." She

nibbled on her bottom lip.

Griffin roared with laughter. "I aim to please."

"Oh?" Her eyebrow rose curiously.

"How can I service you, my lady?" he asked her as his lips trailed kisses down her cheek. He jerked away and looked down at his arm. "Shit!"

Out of the haze, Caylin realized that her arm was also trying to get her attention. "Well, at least we got to have a little fun before. Could have been worse."

"How's that?"

"They could have caught us right in the act, and you wouldn't have been able to finish," she teased him.

"I would have wrapped it up much faster." He smacked her ass with his hand. "Get dressed. I'll see you down there."

Caylin watched him walk across her room in his naked glory. She was tempted to jump him from behind and drag him back to bed, summons be damned. Sighing, she went to retrieve her clothes. He had left long before she had restored herself. She refused to go down until she could conceal the blush that was still covering her face.

Chapter 18

When Caylin finally made her way to the meeting room, she was still worried the others would see her flushed face. Not that she should be embarrassed by what had just happened. It was definitely something she wouldn't mind repeating. Parts of her were still tingling. As she sat down at the table, she refused to look over at Griffin. She was fairly certain while he had enjoyed himself, it wasn't a life altering event for him. The same could not be said for Caylin.

Caylin waited to see what the big deal was that they were summoned so soon after the last meeting. Something had to be up. Part of her wanted to demand an explanation, mostly because she was supposed to be working on shielding herself right now, but she waited as patiently as she could. She did not have to wait long.

"Sector Eight has called for reinforcements. They wanted us to be ready to join them at the portal tonight." Campbell waved his hand over the spinning globe on the table. A black vortex appeared before them. He moved his fingers together and slid them apart to expand the image.

"What is that?" Lia asked curiously.

"We're not entirely sure." Campbell had a perplexed look

on his face.

"Looks like a mega portal." Bryce looked thoughtful. "I think we've been in one before."

"When you were in Sector Twenty?" asked Devon.

"Yeah. It's the reason why our sector disbanded." Bryce looked down at the table and shook his head. "That's bad mojo right there."

"What happened?" Caylin did not have all the pieces to the puzzle that the others did. What had happened to Sector Twenty to tear it apart? Were sectors not kept intact over the years? Caylin had always assumed once you were in one sector, that was it.

"Ten of us went in. Two of us came out." Bryce's voice was cold. "Damn shadows ripped us apart. Never saw anything like it before in my life."

"It took several sectors to destroy that portal." Campbell was solemn. "One of the largest losses ever."

Caylin nibbled on her bottom lip. So these vortexes were more dangerous than the others. That must mean something significant happened within them. They could not afford to ignore it, just because it might be dangerous. "So, Sector Eight wants our help?"

"They do. Five sectors will be working together."

"Will we destroy it?" asked Griffin.

"No. First, we study it." Campbell maximized the view further. "From what we can tell, the Craven have been drawn to this portal. We think the Revenant might be lurking somewhere inside."

"And we're *all* going?" Griffin's eyes looked over at her for the first time as his words hung in the air.

"Yes," Campbell answered.

"She's not ready for that," Griffin cut in.

"She has to be."

"So...let's be clear. When you say *she*, you are referring to me?" Caylin didn't like where this conversation was headed. If Griffin thought she was going to stay behind while everyone got in on the action, he was mistaken. He wasn't the one the Revenant had set its eyes on. She was not going to sit here and do nothing.

"She's not ready for this. If the Revenant is within the portal...." Griffin was clearly worried about her safety.

Caylin should be thrilled he cared enough for her to worry about her, but she was not an infant. She knew how to take care of herself. "I'm able to take care of myself, you know."

"Until you get impetuous," agreed Devon.

Great, so two against one. Caylin looked around at the table to see who else was on the same thought path. They all seemed to be considering his words, except one.

Bryce shook his head. "It doesn't matter how prepared any of us are, we're all in danger in that vortex. Let the Stalker do her job. Maybe she'll find the Revenant."

"Thanks for the vote of confidence." Caylin smiled at him and tried to ignore the way his eyes seemed to run slowly down her body. Bryce was a player from head to toe. She had sensed that a long time ago. The fact that he continued to undress her with his eyes should have bothered her, but Caylin knew she could use that to her advantage. She held her chest up higher, knowing he was watching her every movement. He wasn't the only one.

Griffin cleared his throat. "You know my vote."

Well, now she did. He thought he was going to make her stay here—like hell. He couldn't keep her here if he wanted to. Griffin might think because he mastered her in the bedroom that he was suddenly her keeper. Caylin felt a fury rising inside her. He did NOT get to do that. Her eyes met his, and she knew he did not mistake the anger flashing inside hers. "That's too bad. I'm not staying here, and I can take care of myself."

"Really? So, what happened last night when you decided to throw caution to the wind and touch the orb without any guidance or training?" Griffin was not backing down.

"Why focus on the negative? The second time I found out that the Revenant is having the Craven poison our food source," her voice bit out.

"But you also—"

"Apparently lost my mind afterwards. I'll make sure to keep that in check from here on out." Caylin's voice was ice cold.

Campbell took that moment to put his hands up and redirect them. "The Stalker will be there, as will the Walker. The two of them work well together. Perhaps by putting their heads together, we can find an end to this madness."

"Good. At least she believes in me." Caylin crossed her arms over her chest.

"We'll enter right here." Campbell put his finger on the globe and pointed to a grove of trees. Apparently, the vortex was in the middle of an apple farm somewhere in the middle of Illinois.

"What should we take with us?" Lia asked him.

"Any firepower we have. Speaking of firepower...." Campbell set a silver bag on the table. "Stalker, this bag is lined with hematite granules. It keeps the orb inside from detecting any activity around it. Keep it inside the bag until you are ready to use it."

"You're giving me the orb?" Caylin was surprised he trusted her with it. She knew she had overstepped her bounds the night before. Now that she had learned that the power inside could envelop her own, she had to be careful not to let it extend into her.

"It belongs with you," Campbell answered matter-of-factly. He flicked his wrist and sent the bag floating through the air before her.

"Thank you." Caylin felt humbled. The trust he was showing her, she wasn't entirely sure she deserved it. She saw that the tie around the bag was long enough for her to slide it over her neck. Caylin put it on and let the bag slide under her shirt to rest safely between her breasts. Two pairs of eyes were glued to that spot, and Caylin smirked. Men — easy targets sometimes.

Maybe that's what she needed to do, distract the men with her charms. Bryce would support her, and Griffin would toe the line just to keep Bryce from outranking him. Any minute now, she expected him to leap over the table and charge at Bryce like a stag fighting to impress his mate. The problem was, Caylin was not impressed. She was annoyed at him for acting like a possessive jackass right now, whether he realized he was doing it or not. Caylin thought about giving him a piece of her mind later, but she was afraid that would be a waste of her time. Right now, she had to focus on the task at hand.

"So, what's the plan?" Lia furthered the conversation.

"We'll be gathering here at dusk, then we'll teleport there. We'll be entering the portal in pairs."

"Why pairs?" Caylin was not looking forward to going through with anyone else. With her luck, she'd get stuck with Griffin, and right now, she was too annoyed to even want to be in the same room with him. Other women would probably feel flattered to have a man look after their well-being, but not Caylin. She was used to looking out for herself, and even though she found herself forming some kind of attachment to Griffin, she knew she could survive in a world without him too.

Nothing was ever finite, after all. Everything ebbed and flowed as change wove its magic around the world.

"We found in the past that too many going through at a time seemed to draw attention; whereas, entering a few at a time kept us off the radar," Devon explained.

"Oh, that makes sense." Caylin had never been through a portal yet, not in the waking world, so some of this was still new to her. Everyone had to start somewhere, though.

"If you want to familiarize yourself with our research on the portals, there is a binder or two in the library," suggested Lia.

Caylin nodded at her. "Thanks."

Caylin looked over at Griffin and found his face unreadable. She felt like laughing, really. When she had first come to the table, she was worried that they would suspect the relationship forming between them. Those fears had dissipated as soon as Griffin had ruffled her feathers. Was that intentional? Or did he really think she was incapable of protecting herself? Caylin did not need a savior. She had been protecting herself for quite some time, thanks to one man who believed that she was capable of more. Caylin wondered how Remie was faring. She had barely seen him the other day when she had teleported to the Ghost District. Caylin had not realized teleporting could be that easy. She made a promise to herself to check on him soon. Then he could maybe update her on the ladies she had been keeping an eye on.

Part of her felt guilty for leaving them without her protection. Maybe she could venture out to help them from time to time. She had tried to teach them to be safer, to make wiser choices, but some of them were so far gone, they saw no way out of the life they were living. Circumstances often dictated one's actions or lack of them. Caylin had tired of that cycle long ago.

The other ladies did not have the same magic running through their veins, though. Their purpose was undetectable. Hers had been ingrained in her soul for centuries. All she needed to do was stay focused, which might mean distancing herself from Griffin.

Distance. Emptiness. The two seemed implicit. Did she have to go back to that? Who said she couldn't have it all? Perhaps she could, but this moment was not the time to get lost in it. As the others rose from the table, so did Caylin. She was not going to go into the fight unprepared. Caylin didn't even say a word to anyone else as she headed for the library. It was time to put her mind to the task at hand. Portals, shadows, Revenant. Anything she could find would only help her be more successful. Throw in a little more on stronger shields, and Caylin knew she would have the recipe for success.

Chapter 19

When dusk came, Caylin was more than ready to meet the others. She hadn't moved far from the library for the rest of the day, only leaving long enough to eat. Caylin wasn't sure what Griffin's problem actually was. The fact that she was a little headstrong and sure of herself, or that he was afraid of the attachment growing between them? He had assured her there was no one else, but that didn't mean she was his one and only. Caylin had no expectations, mostly because they never really talked about any of it.

Talk was cheap. At least that's what she used to think. If they had more than a few words between them, then maybe she wouldn't have to read his mind. Not that she could read his mind. Like Caylin, he had it on lockdown. It made her wonder what he was hiding about himself. She'd seen men hide many things in their lifetimes. Speculating could make her conjure any fantasy in her head.

Caylin walked into the meeting room and waited for the others. She was sure they would be there any time now. When Griffin was the first that walked in, she was half-tempted to walk out. She couldn't even look at him. Did he know his doubt was very much like a betrayal?

"Caylin...." His voice was soft and probing

"What?" Still, she looked at the floor, the wall, anywhere but him.

"I wasn't trying to make it sound like you couldn't take care of yourself."

That wasn't even an apology. Not really. She rolled her eyes and gave him an eat shit glare. "That's nice."

He continued to dig his hole further. "You're too important to the Watch Tower."

To the Watch Tower. Got it. This had nothing to do with how he may or may not feel. That was good to know. She didn't want manufactured emotions anyway. "I see. Well, if the rest of the Watch Tower seems to think my presence is required, perhaps you should get on board with it."

"Caylin...don't be like that." His voice was a little gruff.

"Like what? Do tell? How am I being? I was good enough for a quick lay, but not good enough to fulfill my destiny?"

"Is that what you think it was?" He moved closer to her, and his hands reached around her. "Even if we had never slept together, I would be worried about you. Our souls are intertwined."

"Whether we want them to be or not?" she challenged him. Caylin didn't know why she was pushing it right now. Emotions had never been her strong suit. She had her finger on the quickdraw, ready to summon the boiling anger that had fueled her life, and she knew it.

The swoosh of air indicated that the others were arriving. Griffin removed his hands and stepped away from her. Caylin sniffed in irritation. "Right. That was the only answer I needed."

"Caylin...."

"Are we interrupting?" Lia asked.

"Not at all." Caylin moved further away from him and

refused to look at him. Closing her eyes for a brief moment, she tried to slow the thoughts in her head. It was time to focus on the task at hand, not on whether or not she had any facsimile of a relationship with Griffin. If she let her emotions rule her head right now, she might do something that would dismantle her entire existence. Like, touch an orb without thinking. She knew that was the wrong thing to have done. Being a hothead was not going to help any of them.

"Ready?" Campbell waited for the others to reply. "To the meeting point. Then we'll pair up to go in."

Caylin took a deep breath and focused on her destination. She certainly did not want to end up in cornfield miles from the orchard. That would be totally embarrassing. Whisking her hands in front of her, she zipped through the air. This time she kept her eyes open and was in awe of the swirling colors that rotated around her. The colors constantly changed each time she teleported. Part of her wondered if there was some kind of pattern behind it. What were the mechanics of it all? Was it measurable or simply an occurrence of chance?

Caylin did not have time to really get into it, though, for as the last thought trickled into her head, her feet had already touched down on the ground. She found herself surrounded by several other Guardians, most of whom she had never seen before. Her sector was standing closer to the trees already. Caylin walked over to them and stood closer to Bryce. She knew it would piss Griffin off, but she didn't care at this particular point in time. The further she was from him, the easier it would be to concentrate on the task at hand.

"Well, hello, sunshine," Bryce greeted her with a grin on his face.

If Caylin was the sort to fall for the playboy cover, she would have been intrigued with him. His dark hair was styled better than most women's, making him look like a rock star of sorts, all the way down to his glittering eyes and pout-shaped lips. Caylin had met many men like him in her lifetime, and most of them were compensating for something.

"Cut it out, Bryce," Griffin's steely voice bit out.

"What?" Bryce gave him an innocent smile. "I'm just being social."

"She's not interested." Griffin seemed to puff out even further.

Caylin rolled her eyes and fought the urge to stomp her foot. Instead, she turned to find someone else to stand next to. "Excuse me, *boys.*"

Both of them were surprised to see her walk away from them. Caylin headed over to where Lyssa stood. "Walker."

"Hello, Caylin. Are you ready?"

"Yes. I've got the orb." She gestured to the pouch hidden under her grey shirt. Caylin had dressed minimally today. Not knowing what kind of action they would get into, she wore a pair of black jeans and a grey T-shirt under a charcoal grey sweater with a hood.

"Good. And the granules are working."

"Perfectly. Thank you." Caylin nodded at her. "How about you? Are you ready?"

"As ready as anyone ever can be. We should stick together," Lyssa suggested.

"I think I'd like that." At least if she stood by Lyssa, she would not have to deal with either one of the men who were acting like children. Caylin was going to have to set Griffin straight at some point. Sex did not imply ownership. This was not the middle ages. Women were allowed to sleep with whoever they wanted to, no matter how society looked upon it.

"Good, you can pair up with me. We'll go in first."

"Ready any time you are." Caylin tried to mentally prepare herself for the Land of the Shadows. Her only experience with it was from her dream state. If it was just like her dream, she had her work cut out for her. Caylin couldn't see the portal in front of her, but from her reading, she knew this was typical. The portals were hidden from the visual realm, but they could still be felt. The closer she walked to it, the more the air around her seemed to feel pressurized, as if a heavy storm were about to roll in over her head at any moment.

Caylin had felt this many times in her life, but any time she ventured near somewhere with this feeling, she had turned around and gone the other direction. Most people had this same sensation. Whenever they were somewhere that made them feel uncomfortable, natural instinct kicked in, and they would avoid those places. Anytime the shadows came near a group of people, they always went after the ones that were most sensitive to their energy. Apparently, Caylin was one of those people, for she had sensed them for longer than she cared to remember, and she did not think this was just because she had been chosen to destroy as many of them as she could.

"Are you ready?" Lyssa looked at her as if she could read the hesitation that crossed her mind.

"Yes. We have a job to do." Too many jobs to count. Destroy the Revenant, take out the shadows and their power source, and keep the Craven from overrunning their world. Caylin's main objective was to rid the world of the puppet master who seemed to control all of the shadows from his dark perch inside the Land of the Shadows. Part of her wondered if she would recognize him if she saw him. His energy she would know immediately that she was sure of.

Caylin followed Lyssa into the portal. The minute her body fell into it, she felt like she was being tossed around the eye of a tornado. Closing her eyes, she held up her hand and cast a shield over herself, afraid of what they would fall into when they landed on the ground. When the fierce winds cut back, Caylin felt like she was free falling into an abyss.

When her feet finally touched the ground, she landed so hard she fell forward, saving herself in a small roll forward. That was probably a good thing considering that pairs of people were coming right after them. Caylin walked over to where Lyssa stood and started to look around them. The world was shades of grey all around. They were standing in the middle of what looked like a dry, cracked reservoir that hadn't seen water in quite some time. The sky above was almost white, resembling a world covered completely in cloudy smoke.

As Griffin made it through the portal, she put her emotions on lockdown. She was here to do a job, and that was what she would do. Caylin could not afford the distraction, even though his eyes sought hers out. She turned away from him before he could try to communicate any of his thoughts to her. Caylin already knew he didn't believe she could take care of herself. She would prove him wrong if it was the last thing she did.

"Look out there." Lyssa pointed to something that stood out far on the horizon.

There were large stone structures further ahead, standing near a small mountain that Caylin could barely make out. As they stood there watching it, a bolt of lightning shot down from the sky and seared the ground near the stones.

"Hmm...looks a little sketchy."

"Probably right where we need to be." Lyssa took a deep breath as if gathering her resolve.

"I'm game if you are." Caylin gave her a half-smile.

Lyssa turned around to the others. "We'll port ahead, a few at a time. Looks like there are a few places to take cover."

The decision was made quickly, and Caylin didn't turn to look at Griffin. She could feel his eyes on her skin. The man really couldn't seem to control himself. Caylin shook her head slightly and took a deep breath. When Lyssa ported, Caylin followed her. In the Land of the Shadows, if you could see where you were teleporting, or if you had been there before, teleportation was not that difficult. But, unlike their own world, the Land of the Shadows was much harder to travel inside due to all the unchartered territory. Everything on Earth they could reach just by willing it so. That will did not always apply to this realm.

"Let's do it." Caylin nodded to Lyssa. The two of them ported to just a few feet behind the first stone. Caylin was surprised to see that the structure they had seen was closer to a modern-day Stonehenge fashioned of dark black metal that shimmered even with the lack of light overhead. There were five henges total, and each one had a visible portal inside. The portals were the only hint of color in this world, which was strange in itself.

"Interesting. Color is rare down here." Lyssa stepped closer and put her hand up to feel the energy coming off the portal.

"Is that safe?" Caylin cautioned her, which in itself was pure irony. She was usually the first to head into the fray without giving much thought to her actions whatsoever.

"It's the same energy as all the other portals, but you are right to be wary. You try," Lyssa suggested.

Caylin walked closer to Lyssa and put her hand in front of the orange portal. She felt the wave of energy ebb and flow before her.

To her, the energy was different from the other portals, only because she had a piece of the puzzle that was missing to Lyssa. Caylin was looking for the Revenant. That was her number one goal. She wanted to find him more than anything else. She believed him to be the root cause of all the darkness that floated over their world, like invisible reapers to the rest of humankind. Those who were not in tune with the elements around them never saw these creatures coming. The darkness seeped into their hearts and overrode every part of their existence.

"What is our goal here?" Caylin asked her.

Lyssa looked at her thoughtfully. "We're to explore the area."

"That's fine and dandy and all that, but as you can see, there are five portals we can choose from. Which one should we start with? And what are we looking for?" Caylin wanted to make sure their missions aligned.

"Our goal is to find the Revenant." Lyssa looked back at the others. "He's a nasty prick."

"You have experience with him?" Caylin was surprised. So far, the Revenant had made it seem like he wanted to get his hands on her and her alone, but apparently, Lyssa had some experience with him too.

"I do. Not the kind I'd like to repeat, but I'm not about to let my fear hold me back." Lyssa took in a deep breath as if gathering her pure will to continue.

"Fear is for the weak. We don't have time for it. I suggest we pick the portal that resonates more with what we've come to feel from him," Caylin suggested. With him being so hell-bent on finding Caylin, she was a little worried that he might be lying in wait for her, but she couldn't afford to let that keep her down.

"Which portal do you suggest?" Lyssa asked her.

A few other Guardians had gathered around them. Caylin looked at each of them and wondered how brave they felt. So far, this vortex portal had not shown them much of a problem, but that didn't mean there wasn't something inside one of these portals that would take them out. They could become easy pickings. Caylin looked over at Lyssa. "Honestly...."

"What are you thinking, Stalker?"

"That we are in more danger with these numbers than if you and I were to just enter on our own." Caylin knew her words wouldn't make Griffin happy, but she wasn't here to keep him reassured. They were here to find the Revenant. Whether that aligned with her having a future after this point, Caylin couldn't know for sure. Nothing was ever set in stone.

"I agree, but I think it might be prudent to send a few of the Guardians into each portal. That way, they can take a look around those, while you and I go into our portal."

Lyssa walked away from the orange portal and started to put her hands in front of some of the others. Caylin did the same, but she walked in the opposite direction. There were five colors represented in the henge: orange, green, yellow, red, and blue. The orange one was giving off a few warning signs, but not enough for her to truly be concerned about entering it. That portal would be acceptable for the others, no problem, but it didn't contain the energy she was looking for. That much she knew for sure.

When she put her hand over the blue portal, Caylin felt a jolt of electricity. The energy from it did not match the darkness of the Revenant, but it was harrowing nonetheless. She turned to Lyssa. "The blue one is a trap."

"Let me feel." Lyssa walked over to the blue portal and placed her hand near it. She only held it there a few seconds before she jerked her hand away. She called to the others. "Stay out of the blue portal."

"Told you," grinned Caylin.

"It kind of feels like...." Lyssa looked as if she was looking for the right words.

"Sudden death?" suggested Caylin. She felt like if anyone went into the portal, they might be extinguished before they ever made it to the other side. Death, destruction, but still missing the darkness that seemed to corrode the air of anywhere the Revenant touched.

"Precisely. Have a go on the green one," Lyssa suggested.

"On it." Caylin walked over to the green portal and waved her fingers over it. She closed her eyes and waited for some kind of impression. The light rippled as if it sensed her movements. "This one could be interesting, but not for us. We're looking for the Revenant. He's not there."

"The others might be able to investigate this one." Lyssa looked at Caylin for agreement.

Caylin was finding this particular predicament interesting. Never one to be part of a group, here she was part of a large magical order of Guardians that were destined to restore the balance of good and evil in their world. Not only that, they were looking to her for guidance. She was the one who could hunt evil down and bring a final reckoning to him. Caylin looked around her, watching the others take in their directions with little argument.

When her eyes met Griffin's, she was surprised to see respect hidden in their depths. Had something changed? He had gone from treating her like she couldn't take care of herself to giving her space. Or was she overanalyzing everything? Potentially. Nasty habit, really. That was why it was often easier to just let go and deal with the consequences at a later time. Not the ideal way to run her life, but it had gotten her this far.

Caylin continued to the yellow portal. When her fingers came closer, she was almost sucked into it. Something was drawing her closer, but she wasn't convinced the Revenant was inside. In fact, it felt like a decoy of sorts. "I'm not sure I would trust this one either."

"I agree. Try red. I think you'll find it interesting." Lyssa nodded to the portal behind them.

Caylin approached the portal as slowly as possible. For some reason, she already knew this would be an important portal to check into. Red, like his eyes, the same crimson the shadows had within their own eyes right now. Over the years, she had seen their eyes turn from yellow to red as they continued to evolve from one stage to the next.

As her fingers drifted over the portal, she felt the chain in her necklace jerk up slightly. "This is it. I'm not sure if we will find him inside, but we will find something."

"All right. So you and me...perhaps two others?" Lyssa turned to look at the Guardians standing near them. "I need two—"

"I'll go," Griffin answered first.

Of course, he would. Caylin fought the urge to roll her eyes. When Bryce stepped forward to comment too, Caylin was actually relieved when Campbell beat him to it.

"Me too." Campbell nodded to Caylin.

"Okay. The rest of you can divide yourselves up between the orange and green portals. Stay out of the others. If you find yourself in trouble that you can't get out of, teleport out. No fight is worth a life today. Report back to the Watch Tower with what you find. We'll do the same."

Caylin heard a murmur of approval erupt around them. She was thankful that she had aligned herself with Lyssa. It was clear the Shadow Walker had earned the respect of every Guardian here. Would she be able to do that someday? If she learned to hone her skills and keep her impulses at a bare minimum?

Maybe being part of something bigger was what she had been missing all her life. She looked over at the others. "Are we ready?"

"As ready as we're going to be," Campbell replied.

"Lead the way, Caylin." Griffin's voice was soft and determined. He seemed to be getting his game face on finally.

Good. If he focused on the task at hand, then Caylin wouldn't have to worry about him getting all emotional during a fight. She was still a little worried that he might get distracted if any sign of harm came to her. Shaking off her thoughts, she prepared to enter the portal. Looking over at Lyssa, she gave her a quick nod of the head. "Let's go."

Chapter 20

The portal was not nearly as scary as the vortex they had come out of earlier. The winds were barely even felt as she zipped through them. Nevertheless, Caylin threw up a shield. She didn't want to be caught unprepared. Anything could happen on the other side, after all, with the magic that seemed to fill up the time and space around them all the time. The Guardians manipulated it to fix the balance the Craven had helped destroy on their world.

The Craven was a sect of people who dabbled in the darkest of magics. Caylin had limited experience with them, as she usually spent her time taking down the shadows. It wasn't until recently that she had seen them. That was probably when the Revenant had started to send them after her. Just before coming to the Watch Tower, Caylin was starting to become curious about them. After spending some time in the library, she had come to learn that the Craven were mortals, just like each of the Guardians. Their powers came from the elements around them too, but the way they used them was entirely different. Born corrupt and greedy, the members of the Craven were easy targets. They dwelt within the shadows, taking anything they wanted without thinking of the consequences. Long ago, their leader had stumbled upon the magic that opened up the realm of the Land of the Shadows. In doing so, it exposed their world to the darkness that came with them. It was no surprise that they continued to work for the same power and corruption. The Revenant must have promised them power beyond measure to keep them motivated.

As her feet landed on the ground, Caylin took a look around her. They appeared to be in a desert, one filled with natural light and golden sands. This was at odds with the rest of what she'd seen before. "Where are we?"

Lyssa turned to her. "I'm not sure. This doesn't look like the Land of the Shadows."

"I figured as much. Is it always monotone?" Caylin had not been able to read about every portal they had ever entered. The ones she had read about seemed to be lacking light and color of any kind.

"Not always, but this just feels different," Lyssa concluded.

"I agree. We're not there, but we're not here," Caylin whispered.

"What do you mean?" Griffin asked her.

"That something isn't right." Lyssa scanned the sands for any danger heading their way.

"We're lost in a world that's nothing like our own, yet it's not theirs either. I can't explain it. And the power here...it's not his, yet it's not good either."

His words actually surprised her. "This is what we came for. I think we should explore further."

He did? Color her surprised. Maybe he had come to realize that their job was more important than how they did or did not feel about each other. Now was not the time to muddle through those emotions. They needed to be resolved to finding out more, especially if they wanted to help others. "I agree with

Griffin. This place, it's important to the Revenant, even if he's not here right now."

"Is it possible he does come here?" asked Campbell.

Lyssa and Caylin exchanged a glance. The two of them were the only people who had experience with him. The rest of them had no idea how all-consuming the darkness was from him. It scared Caylin to think he might someday get his hooks in her. She might be strong and try to pretend fear did not exist in her, but the truth was Caylin had all the emotions typical humans had. Her anger helped mask every other emotion, but it worked double-time where fear was concerned, for sure.

She considered Campbell's question for a moment. Did the Revenant come here? She was pretty sure he did because his energy had marked the portal. Did he enter it the same way they had or was it just a remnant of his exposure here? That she could not answer. "His energy is always here, but how I'm not sure. That we have yet to determine."

"Well, shall we walk, or port?" asked Lyssa.

"I know that teleporting would be faster, but I think walking would be safer." Caylin did not want to teleport into something that could be potentially dangerous. That would not benefit any of them, especially if they were discovered because of it.

"I agree with Caylin." Again Griffin sided with her.

Caylin gave him a small smile, which seemed out of place in the world around them. The hot blazing sun in the sky was nothing compared to the sand that could eat human flesh. A shiver ran down her spine. If they did end up in a battle of any kind, they would have to keep their bodies shielded during the fight. If they fell onto this sand, it could be the end for them. Caylin wondered if this is what had happened to Sector Twenty. Bryce had not been all that forthcoming with details, and even though she had tried to look it up in research, that particular battle was not listed within the pages. Caylin could understand that, though. She imaged the details were too horrific to be written between the pages.

"Then walk, we shall." Lyssa started to move forward.

Caylin fell in behind her and tried to remind herself to breathe. She could very well be approaching impending doom. They all could die. She felt fingers brush against hers and jerked her head over to see Griffin walking by her side. His face was determined, but his eyes were soft as if he were trying to apologize for his behavior. Caylin gave him a half-smile and wrinkled her nose. She would forgive him for now, but if he did it again, she would probably lay him flat.

I won't.

Caylin blinked. Had he just spoken to her? How was that even possible? She realized in her distraction she'd let the guard over her thoughts down. Did that mean they could communicate? *Griffin?*

Yes. He smiled at her and winked slightly.

How silly she felt to be walking into who knows what with a handsome man winking at her along the way. *Be careful, Griffin.*

I will if you do.

Promise. She meant it too. Caylin would be careful. She would not allow this world to take her down. One foot in front of the other, she continued to move forward. Her fingers brushed against his every few steps. *I'm sorry, Griffin.*

I know. Me too.

Caylin knew she could be a hard ass. It wasn't her best trait, but it was what life had handed her. Her one coping mechanism, it served as a shield to keep others from hurting her. Caylin knew she had probably jumped on him without truly understanding what his concerns were. She had immediately thought he was second guessing her abilities, but that wasn't it. Not really. Caylin was still working through those things, but right now, she had to focus on the walk that seemed to take forever.

The farther they walked, the more parched she started to feel. She started to wish she had brought some water with her. Sweat poured down her face, and she was not surprised to see the others having the same problem.

"It's not even that hot." Caylin shook her head.

"It must be the elements pulling it out of us," suggested Campbell.

"If that's the case, we can't be here for too long. This place will suck us dry." Caylin looked up at Griffin and saw he was trying to conceal a grin on his face.

Get your mind out of the gutter.

Sorry, but that particular image —

Not the time or the place. Caylin could not believe he was thinking about sex at a time like this. What was wrong with him? How could he be thinking of her going down on him now? Not that the idea itself didn't hold merit. He was pretty well endowed. Caylin wouldn't mind doing that at all, but —

Now, whose mind is in the gutter? His eyes had a merry twinkle to them.

Shut it. Caylin sent him a pointed glare.

Lyssa called back to them. "We'll be there soon. Just hang in there. I think if we can just get over this hill, we'll be all right."

Caylin certainly hoped so. She didn't want to think about what else could be there instead. From here, she could see the shadowy figures moving closer. This time she realized that they weren't moving in the same direction they were. Caylin had thought they were heading toward a place ahead of them, but rather they seemed to be moving away from it.

They continued to move in silence. By the time they were closer, Caylin could see the terrain was changing slightly. The sand was drifting away slightly, changing from sand to small, gritty rocks that reminded her of a gravel road. She reached down to test them and found they stung a lot less against her flesh. So, the sand had been there to keep life from this place. Interesting. "We're a little safer here."

"Yes, but remember nothing is as it seems. Even more so in these lands," cautioned Lyssa.

"Don't worry. I don't plan on dropping my guard at any time." In fact, Caylin cast a shield around her. For some reason, she felt the added protection might be necessary.

As they continued through the rocks, they came to a path surrounded by water. Caylin looked down into its depths and shivered. The waters were dark and murky, but just beneath the surface, she could see skeletons floating to the surface. Caylin picked up one of the rocks and let it drop into the water. Large bubbles formed on the surface as the liquid sizzled, burning the rock on contact.

"Don't touch the water," warned Caylin. First sand, now water. They were clearly not going to be safe anywhere in this realm — surprise, surprise.

"Look!" Campbell directed their attention to something forming on the surface further away from them.

At first, it looked like dark oil rising from the water. As it drifted up further, it floated across the surface, an oozy pile of something that was being drawn from the depths of the water. As it moved, it continued to grow, and Caylin heard loud screams echoing inside her mind. Turning to the others, she saw they were afflicted as well. The screams were those of souls being tortured. Caylin turned and looked to the right. She saw a body writhing in agony just beneath the surface and was almost ready to dive within the depths to save the soul inside it.

Griffin grabbed her arm. "It's a trick, Caylin."

"It's not a trick, Griffin. They're feeding off of them. We have to stop this." Caylin felt liquid falling on her face and was surprised. Her hand reached up to touch her face, and she realized it wasn't sweat. Numb tears fell from her face as she realized this was a place of death and decay. There were real people under those depths, or they had been at one point or another.

"We will," he promised her. "When we bring the Revenant down, we can put an end to this."

If only it were that easy. One thing was clear, they had found another power source for the shadows. Not only were they using the obsidian stones, apparently they were using water too. And if that were the case, were they using all the elements to create newer upgraded versions of themselves? Caylin shivered as a cold wind came down around them.

"We need to head back, now!" Caylin felt the hair rise on the back of her neck. She turned around to find shadows pooling around them. If they tried to fight it out on this tiny little inlet of gravel while they were surrounded by this life-debilitating water, it was possible that none of them would make it back.

"Agreed. We'll fight another day. The next time we come in this portal, we'll teleport to the other side there." Lyssa pointed to where the water ended, and a dirt road began.

Caylin shivered slightly. She knew that road. It was burned into every inch of her mind and not something she was looking forward to at all, but she would not let fear keep her from her mission.

"Let's go." Caylin watched the others teleport out and looked around her one last time. Before she could leave, she felt something hot slice against her arm. Caylin grimaced slightly and turned to face the shadows that were surrounding her. Throwing up the brightest shield she could, she kept them off her long enough to teleport.

As Caylin teleported away, she found herself spiraling out of control. She was trying to make her way back to the Watch Tower, where Sector Fifteen would be waiting for her, but she couldn't seem to focus on the location. She continued to float around aimlessly, trying to concentrate on her mark. The pain in her arm started to emanate all through her body. She reached down to console the pain and found a wet liquid dripping from the wound. What the hell had happened to her? Shadows had never done this much damage before. Was this another form of their evolution?

Caylin winced as pain sliced through her body. She heard a loud cackle in her head and knew at once that the Revenant was trying to reach out to her. Caylin didn't think he could break into her teleportation, but at this point, anything was possible. The pain was a reminder that she was too pigheaded for her own good. She should have left with the others instead of waiting around those last few seconds.

Panic filled her. She reached out with her mind, knowing she wouldn't be able to get anywhere like this. *Griffin.* As she continued to fall through time and space, Caylin prayed that he could hear her words from so far away. *Please find me.*

Two strong arms wrapped around her and pulled her tight against him. "Always."

"Thank you," she whispered. Caylin relaxed in his arms, and the world went black around her as the rest of her energy seemed to fade.

Chapter 21

When Caylin finally woke from the darkness, she saw a very worried Griffin sitting next to her bed. She tried to call out to him, but her mouth didn't seem to work. Her lips were parched as if she hadn't had water in weeks. Squeezing her eyes shut, she tried to get a message to him the only way she knew how. *Griffin?*

His eyes flew open, and he moved closer to her. "Thank God. I thought we'd lost you."

We...not him. He spoke for the collective organization, not for himself. She tried not to feel hurt by that, but it was growing increasingly difficult each second he sat there next to her. Caylin tried to form more words with her mouth, but they just would not come. *Water.*

"We've tried that, but water seems to make you worse." Griffin reached over for a slice of cactus. "This is the only thing that seems to work."

What happened?

"You were marked by one of the shadows."

That's not the first time. Why was this different?

"We're still trying to figure that out. Right now, the best thing you can do is rest."

Rest? He had to be kidding her. She tried to push up in the bed but realized the moment her body slumped back down that his words were spot on. Caylin wasn't going to be able to do anything at the moment. Her body would not cooperate, no matter how much she wanted it to. Anger grew inside her. Why had she been so stupid? Now she would be out of commission for who knows how long.

How long have I been like this?

Griffin refused to meet her eyes. What was he hiding from her? Something was definitely wrong. Not only that, he was shutting her out of his mind completely. What had happened to make him keep his thoughts on lockdown? What didn't he want her to know? She wanted to throw something at him. Caylin settled for trying to get his attention right back on her. "Gr...ii—"

"Don't, Caylin. You'll only hurt yourself."

Then tell me what the hell is going on. Her eyes accused him of more than holding out on her. If it had been him on the other end of it, she would have told him right away. How could he keep that from her?

"You've been half-dead for almost a year now, Caylin."

What the actual fuck? She felt her heart race fast in her chest, and her breathing came in shallow gasps as panic took over her.

"Calm down, Caylin. Please." His eyes started to water.

A tear slid down his face, and Caylin felt confused by its presence. Why was he crying? She wanted to reach out to him, to console him even though she didn't understand what he was going through. Caylin calmed her breathing the best she could. *What's going on?*

You've died five times already, Caylin. Please don't die again.

I don't plan on dying. Caylin couldn't believe what he was telling her. She had died? Then what was she doing here still? When Griffin reached over to touch her, Caylin almost jerked away. Her skin was on fire the second he touched her. Writhing in pain, her eyes flew to his. He removed his hand, and she heard him curse softly.

How long do I have? If she was going to die, Caylin felt like she had the right to know. She did not remember waking up before, but if she had woken to this pain, Caylin would have begged them to kill her.

"You are *not* going to die." Griffin tensed up and pulled away again.

You're upset. Caylin surmised. She pushed past the pain to try to bring some kind of reason to the forefront of her mind.

"I can't even touch you." His face looked so tortured.

It's okay, Griffin.

"You shouldn't be comforting me. You're the one in pain." He put his head in his hands and let out a frustrated breath.

You're hurting too.

"It's nothing compared to what you're going through." He looked at a loss for words.

What she was going through? Honestly, Caylin wasn't entirely sure what she had been through since most of the time, she had been asleep. She could only imagine what they had been through. How much time had they wasted on her? What had they been doing over that time?

"There's a lot to tell you, but right now, I'm going to get the healers."

Caylin wanted to beg him to stay. For some reason, his presence brought her comfort. At the moment, she felt incredibly weak. If she had been asleep all this time, did that mean she was going to start getting better? Or did this mean something else entirely? Caylin felt gloom and doom surrounding her.

A glimmer of light flashed around her, and Caylin closed her eyes against its brightness. She couldn't understand what was going on until six pairs of hands floated above her. The healers were standing over her, sending their healing energy into her body. Caylin felt the conflict inside her as the darkness coiled like a snake ready to attack. Her stomach clenched painfully as they tried to draw the poison out.

"You're hurting her!" Griffin accused them as he fought through those that were surrounding her.

"We have to get it out of her," one of them proclaimed.

Caylin felt her arm start to burn like it was on fire. She looked over and saw that one of the healers had sliced her arm open. Caylin bit her lip as blood trickled down her arm. She wondered how many times they had bled her out before. Was that why she had died? Or was something else the culprit?

"Breathe, Stalker," another voice told her.

Had she stopped breathing? She tried to focus on taking small breaths, but the pain was almost too much to bear. Closing her eyes, she tried to keep herself awake. She wanted to remember what happened. How many times had they done this before?

Caylin.

Griffin?

Just hold on a little bit longer.

I don't think I can. It was the truth too. Sometimes death was easier to handle. This was one of those times. Caylin wasn't sure she could take much more of this. Her head pounded furiously as dizziness started to take over. She felt like she had been sliced open from the inside out. Every inch of her felt like she was on fire.

Then Caylin realized she was. Closing her eyes, she could feel the flames ripping into every inch of her body. In her semiconscious state, Caylin reverted back to a time and place that had existed long ago.

There she stood, tied to a pyre with wood stacked all around her. Caylin struggled against her restraints.

"Witch! Witch!" shouted the crowd around her.

Caylin screamed at them. "Don't do this."

"Burn her! Break the curse!" They threw rotten tomatoes at her face, and Caylin tried to dodge them.

"I didn't curse anything!" The people had blamed her for the crops failing. The summer had been scorching hot, drier than most deserts. Even if the rain would come, it would barely soothe the parched cracking lands. When they could not figure out why the rain would not come, they blamed her for it. She had married their master, she had to be the root cause, for she was the only new piece of the equation. Everything had been fine up to that point.

Caylin searched the crowd, wanting more than anything to see the pair of eyes that would help set her free, but her husband was away when the crowds had taken over the keep.

When the first one tossed the torch to the dried grass below, it caught faster than anyone could have anticipated. As the first flames touched her skin, she had screamed in agony.

It was then that Griffin broke through the crowd. He pushed past them, trying to get to her, but a few men held him just a few feet before her.

Caylin....

His words caught her attention. Her eyes flew to his, just as they had when the fires had devoured every inch of her flesh.

Don't leave me.

Never again.

I can't....

Look at me. Just look at me.

Caylin remembered the moment, tattooed on her soul for so long it had almost forgotten. Griffin had been with her at the end, to soothe her through her transition. What happened when her body had taken its last breath had been lost to her until now? His eyes filled in the blanks. She could see him gathering enough strength to push an army away from him and leap into the flames. Even though the flames melted through his flesh, he ripped her down from the pyre. His people had put the fire out around him, but he had not noticed. His agony came not from the painful burns but from the loss of the only person he had ever truly cared about. He shook as sobs took over his body.

Caylin wanted to reach out to him, to tell him it would all be okay, but the pain slicing through her was hard to push through. All she wanted was to feel his touch. To know he was all right, even though she felt like she was dying inside and out. Caylin knew he was part of the answer.

Griffin.... She turned to look for him through the people that were crowding around them. When she finally found his eyes, she tried to reach for him, but there were too many people in the way.

Just a little longer, Caylin. Hold on.

Hold me, she begged him. Please, she wanted to beg him. For him, it had been a year since they last had any kind of contact. For her, it was just like yesterday. The last thing she remembered was being angry at him for what she couldn't recall. It all seemed pointless right now. Never in this lifetime had she wanted someone to be close to her so badly.

I can't.

Please. Tears fell down her face. How she wasn't entirely sure as her body had been so parched. When Griffin saw the tears, he pushed past them and ignored the blast of light flowing around him. He gathered her in his arms and held her tightly against him.

Caylin sobbed against his chest as he cradled her head against him. His hands stroked her hair softly as he whispered sweet words in her ear, none of which she could actually make out. That didn't matter, though. His love was flowing around her, and Caylin finally understood what that meant. To sacrifice everything for something so pure, so raw, it was the highest power of the universe. He had done that for her before; she knew he would do it again.

Caylin felt him tense under her, and she realized that was exactly what was happening. Their two bodies seemed to melt together, not in body, but in mind. Their souls were coming together the way they were always meant to, without fear or reservations.

Caylin's tears dried as the beautiful white light he had always shared with her in her dreams now revolved around her. She was warm and safe in his arms, where she should have been all along. Caylin reached up to touch his face and smiled when she saw him look at her in surprise.

You're okay.

So are you.

Caylin closed her eyes when he brought his mouth down to hers. She didn't care if anyone else saw the display of affection. None of that mattered now. Her past couldn't come up and taint this moment anymore. The moment his mouth touched hers, Caylin felt lights explode behind her eyes.

She screamed as pain beyond belief ripped through her. The man kissing her — was Griffin an illusion? Did any of this exist? She tried to shove him away, but he shifted in her arms.

What's the matter, Stalker? Was it something I said?

"No, get out of my head!" she shouted. Her arms fought, her nails digging into anything tangible.

Never! the evil voice hissed in her head.

Caylin.... Griffin's voice sounded as if he were ready to give up.

There it was again. She blinked and shook her head. Two men, at once. Not at once? Was it in her head? What was going on? She was being pulled in two directions. The pain of her past was an easy target for the darkness that lured her in. She needed to fight against it. Caylin knew there could be more to life. There had to be. Her hands grabbed whatever she could reach and held onto it for her life. She pulled him closer to her, so he was just inches away from her face. *Don't give up on me, Griffin.*

His face was right in front of her. She could see every inch. The roar of anger circling inside her head told her she had chosen well. The Revenant was losing his touch, and he knew it. As the healers siphoned the rest of the poison from her system, she stared into Griffin's eyes, letting his soul lead her down the right path. When they were finished, she drifted off into a deep sleep.

Chapter 22

The next time Caylin woke up, she was in a fair amount of pain. Her head felt like a jackhammer was chipping away at it. She tried to open her eyes, but they felt like they were glued shut. Caylin moved her arms and found they were held down. What was going on? Where was she? What happened to her?

"Griffin?" she whispered.

"I'm here, Caylin," his voice answered.

The last time she had woken up, he had told her she was out for almost a year. How long was she out this time? "I can't move my arms."

"We had to tie you down. You started to attack yourself."

Why would she do that? That was crazy. What had that shadow put into her when he had attacked her in the portal? Was this what had happened to Sector Twenty? Had they gone crazy and self-destructed too, or was she the only lucky one? So many questions, all of which she would probably never have the answer to. Everything was so distorted. "I can't open my eyes."

Caylin felt a wet cloth run across her eyes, followed by Griffin's gentle touch. He worked the crust away from her lids and helped to pry her eyes open. When she could finally see, everything around her was blurry. She tried to focus, but she was having a lot of trouble doing so. "What happened?"

"We got it out of you."

"What was it?"

"The shadows left an imprint in you. It was like they injected themselves into your core," Griffin explained slowly.

Injected something into her? She remembered the pain that had sliced through her when she had tried to leave the portal. "Did I die again?" Griffin couldn't meet her eyes. Was he afraid to tell her? "Griffin, tell me."

"Two more times. We fought like hell to keep you from passing over."

Caylin couldn't even imagine what it had felt like to lose her seven times over. "I'm sorry, Griffin."

She could see him clearly now. His face was haggard as if he hadn't been taking care of himself at all.

"Untie me, please."

Griffin looked reluctant. "I've already done that five times before."

"I'm okay," Caylin promised him.

"That's what you always say, Caylin." Griffin was definitely haunted by memories they didn't seem to share. "And every time he comes back through you."

"What are you talking about?" Caylin struggled against her ties.

"The Revenant. He has his hooks in you, Caylin." Griffin ran his hands through his hair.

"You should have let me die then." Her voice was cold, unfeeling. She didn't want to exist in a world that the Revenant controlled.

"Never again." His words were filled with a bitter promise.

"Fine." Caylin closed her eyes and willed herself away from

the room. She shimmered slightly against the ties that held her tight.

"You've tried that too." He smirked at her.

Caylin sighed. She couldn't stay here. This was no way for her to live, no way for either one of them to exist. There was only one thing to do. Caylin closed her eyes and willed for the end to come. Let her die, so he could live again. A sadness erupted from inside her at the thought of never seeing his face again. Her feelings from long ago echoed around in her head, and she had trouble pushing them to the side. Caylin held her breath, hoping she could be resolved enough to finish this up.

"Caylin...what are you doing?"

She refused to answer him. Tears fell down her face as she tried to say goodbye without speaking. As she slipped out of consciousness, Caylin had no idea if she had succeeded or not.

When she woke again, Caylin found her restraints had been removed. Griffin was nowhere to be seen, which made her think she had succeeded. She was surprised to find someone else in the room in his place.

"Stalker."

"Walker?" Caylin squinted slightly. "Where am I?"

"At the Watch Tower, where I can keep a closer eye on you." She smiled at her. "Do you want a drink?"

Caylin looked at the water on the table. She wasn't sure what to think right now. Was any of this actually happening to her? That was when Caylin figured out the missing piece to the puzzle. "I don't think so. You're not who you say you are."

"What do you mean?" Lyssa's eyebrows rose curiously.

"You aren't the Shadow Walker." Caylin sat up in bed and glared at her. "What did you do with my friends, Revenant?"

Lyssa cackled momentarily before shifting into another figure completely. Darker than the darkest night, his shape was like any human's, but he didn't appear to actually have skin. A normal person had wrinkles, pores, and cracks. He was smooth, like a black marble carving. His eyes were red, but she could see black pupils inside them.

"How did you know?" he asked her curiously.

"Because Griffin would not have let me suffer so many times, no matter how much he wanted to keep me in his life. Humans don't get off on suffering. Only the wicked do." Caylin waited to see what the Revenant would do. Sadness filled her to think that the Griffin in her nightmares did not exist, even though she wanted that one in her life. Where was he? Did he worry about her? Was he upset? Was he hurt? There were so many questions rotating through her head at once, but the only thing that mattered was that she was face to face with the one being she had promised to destroy.

"Very intuitive, Stalker. No other has fought against our procedures the way you have."

Caylin knew that the Griffin she had seen all the times before was a facsimile, created by the Revenant's corruption over her mind. Her mind flashed back to when she had teleported away from the new realm. She had thought Griffin was the one who had pulled her out, but now she knew that had been a lie, a dark fantasy concocted by the very being who was enjoying her torture wherever he was keeping her.

Nothing was as it seemed. There was no telling how long she had been in this private version of hell, or what he had done to her while she was here. Caylin shivered as horrible images entered her head. The probing, prodding. She had not been awake for it, but the pain had been real as the Revenant, and his lackeys had drained everything they could from her. Caylin would not rest until he was exterminated. Even now, she was trying to come up with a way to kill him.

"Why do you want me so badly?" Caylin asked him. There was nothing to lose in doing so. Not that she was even remotely sure he would tell her the truth.

"You have been a thorn in our side for far too long."

"Liar. That's not it at all." Caylin refused to believe that. She had hardly done anything but kill a few shadows. Her job had only just begun. There had to be some other reason that they were keeping her here.

"You're right. Let's just say, you hold something important."

If the dark creature could smile, Caylin knew he would. She stood up from the bed and walked over to him. Fury raced through every inch of her body. "Let me go."

"And if I don't?" he asked her.

"I'll kill you," she threatened him. Her hair rose around her angrily, and the energy inside her started to pick up. Caylin tried to conjure anything that would destroy him, but very little would rise to the surface. They had drained her for far too long. What were they going to do with what they had taken? Was there actually something missing?

"I'm not afraid of a puny woman, Stalker."

"Then why were you looking for me?"

"The answer lies inside you." The Revenant pointed to her belly.

"What did you do?" Caylin put a hand to her stomach and worried that something could be growing inside her. How long had she been here? Had they planted a pseudo-human inside her?

"Oh, not to worry, Stalker. You've not been molested. I've no taste for human desires." His voice was taunting her.

"Then why did you kiss me?" Caylin refused to believe him. He had a desire for her, whether he wanted to admit it or not. Some day she could use that to her advantage, but today was not one of those days. Today, she chose to fight her way out of this place.

"There is darkness brewing inside you, Caylin. Darkness, you will not be able to fight once it consumes you. Then you'll be working for me."

"Never!" Caylin would not turn to the dark side, no matter how much this creature thought he could manipulate and control her. She would die first.

"Suit yourself, Stalker." The Revenant waved his hands, and several shadows entered the room. They surrounded her before she could move.

"Let go of me!" Caylin tried to fight them off, but there was nothing she could do. There were far too many of them to take on, and her body did not work the way it had before. Before she knew it, they were whisking her out of sight.

A whoosh of air pushed past her, and she realized that the shadows were teleporting her somewhere else. She tried to break free from their grip, but they held her so tight, her skin started to hurt from the bruises that were forming. When they landed on the ground, Caylin was surprised to find they had left her by herself. Something wasn't right. Why would they just let her go? None of this made any sense. The only thing she knew right now was that she would be a danger to them if she returned to the Watch Tower. Caylin sensed they would follow her wherever she went, so she would have to choose wisely, wherever she decided to go.

Reaching behind her, she was sad to feel her beloved athame was no longer in its sheath. Caylin knew she could fight without it, but it was her only connection to a time that was clearer in her mind. She closed her eyes briefly and tried to formulate a plan of action. From here on out, she would have to be one with the shadows if she were going to protect the ones who were trying to save the rest of the world. That meant she couldn't even return to the Ghost District, where Remie would welcome her with open arms. Not if she wanted to keep him safe.

Where could she hide where the shadows couldn't sense her? For now, the only place that seemed rational was somewhere farther away from the life she had created. She had only one place to go, and it was somewhere she had promised she would never return to—home.

Chapter 23

The path home was never one that was easy to travel, especially considering the circumstances for her departure. Caylin wasn't even sure home was there anymore. She turned down the alley that led to the old brick house she had known so long ago. It had been her mother's house, passed down from generation to generation. With only a small alley leading to the back entrance, Caylin continued down the old worn-down muddy path.

When she saw the house, Caylin felt her insides twist painfully. All these years, she had refused to think about what it meant that her mother had wanted to have her committed. All those years when she could have used a mother to rely on, someone to nurture her when she was bruised and broken. That was something she had tried to pretend didn't matter all those years ago, but the truth was it did. It always had. There were so many questions she had for her mother, so many things she had wondered all these years.

Caylin took a deep breath and took in the brick building before her. The red brick seemed just a little faded, but the roof looked like it had been replaced recently. The gutters were clean, something her mother had always made sure to do. Did that mean she still lived inside the two-story house? She walked up the sidewalk leading to the porch and took a deep breath. She couldn't figure out if she wanted her mom to be there still, or if she was hoping she had long gone. But if that were the case, she would have to go somewhere else.

Sticking her finger out, she pressed the doorbell and heard the haunting ding that had always been there. Holding her breath, she was unsure what would happen next. All she knew was she really had nowhere else to go. She waited there only a few seconds, seconds that felt like an eternity unto itself. When the door opened, Caylin heard a distinct gasp.

"Caylin?"

Caylin looked up, and her eyes met the face that had haunted her dreams so many times. Her mother had aged much more than decades. Her face was wrinkled and spotted with age. Her hair was pulled back into a bun at the top of her head, the blonde streaks intermingling with silver. Her mother fell to her knees and started to sob hysterically.

Caylin rushed over to her. "Mom, it's okay."

"I thought you were dead." Her mother reached out to her, and her arms held her tightly against her. The second she did, Caylin felt dripping ice enter her skin before the nails bit into her flesh. "Why can't you just die?"

Caylin pried her fingers off her and saw the dark black eyes that were peering out at her. Her mother was not herself—the shadows had taken over her. She could see that clearly now. Stepping away from her, Caylin shook her head sorrowfully. "I'm so sorry, Mom. If I had known they would come for you, I would have stopped them."

"You always were an ungrateful child," the woman hurled at her hysterically as Caylin walked away from the house.

Caylin felt tears falling down her checks as she looked at

her childhood home one last time. Sometimes you couldn't go home again. She tried to find a safe place for her to travel to, where the shadows and the Guardians would not come looking for her. There was really only one thing to do. Caylin would have to take her chances at the one place she had promised not to return to.

Whisking her hands in front of her, she put all her concentration into returning to the one place her heart ached for. She pictured him with her mind as she closed her eyes. Caylin could see him clear as day as if she had never left his side. Her heart beat fast in her chest—she was half-afraid the Watch Tower would turn her away. When she pushed past her fear, Caylin was surprised to find herself inside a bright white room.

"Hello?" she called out to the emptiness.

"Caylin?" A groggy voice answered her.

"Griffin? Where are you?" She couldn't see a thing with the white illuminating around her. The light started to dim slightly, and Caylin found herself standing inside a room, much like the one she had at Sector Fifteen.

"Caylin, is that you?" He looked up from his bed, his eyes still showing signs of sleep. Something else stirred beside him.

"What's going on, Griffin?" a female voice called out from under the blankets.

Caylin sucked in her breath. "Oh. I'm...I'm so sorry. I didn't mean to...."

Caylin closed her eyes, wishing she could disappear on the spot. If only that were possible. She was about to wave a hand in front of her when Griffin leapt from the bed and grabbed her hand to stop her.

"Don't go, Caylin."

"I'm interrupting." Tears were now free falling of their

own accord. She pulled her arm away and sent herself through time and space yet again. At least she had made it to the Watch Tower. This time, she forced her way to the only other person she trusted in this lifetime.

Caylin stood outside the meeting room of Sector Four. She heard voices inside and knocked tentatively. When the door opened, she was relieved to see the one person who might be able to help her.

"Caylin."

"I need your help, Shadow Walker," she whispered as the tears continued to fall down her face.

"Come in." Lyssa ushered her inside. "It's good to see your face. We've been looking for you ever since that day."

"I know. A lot has happened. You need to lock me up right away." All Caylin could do now was wait to see what the Watch Tower would do with her. If there was something evil brewing inside her, they were the only ones who could help her.

"Lock you up? What are you talking about, Caylin?"

"The Revenant had me," Caylin tried to explain. One word seemed to do the trick.

"I suspected as much." Lyssa gestured for her to have a seat.

"You don't want me to just sit down here, Lyssa. Do something. Bind me if you have to, but something is terribly wrong with me."

At this point, everything in her brain all came crashing down at once. Being taken from her life and tortured under duress wasn't something that she wanted to think about. It wasn't even that which made her so upset. They had taken everything from her. Her mother, even though she had been out of her life for so long, and the one glimmering hope of a future with Griffin. That was shot to hell. He had already moved on.

Everything was a mess. There was no other way to describe it. At one point in her life, Caylin had a handle on everything. Now, everything was out of her control. What was she going to do? How was she going to survive this? The bitter anger she had always held onto was weakened with defeat. This was not the woman she'd created, not the path she had carved out for herself so long ago. Was she destined to always walk alone?

"If it makes you feel better." Lyssa cast a net of light around her where she sat. "Now, tell me what's going on."

"I don't know where to start."

"Start with what you remember," Lyssa suggested patiently.

First thing first. "How do I know this is the Watch Tower?"

Lyssa looked at her with a blank stare on her face. "Wow, you've really been through something. How about you ask me something only I would know?"

"How is your daughter?" Caylin asked her. It was a trick question, really. Not something the Revenant would have probed for, because it wasn't something that Caylin found pertinent to the Shadow Walker.

"My *son* is fine. Thank you for asking." Lyssa winked at her and sat down across from her. "Anything else you'd like to know?"

"Your husband, Lincoln. How is he?" Another half-truth.

"Hunter is fine. Although the terrible threes are hitting us, so he's been trying not to pull out all his hair from chasing after our son."

Caylin let out a sigh of relief. "That's not something they would know, right?"

Lyssa smiled at her. "First you come in here and demand I tie you up, and now you're worried I am on the other side? You really can't have it both ways, Caylin."

Caylin put her head down on the table and tried to still the emotions that were ripping through her. How in the world was she going to be okay, when every piece of her felt like it had been ripped out of her chest? Caylin almost wished the Revenant had been successful in killing her. At least she wouldn't have to live this life.

Lyssa's hand reached out for hers. "It's okay, Caylin."

"It's not. They've taken *everything* from me. My family, my life, my...." Caylin stopped. She was about to say her love, but had she really known Griffin long enough to consider him that? All the time on the other side, she had felt like he was there with her. And then suddenly, she finds out that not only was he not there, he was now with someone else.

"It's okay, Caylin. Let it out. I can see you've been through quite a bit." Lyssa's blue eyes were filled with concern.

Caylin stared at them. They were the key this whole time. If she had paid more attention to Griffin, then she would have known he was just a projection. Nothing more. And she was nothing less to him. "It *is* you."

"I'm glad we've established that finally. Now, you came here for help, desperate for me to tie you down because you were afraid of what you might do to us."

"How long have I been gone?" Caylin whispered.

"Fourteen months," Lyssa answered her solemnly.

"How is that possible?" Caylin couldn't believe her life had been on pause for so long. She looked down at her hands and found they looked just as they would have if nothing had happened to her.

"With magic, even dark magic, anything is possible. When you didn't come back, we searched for you. Your light seemed to have faded. We thought you were gone," Lyssa tried to explain.

"I was, several times over. At least that was what *he* told me. I was stuck in a room, held down to the bed. He pretended to be...."

"Griffin?" suggested Lyssa.

"How did you know?" Caylin asked her suspiciously.

"Because he was devastated when you didn't come back. He's only just...."

"Moved on." Caylin's voice was hollow.

"It might seem that way, but I wouldn't put too much into that relationship. He was looking for you, and I'm pretty sure he didn't find that in her."

Caylin shook her head and looked away from Lyssa. "I went there first. They were in bed together."

Lyssa sighed. "I'm so sorry, Caylin. I know you cared about him."

"How did you know that? I never said a thing, not even to him, really."

"I have a soulmate too, Caylin. I know the signs." Lyssa patted her hand. "Don't give up on that."

"I have to, he deserves better." A tear fell down her face, and Caylin closed her eyes. "That's not important right now, though. You have to listen to me."

"I'm listening." Lyssa released her hands and nodded her head. "Go on."

"I was asleep for most of it. I'm not even sure what they did to me while I was out. At one point, the minute they touched me, I felt like my skin would melt off my bones. The water poisoned me. I couldn't eat or drink. They killed me seven times before I finally broke free."

"And how did you break free?"

"That's the thing. He just let me go. He told me I now had something dark brewing inside me. I almost thought he impregnated me, but he assured me I was not molested. I think they are going to use me to get to you all." Caylin felt guilt rise through every inch of her.

"And you came here?" Lyssa asked her.

"Not at first, but I didn't know what else to do. First, I went home thinking I could hide out from their control, but they have my mom under their thumb. She was no longer herself. I'm not even sure she was actually alive."

"They can do horribly wicked things," Lyssa interjected. "I'm sorry that happened to you. I know what it's like to get over those wounds. I was injured once; their magic sliced inside me and almost poisoned me from the inside out. I know what that's like."

"Then I went to Griffin—I didn't know what else to do. I thought he would be able to save me, but...."

"Strike two." Lyssa looked at her sadly. "I can feel your pain, Caylin. No one should hurt like that."

Caylin tried to pull her arms tight around her, but they were caught tight in the magical binding. She fought through her melancholy. "I'll be fine. I always am. It's the Watch Tower I'm worried about. I may be the weapon he wants to use against you. I figured if you could pull it out of me, you could figure out how to defeat him."

"That's not a bad idea, but what if we can't?"

"Then I need you to kill me."

"Excuse me?" Lyssa looked at her like she had lost her mind.

"I tried to kill myself, but it didn't take. I need someone to finish the job. Whatever is growing inside me needs to die." Caylin was dead serious. She did not want to be the cause of more darkness.

"I won't promise that," Lyssa told her.

"Then, I need to leave."

"Too late for that. I'm not going to let you go anywhere." Lyssa pointed to the nets that held her tight.

"You can't let me hurt you," Caylin pleaded with her.

"Don't worry. You won't. Sit tight. I'm going to get some help," Lyssa promised her.

Caylin watched her leave and tried to break free from her restraints. She should never have come here. Doing so had put them all at risk. Even now, the Revenant could be using her to find their location. How could she be so foolish? Caylin looked down at the table and felt misery swirling inside her. If they couldn't help her, Caylin didn't know what she was going to do with herself.

Chapter 24

When Lyssa returned, she was not alone. She had brought several of the other Guardians with her. Caylin could barely look at them, so deep was the shame she felt for having come to their door. The problem was if she hadn't come here, there was no telling what she would have done to the outside world. She could be equally dangerous out there. It would have been so much easier if the Revenant had just killed her.

"We've got an idea, but you're not going to like it." Lyssa's eyes met hers.

"Will it keep you all safe from whatever's lurking inside me?" Caylin asked her.

"We believe so, but it could come at a great cost to you." Lyssa was clearly not mincing words.

"That doesn't matter so much." Caylin didn't really care what happened to her. She just wanted to do what she had been put on this planet to do. Right now, she was not capable of fulfilling that destiny. Her life was not as important as keeping the darkness at bay.

"I beg to differ." Griffin had just entered the room. His eyes were bloodshot, and he was thoroughly upset.

Caylin looked away from him. Even now, she memorized

the details she had forgotten to hold onto before. She looked down at the ground. "Whatever it is, I'll do it."

"Caylin...." His voice had the air of someone who was haunted by grief. "Can we have a moment?"

The others were preparing to give them space, but Caylin put a stop to it. "There's nothing left to say. Take me where we need to go, but don't loosen these ties."

"As you wish." Lyssa waved her hand, and Caylin's body started to rise from the chair.

"You can't be serious. She doesn't even know what she's getting herself into...you have to at least tell her." Griffin was almost frantic.

"She's already faced it once before, Griffin. She can face it again." Lyssa nodded for the others to take Caylin on. "It's best if you wait here, Griffin. I think she might need some space."

"I thought she was...." Griffin sat down at the table, and his head sunk into his hands.

Caylin turned her head and saw the anguish trapped on his face. It tore her into millions of pieces inside to see him hurting, a pain that she had inevitably caused. Maybe that was what all those lifetimes had been about. As much as they were thrown together, they always seemed to be ripped apart. They were no good for each other, no matter how much they fought against it.

Caylin closed her eyes and let the Guardians levitate her through the air. She had heard Lyssa's words. They were taking her to something she had already faced before. One thing came to mind, and the last time she had been upon it, she had felt like her entire body was being ripped apart. The Altar of Azure—it had stripped away the darkness that had been bleeding through her veins. This time, it would have to take even more if they were going to break the Revenant's hold over her. Caylin almost hoped the darkness seeping through her would take her life once and for all this time. Then the Revenant would no longer have control. They would have to find another Shadow Stalker to complete the final task of removing the Revenant completely. Caylin was no longer sure she was good enough for the task.

Caylin was surprised to find they were being led down a long hallway that seemed to go nowhere. Somehow they had left Sector Four behind, that she was sure of. They must be traveling to where the Altar of Azure was housed when it was not in use.

When they finally stopped before a wooden door, Caylin shivered slightly. It looked very much like the door at Sector Fifteen. Whatever happened next would probably stay with her for the rest of her life if she continued to live after it. As the door opened, a blast of white light greeted them. While it should make her feel calm, her insides were starting to bunch up painfully. It was as if whatever was spawning inside her suspected the purpose of this room. She fought the urge to buck against the ties that bound her. Caylin squeezed her eyes shut and tried to shut out the silent screams inside her.

"Relax, Caylin." Lyssa's hand touched hers, and Caylin felt light enter her body. Lyssa waved her arms, and Caylin's clothing was reduced to her undergarments. She should have felt half-naked in front of them, but Caylin ignored it.

"Let's get this over with." Caylin clenched her teeth as they lowered her down to the altar. She felt the icy threads of light starting to twist around her. This time, they locked into her flesh like screws that held a bone into place. She screamed against the pain and closed her eyes.

The tight energy net that Lyssa had cast over her melded into the stone of the altar beneath her, attaching like it had always belonged. This time, she was sure the ties were slicing into her skin. She could feel the blood seeping from her skin, but refused to look down at it. A misty fog resonated around her, but Caylin knew she was not alone. The Guardians stood near her, their eyes closed as they sent their light into the altar beneath her.

Caylin heard them hum gently as they sent their voices to guide their light. She felt the altar send a wave of electricity through her, and her body jolted in reflex. Low chanting picked up around her as they blessed her body with their light. Caylin closed her eyes and felt something slithering inside her, almost like a snake had been trapped within. She knew it was his touch, the very thing that could bring him barreling down upon the Watch Tower.

"Get it out!" she screamed at them, as it started to thrash inside her. Tight pains ripped through her as the darkness fought against the light. The Revenant's darkness did not want to let go of its control over her. Caylin had never felt so much pain in her life. She prayed for the end if it would erase this pain from her.

But what would happen to the darkness if she went? Would it filter into one of the others? She had not thought of that before. That could have been his plan all along. Caylin tried to take a deep breath, but the spasms in her body came in quick little spurts, making it impossible to focus on anything but the devastation destroying every inch of her body. Oh, make it stop, she wanted to scream, but she bit her lip to keep from screaming out. If the Altar of Azure was the only thing that would delete the darkness that corroded her veins, then she would remain in place, holding on to life until the last drop left her body. She had very little to live for, but she didn't want her legacy to be passed on to any of the innocents in this room.

Just when she thought she could stand no more, she heard a voice whisper inside her head.

Hold on, Caylin.

Tears pooled in her eyes. What good would that do? There was nothing left on that road. He had already replaced her in his life, which was his right considering the crap she had put him through when she disappeared. That seemed to be the only thing she was good at in her life, causing pain and destruction.

Caylin? he called out to her.

Caylin refused to answer him. She didn't want him to think he needed to be here for her right now. His priorities should be somewhere else.

Answer me, damn it.

Go away. She didn't want him in her head. Caylin was trying to focus on sending the darkness back to the hell it had come from. She did not have time to deal with him. The more he reached out to her, the angrier she became.

I won't go away.

Another burst of pain shot through her, and she felt like she'd been hit with a sawed-off shotgun. Her stomach was writhing in pain as she struggled against the bonds that held her tight. She looked down and saw the blood trickling down her skin was not the bright red she expected to see. Instead, an oily black mass was sliding down her flesh and being siphoned into the altar below her. Caylin felt bile rise at the back of her throat. Was that what was making her feel so sick? Did she even have blood in her system at all? Had they turned her into one of those *things*? If she was a shadowed creation, would she have knowledge of it?

Closing her eyes, she tried to put herself in a higher place, any plateau that would help her rise above the pain that ate through every inch of her body.

Caylin?

Griffin.... There was so much she wanted to say to him. To tell him to go, to ask his forgiveness, to go jump off a bridge. Her emotions were unstable. It was not the time to tackle this particular issue, but one thought still rose from inside the depths, one that she had not ever expected. *I love you.*

At that moment, a tremor started in her body, one that she could not shake. It quickly turned into a spastic attack. Her eyes rolled back in her head as she heard an angry scream inside her that broke free from her own mouth. "No!"

"Don't listen to her. It's his control. Keep going," Lyssa ordered them.

Caylin's eyes snapped open, and she looked over at Lyssa. She tried to communicate what she could not say. They were not to stop, no matter what it took. Lyssa nodded her understanding. Something beat against her stomach, darkness wanting to eat its way out. "Don't let it go into anyone else."

"You heard her. That thing has to come out, but don't let it go anywhere but the altar."

Caylin braced herself for what had to come next. "You have to remove it."

Lyssa did not seem happy with her request. "Caylin—"

"Please. It's going to slice me open anyway, might as well get on with it." Caylin's eyes pleaded with her. She wanted this to be over once and for all. Every ounce of him had to be removed this time. If there was any left, she would never be free of him. When it was gone, then she might be able to do something else with her life. Staying here at the Watch Tower would only be an option for her if she could find a new sector to work within. Caylin was too proud to admit it, but she was suffering from more than the pain the altar was inflicting on her. She had a broken heart that might never be repaired. She had told him three words that she had never told anyone else before. He hadn't even bothered with a reply. She couldn't really blame him, though. He had moved on.

As an athame was brought over her stomach, Caylin closed her eyes and prepared for the pain that was yet to come. She felt the first slice of metal into flesh and tried to stay conscious for it, but the pain was too great. One last scream left her mouth as the dark, bubbling oily creature inside her pushed its way out. What happened next, Caylin did not know. She was lost to the dark dream world that had been her friend for far too long.

Chapter 25

When Caylin awoke next, she was inside her room at Sector Fifteen. Her entire body was raw and sore. She let her hand slide to her belly and felt the stitches that lined it. So, it hadn't been a dream this time. She tried to sit up, but none of her muscles could comply. She lay there, completely aware that she needed to use the restroom. Forcing herself to sit up, she flinched as one of the stitches pulled tight.

"What are you doing?" Griffin entered the room and gave her a shake of his head. "You should be resting."

"What are you doing here?" she asked him as she tried to rise from the bed.

"Caylin, stop. You're going to hurt yourself."

"Then help me, for fuck's sake. I have to pee." She ignored the mortified blush that rushed to her face.

Griffin rushed over, and when she thought he was going to help her walk to the restroom, he scooped her up in his arms. Her heart beat in her chest, just being near him. How was this even fair? She closed her eyes and refused to look at him as he carried her to the toilet.

"Hang on here," he suggested.

Caylin was thankful that the sink was close enough to the

toilet to support her weight. "A little privacy, please?"

"Of course." Griffin stepped out of the room, but she could tell he didn't go very far.

Caylin did her best to take care of business without making a mess. When she was done and made sure her clothing was back in the proper place, she called out for him. "Would you mind helping me back to bed now?"

Griffin stepped into the bathroom with a slightly lecherous grin on his face. "I can do that."

Caylin looked away from him, now feeling uncomfortable around him. When he scooped her up in his arms, her eyes met his. Caylin could not look away, no matter how hard she tried. The message inside was lost on her. She had given up mind reading a long time ago, and at this moment, she had every part of herself on lockdown. She did not want him to know the pain that had settled in her heart. When other people knew her weaknesses, it only served to further her self-destruction. The longer she looked in his eyes, the more pain she felt. She didn't want to see the light inside them. It only reminded her of everything she had lost. Closing her eyes, she fought the wave of sadness that rippled through her. It was clear, now more than ever, that she could not stay here, not when the one thing she wanted was so close yet so far out of her reach.

When he lowered her to the bed, Caylin whispered, "Thank you."

"Any time. Do you need anything? Are you hungry?"

"I'm sure you have other things to attend to. Someone else can help me." She wanted to shoe him away.

"I'm not going anywhere." His voice was soft, yet firm at the same time. "And since you can't move very far, you're stuck with me."

"Damn it," she muttered.

He chuckled at her anger. "That's my girl."

"I'm not *your* girl." Tears fell down her face, the traitorous bastards.

"Caylin...." His voice was soft as his mouth kissed the tears off her face.

"Stop it, Griffin. We're not...." She couldn't even finish the sentence, mostly because they had never determined they were together in the first place. There had been no promises between them, only a passion that had sparked the first time she laid eyes on him. The past was a distant memory, each life, one right after the other. All of those had ended with pain and misery. If there was a chance that it would turn out different for him this time around, he should take it. Caylin was quite prepared to live a solitary life.

"I thought you were dead, Caylin. Do you even know what that did to me?"

Her eyes met his, and she saw the pain shuttered inside them as if he were still mourning her loss. Part of her wanted to throw the woman in his bed in his face just to keep him distracted from whatever it was he was trying to achieve here.

"I was dead."

"What?"

"Technically, seven times over, but they just wouldn't let me go." Would the shock factor get him to change the subject? If her torturous treatment would get him to focus on something else, then she would keep it going that route.

"*Caylin.*"

"I'm alive, Griffin. At least I think I am. Is this a dream?" she asked him. At this point, she wasn't really sure where reality existed. Too many things had happened in the past year for her to really know for sure.

"No, this isn't a dream."

"What happened on the altar?" Caylin asked him.

"You told me you loved me," he answered her matter-of-factly.

Caylin sighed and tried to turn the conversation around. She didn't need to be reminded of her moment of weakness. It hurt far too much. "What happened when they cut me open, Griffin? I don't remember what happened after."

"From what Lyssa said, something like a shadow was sucked out of you."

"Did the altar take it?" Caylin prayed that the creature did not take over anyone else. If it did, she would never forgive herself.

"Yes, and it cracked in two right after."

"Will they be able to fix it?" Caylin asked him. What would they do if it happened again? The Revenant could try to take over any of them at any time. His magic was far more powerful than they had assumed at first. To bring him down, it would take an entire army.

"I hope not. That torture chamber needs to be recycled to whichever hell it came from."

"I'm fine, Griffin. There are far greater things you should worry about."

"But it's my job to worry about you, Caylin." He stroked her cheek with his hand.

"Why?" she asked him. Did she really want to know the answer to that? Perhaps it was guilt, a personal assignment. All of those things were rational. Though, the answer he gave her made absolutely no sense to her considering the circumstances of their relationship.

"Because I love you, Caylin. For all eternity."

"What about the other woman?"

"She ceased to exist the moment you came back into my

life."

His mouth was now very close to hers, so close she would only have to move an inch or so to feel its taste upon her lips. She wanted to, but her heart was fragile. Caylin was not used to feeling so raw and exposed. He bridged the gap and kissed her gently. Something happened, something Caylin did not expect. A peaceful feeling unfurled inside her, like a gentle rose opening its petals to the light of the sun above. Natural wonders were nothing compared to the love that she felt traveling through her. He loved her, and with his love, Caylin felt anything could be possible.

When he removed his mouth from hers, his head rested against her forehead; a lifetime of sadness oozed from inside her. To feel something so cleansing and pure, was at odds with the darkness that had touched every part of her life. Tears poured from her eyes. They were the tears of a daughter who had to survive without a mother who cared for her. They were the tears of a young woman being ripped into tiny pieces, segmented over and over any time she gave a part of herself away just to survive. They were the tears of a woman too cold and hard to realize that love was one of the most powerful emotions that existed. No darkness could taint it when it was nurtured enough to grow strong. Caylin realized everything she had fought so hard against her entire life was right here in her arms, and while she was terrified of what that meant for her future, she found strength in his arms as he pulled her gently into them.

She sobbed uncontrollably against his chest. If he only knew how hard it was to imagine that anyone could love her when she had never been able to manufacture that feeling for herself.

"Shhh," he soothed her as he stroked her hair gently.

"I don't deserve this." Caylin tried to push him away from

her.

"My love?" Griffin asked her.

"Any love." Caylin sniffled and tried to stop the tears. Her stomach started to hurt slightly from crying so hard.

"Stop that right now. I've never seen someone more pigheaded and resolved than you."

Caylin snorted. "Right."

"You put your life on the line just to protect us all, Caylin. You knew what you were walking into when you went to the altar."

"Honestly, I hoped that I would die. How is that strong?" Caylin challenged him. Death had never been something she welcomed before. Caylin had been a fighter, but the Revenant had sunk his teeth into her body, and his hold had made her a weakened version of herself. She had very little fight left.

"But, you didn't." He pulled her closer, careful not to hurt her stitches. "Get some rest, Caylin. You're still healing."

She felt his white light surrounding her again and snuggled against him. Caylin had missed his energy, his touch. She hadn't thought she would ever feel him again, but here he was. Or was he? Caylin pinched him hard on the arm

"Ouch!" he complained. "What was that for?"

"To make sure you were real this time."

"This time?" he asked her curiously.

"For the first year, you were by my side, trying to bring me back from oblivion, but it wasn't you. It was him."

"I couldn't find you, Caylin." His voice seemed tortured, even now.

"I'm here, Griffin." She rubbed her face against his chest.

"You better stay here, Caylin. I can't lose you again."

"I know."

And she did know. Caylin never wanted to lose him either.

Unfortunately, she couldn't stay here in the safety of his arms forever. The Revenant was still out there, and Caylin knew how to defeat him. It had been right there in front of her the whole time. She just hadn't recognized it. She would have to heal before she could even attempt the next leg of the journey. For now, though, she would stay in the safety of his arms. Her eyes drifted shut as a slow yawn worked its way out of her mouth. She fell asleep with the steady beat of his heart, reminding her that the flesh and blood beneath her was the man she had fallen deeply in love with no matter how hard she had fought against it.

Chapter 26

Time turned slowly for Caylin as she tried to recover from her wounds. The healers at the Watch Tower had done as much as possible to bring relief from the pains. Her stomach wound was healing well—it was the rips and tears from the shadowy substance that refused to cooperate with her treatments. It made sense that something so corrupt could corrode the physical body if taken in too long. Caylin had been taking it in for over a year, an experiment to human frailty that the Revenant had taken great pleasure in conducting.

A firebolt shot over her head, and Caylin ducked. It would have been far easier to deflect it if her muscles weren't so stiff. Even with the energy massages she had been getting, Caylin was having trouble rediscovering movement without pain. She pushed through it, though, because her destiny had not yet been fulfilled.

"Better," Griffin complimented her.

Caylin smiled weakly. He had not left her side since she had come back. That was three months ago. Even when the others had gone out on their missions, Griffin was loathed to leave her. Someday she would have to shove him out the door. During the day, they trained together, until Caylin met her physical limits. At night she slept in his arms, but he never made a move towards her sexually. She was starting to get frustrated. Her body still missed his touch. Part of her wondered if he was no longer attracted to her. With everything she had been through, Caylin was no longer the same woman he had met earlier. The way they had clashed together was a magnetic pull. Now it was like they had been married for thirty years, comfortable to be around each other without the drive to perform.

Caylin sighed. She missed the anger. It had fueled her so easily that doing what was required of her had been so much easier, but the Revenant had broken her in ways she might never recover from. She knew how to defeat him, but getting there was half the problem. There would be many shadows along the way, and Caylin would need the stamina to fight them. Her fear was that she had lost her spunk.

"What's wrong, Caylin?"

"Nothing." Maybe if they would just put her into the fray, something would come back to her. She needed the spark, the flame that was extinguished.

"Liar," he baited her. It was like he was trying to pick a fight, something that should have brought her anger to the forefront of her mind.

"I think I need a break," she deflected. Caylin looked down at the floor with her shoulders slumped over. Tears rose without her permission.

"I've got an idea." Griffin looked reflective.

"What?" Caylin was half afraid to hear his next words.

"Why don't you go visit Remie for a little bit?"

"What?" Did he want her to leave him? Was he sending her away?

"I think you could use a break."

What he meant was he could use a break, and that knowledge

made her feel guilty for keeping him attached too closely to her side. He was right. Caylin needed to return to her roots if she were going to find herself again. She hadn't heard the Revenant in her head since the Altar of Azure had ripped the darkness from her body. Still, she felt like a kicked puppy being sent to a dog pound. "You mean you need a break, right?"

"We're out of sync, Caylin." He looked as if he had been debating these words for quite some time.

"We shouldn't have to fight this hard to be around each other, Griffin. I know you love me, but is it enough?" she asked him. They had suffered horrible heartache this time around. Losing each other when they had barely gotten to know each other had almost broken them. And now that they had returned to each other, there was a gentle love between them, but Caylin was afraid that might not be enough. She was not the woman he had met a year ago. That woman could easily have held his attention. This one, she was only a facsimile of herself.

"I don't want you to go, but I can't keep you here. Not like this. You're a caged bird, and I fear you're dying a little more each day that I keep you here."

Caylin felt a tear fall down her face. "Are you saying we're over?"

"No. I don't plan on going anywhere, Caylin. I'll be here when you're ready, but you need to find yourself again."

Caylin wanted to beg him to make her stay, but she knew the words would never leave her mouth. Not because she wanted to stay, but because she felt he wanted her to go. She resolved herself to the regret that had floated up between them. He was right. This was not enough. "Fine."

"Caylin, don't be like that." He stepped toward her as if reading between the lines she hadn't bothered to throw up.

Caylin put her hand up. "Take care of yourself, Griffin."

"I'll check in with you soon, Caylin." His promise was bittersweet because just checking in with her wouldn't be enough for Caylin. She wanted so much more, but she was too tired to fight for it right now.

Caylin didn't even wait to say goodbye. She waved her hand in the air and conjured the magic that would teleport her back to the Ghost District. As she traveled through the air, she was half afraid some unknown entity would reach out for her. The last time she had traveled by herself, that was exactly what had happened. She sighed in relief when her feet touched down outside the old rundown tenement building that she had shared with Remie so long ago.

It had been a lifetime, it seemed, since the last time she had entered this space. Would Remie even want her here? She opened the door and walked up to the door where she had spent several years of her life. Knocking on the door, she stood outside it, waiting to see if he would grant her entrance. When the door did not open, a cold sadness filled her heart. Even this was hard for her, coming back to the darkest part of her life and feeling as if she were completely shut out from it.

"You look well," a soft voice greeted her from behind.

"Remie...." She turned slowly, almost afraid for the look that would be plastered on his face. Would he treat her differently now too? When she looked up at his face, she saw a grin plastered across it. It warmed her heart to see it.

"Let's go inside, shall we?" He waved his hand and the door opened for them.

Caylin sighed in relief. It was possible that some things had not changed. When she stepped inside, a wave of memories started to rotate inside her head. The first time she had come here, Remie had patched her up from a knife wound on the inside of her thigh. Her pimp had paired her up with a man who was particularly fond of inflicting pain on women. Having a higher pain tolerance, Caylin had barely fought the man off, which had enraged him beyond belief. If Remie had not intervened, the man would have killed her. Caylin had been prepared to die.

A tear fell down her face as she sat down at the table they had shared many a meal at. "Why do things have to change so much?"

"Change is constant, Caylin. It is always happening. Nothing ever stays the same." He sat down next to her and conjured a pot of tea with two cups. He poured the tea and handed one to her.

"Thank you." Caylin stared down at her tea. "I feel like I've lost myself, Remie."

"We all get lost from time to time, Caylin."

"I can't afford to lose anymore, Remie. He's still out there." Caylin clenched one of her hands into a fist. Where was the anger? Vengeance, revenge, they should be floating inside her. Instead, Caylin felt numb, as if the only emotion she had left was an even keel version of herself. There was no way she could face the Revenant like this. She would put everyone at risk if she did.

"He is always out there, Caylin." Remie shrugged his shoulders. "The darkness is as it ever was."

"But, it grows stronger."

"That is not your fault," Remie assured her.

"Isn't it? I was there. He had me for a year, Remie. Why didn't I take him out when I had the chance?" There it was. The guilt. Her constant companion that kept her trapped inside its misery. It was a horrible cycle that she could not seem to change.

"Because it was not the time or the place. You have another

challenge to master before you see him again," Remie said thoughtfully.

"And what is that?"

"Remembering who you are. I think this might help."

Remie snapped his fingers to retrieve something else. The second the metal clunked down on the table, Caylin gasped.

"Asodio! Where did you find it?"

"It found me. The day you left." Remie's eyes had grown serious. "I knew something horrible had happened to you if Asodio had left your side."

"I was afraid he had corrupted it." Caylin reached out to touch the athame and felt the gentle hum of purple light touch her fingertips. Asodio...the athame was a symbol of who she had become, the woman with enough fight to bring down a house full of shadows.

"The Revenant could never touch it. This athame works only for one person. I have only been its keeper. The funny thing is, even throughout the time you were gone, Asodio never stopped glowing. That's how I knew you were still alive."

"No one else did." Caylin let her fingers slide over the metal.

"Well, not everyone knows you the way I do." He put his hand over hers. "I'm glad you're back now, Caylin."

"I'm not staying long, Remie," she cautioned him. Caylin didn't want him to make any assumptions. She and Griffin were taking some space, but Caylin knew she would run right back to his arms when she had found herself again if his arms were still there to welcome her.

"I know, Caylin. Your destiny was never here. I just helped it along." His smile was sad. "We've got work to do. Get some rest. Tonight, we hunt."

Caylin nodded to him and rose from the table. She held

Asodio in her hands as she left his apartment. The gentle hum felt so much like a beacon, calling her in from the storm. Tonight, she would get back a part of herself if it killed her.

Chapter 27

Caylin found her apartment was pretty much the way she had left it. A cover of dust seemed to float everywhere she looked. She went to the closet and retrieved bedding that smelled as fresh as the moment she had packed it away. Caylin was thankful for that. Trying to sleep on something covered in dust and mildew was not something she would look forward to. When she made the bed, she was finally ready to get some rest.

She placed Asodio on the floor beneath her bed and tried to get her mind to shut off. That was the problem with brains; they tended to have a mind of their own, especially when it was time to get some sleep. She contemplated her life, where it had gone over the past two years. First, she had found a purpose — to bring down the lead of the dark chaos that had fallen over their world. In doing so, Caylin had met the one man who had been plaguing her dreams for far longer than she cared to admit. Then everything fell to crap because one being decided to take everything she had worked for away from her.

Revenant, destroyer of peace, a wrathful creature who wanted to create a world where his shadows could reign supreme — it was time to have him meet his maker. Anger started to boil inside her, for all that she had lost, all that she had yet to find deep within herself. She would never let any living thing take her will away from her again. Tonight, she would retrieve the part of herself that had been missing far too long—her will to fight.

As Caylin slipped into sleep, she was surrounded by a white light, the same light that had blanketed her over the past few months. Griffin was not with her, but yet she felt his touch as if he were. Her voice called out to him before her brain could stop her. *Griffin.*

I'm here, Caylin.

As if she summoned him into her dream, he materialized before her. His rugged face wore a half-smile as if he had been waiting for her to call him. Caylin knew she was supposed to be taking space, to find who she was without depending on his presence. He needed to have some space to discover what he needed in life too. The problem was, no matter how much she focused on tearing down the Revenant and its cronies, she was still thinking of him far too much, and that was unfair to him. Even in her sleep, she fought the resolve to let him be.

Please don't give up on me.

Never.

His hand reached out and stroked her face. Caylin closed her eyes and sighed softly. His mouth came down to hers, and Caylin melted against him. The moment she did, Caylin fell into a dreamless sleep.

When Caylin woke, she felt a heat beside her as if his energy had held her tight while she slept. Even now, she knew his thoughts were of her. Caylin took a deep breath and rose from the bed. Her joints hurt a little, but they had improved a lot since she had come back from her captivity. Tonight, she would shake the dust off and find a little piece of herself.

Dressing in all black, Caylin pulled her hair back tight behind her head. She looked at the makeup on the stand and gave herself a quick makeover. Tonight, she would be the dark raven who hunted the beasts of the streets, whichever they happened to be. It was time to get back to her roots. That was the only way she could find her way to the other shores. With smoky eyes and ruby lips, Caylin scowled in the mirror. She reached for Asodio and held it in front of her. It glowed in her hands, and Caylin took in its light. Tonight, she was on the prowl. "Look out, world. Something wicked this way comes."

Caylin teleported to Remie's apartment and saw he was already up and preparing for the fight.

"Where to, Remie?"

"B-street."

"Vick's domain?" Her eyebrows rose curiously. "Is he up to his old games?"

"He's got a few new ones now." Remie's nose seemed to twitch as his lips curled into a wicked snarl. "Bout damn time, we take him down, especially considering his new employers."

Vick was one of the pimps of the backstreets. He specialized in fetish life, often making his prostitutes into slaves to anyone who would pay. When they took them under their wings, very little was left when they returned. "I thought we already dealt with him."

"We had until the Craven entered the mix."

"Craven?" Caylin felt her blood boil. They were also on her list. "How many are there?"

"Ten in all, I believe. You up for the challenge?"

"Are you kidding me? That's child's play." Caylin winked at him. She didn't admit to him that it had been a long time since she had actually attacked any living thing. Sparring with Griffin had been different. She knew he was holding back a little each time. That would not help her get back to the way she'd been years before. It was time to jump into the danger zone. Remie was the only living being that believed she could. He had helped create her, after all.

"Good. 'Bout time they stopped coddling you."

Caylin gave him the evil eye. "I'm not coddled."

"Aren't you?" he challenged.

In so many ways, he was right, but she wasn't going to admit that anytime soon. "Porting?"

"Unless you want to take the long road." He half-smiled at her.

"No need to do that if we can cut some corners. Last one there has to take the easy shot." Caylin whisked herself through the air and teleported to B-street. She was standing in the alley just outside Vick's parlor. Two men were guarding the building from intruders.

Remie landed right beside her and shook his head. "I'm not taking the easy shot."

"You lost," she challenged him.

"Says you," he grumbled. Even though he was being slightly snarky, Caylin could tell he was in a good mood.

"You didn't let me win, did you?" Caylin asked him curiously.

"Hell no. Have I ever gone easy on you?"

Caylin remembered back to her very first fight with Remie. Even though she had struggled against her attacker, Remie had refused to help her. His reasoning had been that she would have to learn how to fight for herself. If she always relied on someone else, she would never find the strength and determination she needed to survive in the outside world. At the time, Caylin had no idea he was really getting her ready for a life filled with infinite possibilities.

Caylin heard a scream come from inside the parlor. Her hand gripped Asodio, and a bright flash of red passed behind her eyes. This was what had been missing. She sprung into action, not caring whether the two men at the door notified the occupants inside that they had visitors.

"You're jumping the gun, Caylin," Remie called after her.

"So, sue me." Caylin stood before the men and waited to see who would be the first to take her on.

"Don't worry, Lou. I've got her." The smaller one cracked his knuckles together and sneered at her slightly. "Why don't you put the sword down, honey, before you hurt yourself?"

Caylin chuckled at him. "Why don't you come and get it?"

"Oh, she's got a little bark." One side of his mouth turned up. "I think I'm going to enjoy this."

"I seriously doubt it," Remie called from behind them. He still hadn't moved from his perch, the lazy bastard.

Caylin waited for the man to attack. When he lunged at her, she sidestepped him and slammed the hilt of her sword into his back. He roared and turned to face her. His face was filled with fury when he grabbed her arm. Caylin smiled at him and held her chin up. When their eyes met, Caylin saw that he thought he had the upper hand. She summoned every inch of the energy that had been dormant inside her. Her arm started to glow bright orange, like a blade that had been forged in flames.

The man yanked his hand away, screaming in pain. "What the fuck?!"

"Haven't you learned it's not polite to put your hands on others?" Caylin taunted him. At this point, the other man reached from behind her and pulled her tight against him. Caylin winced as his grip was tight against her healing stomach. A wave of pain raced through her, but Caylin refused to buckle under it. This was why she had come here, after all. The other man tried to pull Asodio from her hands at the same time.

Caylin focused all her energy into a small ball inside her. It grew within seconds, creating a large sphere of crackling energy. She waited until they thought they had the upper hand. Caylin went limp in his arms and heard the chuckle behind her ear.

"That's right, be a good girl now." His breath was at her neck now as his hand reached up to grope her chest.

"I wouldn't do that if I were you," Remie tried to caution him.

It was too late to take any warning into consideration. Her hair crackled around her as the power grew within her. One small burst of light turned into a loud explosion as the powerful burst left her body and sent the two men flying into the air. Their bodies slammed to the ground, and their eyes rolled back in their heads.

"You coming, or am I doing all the work?" Caylin called to Remie.

"God, I missed you." His eyes were filled with admiration for her.

"If you're done crushing, it's time to keep moving." A spark had come back into her. Caylin was ready to burn this place down and bring Vick to his knees. This time, he would be the one begging for mercy. Maybe she'd let his women help.

"After you, my lady." Remie's hands waved before him in a grand bow.

Caylin shook her head as she pushed the doors open. The two men hadn't really given her a second thought when she'd walked up to them. That meant they hadn't even bothered to warn the occupants. This was definitely going to be interesting.

As she walked down the darkened hallways, Caylin was reminded of a time and place she thought no longer existed inside her. Vick had not been in charge of the parlor at the time, but Caylin had been here before. She remembered the dungeons below their feet, where the women were kept in the worst living conditions. They slept in their own filth and never saw the light of day unless they were summoned to be used for the night. Caylin knew the only reason she had gotten out herself was that Remie had posed as a prospective John. The money he had paid for her had allowed him to take her off the property. At the time, she had never understood why he would take such a risk. Now she understood it. When the cause was just, anything was worth the cost.

As she made her way to the blue room, Caylin saw Vick sitting at a table with three women nearby. Two of them recognized Caylin, but they averted their eyes.

"Well, well, what do we have here?" Vick tapped the table with one hand and pushed a button underneath with the other.

"Vick." Caylin nodded to him.

"What brings you to my humble abode?" he asked them.

"You do." Caylin tilted her head and waited to see how many people Vick had summoned. She was no fool. She knew his cronies lurked in the shadows. Some of them were more comfortable there.

"I see. And just what can I do for you?"

Caylin turned to look at Remie. "What do you think, Remie? Left or right?"

Remie looked as if he were trying to decide the answer. Caylin shook her head and swung Asodio through the air, slicing Vick's hands from his body.

"What the fuck?!" The man writhed in pain and convulsed before her.

"I was still thinking," Remie chided her.

"You took too long." Caylin reached forward and slammed

Vick's head on the table. She waved her hands, and his hands flew back to his arms, reattaching themselves as if nothing had ever happened.

"What the hell?" Vick stopped and looked down at his hands. His fingers moved one at a time. He turned to her and shook a finger. "What did you do?"

"Something wrong?" she asked him. "Looks like we have company, Remie."

Three men had come up from the dungeons, and four more had teleported in.

"Aw...only seven?"

"They could have at least given us an even number. Now we'll have to share one." Caylin sighed in disappointment.

In the next few moments, the room was filled with so much activity that Caylin had trouble keeping track of it. Her reflexes seemed to return as if they were back to the second nature they had always been. The first to fall were the three men who thought their physical strength would get them out of this mess. Even with the guns they carried, they were no match for the fury that was rising deep within her. White-hot light seared through her as an angry red started to grow. The two colors wrapped around each other, creating a new breed of champion. Love for the women who had suffered beneath her feet fed the fury that any man thought they could do whatever they wanted without consequence.

When only two Craven remained, Caylin pouted. "Only two left? I thought you promised me a challenge, Remie."

He smirked at her. "I may have over-estimated."

"Men!" Caylin rolled her eyes. The two Craven were conspiring together, and Caylin knew they had to take them down before they summoned more. If they weren't careful, they would summon....

"Well, shit."

"I think you spoke too soon." Remie winked at her as he dispatched the first shadow that was creeping into the room.

Caylin sent a bolt of lightning into the closest man and watched as he writhed in pain. The orb around his neck exploded, taking him with it. She walked over to the other man and got right in his face. With Asodio at his neck, the man refused to move. "You tell him we're coming for him."

"You can't defeat him." The Craven smiled darkly at her.

"Watch me!" She slammed her fist in his face, knocking him unconscious.

Caylin turned to face the shadows now surrounding them. Her hair rose around her, the static electricity flowing through every pore of her body. For the first time in a long time, Caylin felt as if she might be able to carry on. Nothing and no one was going to hold her back. Anger rose inside her as she thought about the desolation these creatures had caused. She took it out on each and every one of them. Sharp bursts of light erupted around her, taking out the rest of the shadows. They incinerated into dark ash on the floor.

"Hmm...why do I think we're forgetting something?" She saw Vick cowering under the table. "Oh, right. The cow shit under the table. Should we take out the trash, Remie?"

"I still think he looked better without his hands." He shrugged his shoulders.

"Hmm...maybe so."

At that moment, Vick knocked the table over and tried to make it to the door. Caylin knew she could take him out, but she didn't feel the need to. She turned to Remie. "You can have him."

Remie gave her a gleeful smile. "Oh, goodie."

Caylin walked away from him and headed down to the

dungeons. When she looked through the rooms, she found three women who were terrified of what might happen next. Caylin opened the bars and waited to see if they would come out. When they didn't move, Caylin knew they were afraid of the consequences. "Ladies, I regret to inform you that you are now unemployed. The benefits of such start immediately."

"Unemployed," whispered one of the girls. She looked to be fifteen, which made Caylin want to kill Vick all over again.

"Yes. Now, get the others and find Madeline on Sixteenth. I'm sure she will help you find your way."

"Is he...?"

"Gone? Yes, and he won't be coming back from that hell any time soon," Caylin promised her.

Caylin smiled as the girls leapt from their prisons. God, she'd missed this. Maybe she wasn't meant to spend the rest of her life within the Watch Tower's walls.

As if Remie understood her thoughts, he put his hand on her shoulder. "You have to go back."

"I know. There is still so much left undone." She smiled. "Thank you, Remie."

"For what?"

"For helping me remember who I am." She turned around and kissed him on the cheek.

"You're leaving again?"

"Yes, but I will come back and visit more often. I promise."

"Good luck, Caylin."

Caylin nodded at him and stepped back. She knew Remie would clean up the mess here. It would look as if no one had ever been here by the time he was done. Maybe he would burn the place down. That would certainly make it harder to use for the same purposes again.

She put Asodio in its sheath and waved her hands to return

back to where she truly belonged.

Chapter 28

When Caylin's feet landed on the floor, she walked over to where Griffin was sleeping in his bed. She smiled to herself. He had no idea what he was about to get up to, but it was about time she made some changes.

Peeling the clothes from her body, she walked across the cold floor naked as the day she was born. She stood over him, waiting to see if he would wake. When he did not, Caylin pulled the covers away from his body. He stirred in his sleep, and his eyes opened.

When he saw her standing over him, his eyes roamed over her body. "Caylin...what are you...?"

"Doing what I should have done a long time ago."

She ran a finger along his stomach and relished the way it shook beneath her. Climbing into the bed, she brought her lips down to his as she held herself over him. Her kiss was tentative at first, as she tried to gauge whether he wanted her to continue or if he would push her away. He had been so considerate of her recovery that he had barely even touched her.

Caylin was surprised to find his lips hard against hers. Yes, he was definitely interested. She plunged her tongue into his mouth, and heat started to rise inside her as their tongues fought for control. When she broke the kiss, her heart was already racing.

"Caylin...."

He was still trying to be the gentleman, but Caylin didn't need a gentleman. She wanted him wild and wicked beneath her as she took every inch of him into her body. The last time they had been together, he had been the one to take what he wanted, and she had loved every minute of it, but right here, right now, this was for her.

"Do you trust me, Griffin?"

"Yes, of course, I do."

"Good." She gave him a wicked smile. "I intend to be very bad...."

He shivered beneath her as the thrill of her words shook through him. "I'm all yours."

"Yes...you are. And I'm going to make sure you never forget it." She moved down to kiss him again, and this time he tried to wrap his arms around her. "Ah-ah. This is my turn."

Caylin conjured a white rope that slowly wrapped around his right wrist and tied it to the post of the bed.

"Caylin...what are you doing?"

"You said you trust me, right?" She reached down and bit his left nipple. Her whole body shivered in anticipation as she did his. "I think you're going to like this, Griffin."

"Oh, I'm pretty sure I already do." He looked down at the erection that was trying to push through his briefs.

"Good, because I intend to take good care of you. After I take care of myself." She licked her lips and taunted him slightly.

His body went taut just imagining what her words might mean. He let her tie his other arm to the bed and waited patiently.

"Hmm...so where do I start?" Caylin whispered in his ear.

Nibbling on it carefully, she was debating what her next move should be. The first thing she would need to do was remove the rest of his clothes. "I think here might be a good place."

Her hand slid down his stomach, and he clenched against her touch.

"You like that, don't you?"

Her fingers massaged his stomach right before they slipped beneath the bands of his briefs. When they brushed against the velvet tip of his cock, she bit his ear again. "So soft and hard at the same time."

His cock jumped at her words, requiring very little coaxing from her. It had been a long time for him too, but she wasn't prepared to end this too fast. She wanted to bring him to the brink and pull him away before he could find bliss. Caylin wanted him wild and crazy, the way they had always been together before. She would erase the wall that had grown between them, and she would have a lot of fun doing it.

Moving away from his ear, she ran hot kisses down his neck as her fingers rubbed against the length of his erection. She could feel the small veins popping along his shaft. He was ripe for the picking for sure, but Caylin wasn't nearly hot enough. She moved down to remove his briefs. When his cock sprung up in front of her, she licked its head. His whole body tensed, and Caylin reveled in the control. She looked up at him and saw the dark desire rippling across his face. It was good to see it still raced through him. That was the Griffin she wanted here and now, not the one who was guilt-ridden and worried about her. She would remind him she was not as breakable as he thought.

Her nails raced along his legs, and she bit the inside of his thigh. She loved the way he flinched beneath her. She straddled him but didn't take him inside her. Instead, she teased him with the idea that she was right there above him, just out of his reach. That was what he had been all these months. Here, but so far away at the same time. She would remind him never to do that again later. For now, it drove her forward. Leaning over, she let her breasts slide against his chest and felt her nipples starting to rise against the slight friction of heat beneath her.

Caylin brought her lips over his and kissed him until he wanted to control it. Then she moved just out of his reach, her mouth so close to his he could feel its heat. Kissing him again, she mastered every inch of his mouth, and when their tongues dueled together, Caylin let his cock rub against her clit. Her breath caught in her mouth, and he sucked her tongue into his mouth.

Sensing the growing need inside her, Griffin rubbed himself against her, and she trembled against him. Pulling away from him, she climbed off him. "Ah, ah. I'm in control."

"As you wish. I'm yours to command." His eyes were filled with a growing desire.

Caylin knew she was playing with fire, but she didn't care. The anger she had unleashed earlier had been a precursor to a need she had been ignoring for far too long. She would make sure neither one forgot it after tonight. Her mouth seared a path down his body, stopping to bite his nipples before sucking them one at a time. She saw him pull against the ropes as he tried to control the madness that was circling inside him. Good, let him suffer. She had wanted this forever and a lifetime, it seemed. As she continued to work on his nipples, her hand reached down and squeezed him hard.

"Caylin...," he almost growled at her.

"Too much, Griffin? Good. Serves you right." She bit his nipple hard, and he moaned.

"What did I do?" he asked her, completely helpless to her

torture.

"It's what you didn't do." She bit the other nipple and almost thought he'd ripped his way out of the ropes. Thankfully, the magic held them tight.

"Tell me...." he begged her.

"Nope. I plan on showing you." She gave him a wicked grin as her hand started to slowly pump up and down over his cock. His breath caught in his chest, and his eyes closed. His face looked like he was caught somewhere between pleasure and pain. Caylin should have pity on him, but she just couldn't bring herself to summon that emotion. Her raw need was taking over as she slid down his body and brought him into her mouth.

"God, Caylin. I'm not sure that's a good idea."

She bit down on his tip, and he writhed beneath her. Pulling her mouth away, she challenged him. "Was that a complaint?"

"No...lord no. I'm just not sure how much I can take." He was getting terribly close to the brink, and Caylin knew it, but still, she pushed him further.

"You're not allowed to finish, do you hear me?" Her eyes narrowed on him and his breath caught in his chest.

"Yes."

He flinched again when she ran her hands between his legs. She massaged against his two engorged sacks as her mouth rose up and down the length of him. The control she wielded over him made her ache for every inch of him. Her own juices were flowing down her leg; she was so hot for him. When she felt his entire body strain beneath her, she gave him a little reprieve.

She licked her lips and looked up at him, raw desire flowing through every inch of her body. How long could she continue this? She was having trouble deciding who was more worked up at that point. Her insides quivered and throbbed as they ached to feel his length inside her.

His eyes were dark, his mouth filled with a need that was so crazed he was having trouble breathing.

"Now, you're listening to me?"

"Yes...what are you...oh god, Caylin, don't do that."

She had taken one of his ball sacks into her mouth and was sucking it like a jawbreaker as she squeezed her hand on the other one.

His legs were pulled taut now as he fought for control over himself. Caylin took pity on him and released him. She slid up the length of his body, enjoying his heat against her. It emanated through her and tickled her senses.

When she brought her mouth down to his, his lips were on hers like a mad man who had no wish to temper himself. Caylin reveled in the feeling. She let her hand run along one of his arms, scraping her nails against his flesh. He sucked her tongue hard into his mouth. Breaking the kiss, it was unclear who was more aroused. Both of them were panting, their skin flushed and sweating, and they had barely begun.

Caylin moved again and opened her legs wide as she slid down his hard cock. She knew she was playing with fire, but she didn't care. Caylin had one life to live, and she was damned if she would let any conventions get in the way. His skin was so hot inside her, she thought she would melt around him. He tried to move, but she pulled out of his reach.

Caylin leaned over and bit his nipple. "Don't move, Griffin."

He growled when she rode him slowly again. She felt his ass tighten under him as he focused on her command. Caylin knew he wanted to move, probably more than he wanted the air he breathed, but she didn't care about that right now. She was taking her turn, bringing him to an ecstasy he would never forget. He was hers, and she was never going to let him go again.

As the desire built inside her, she closed her eyes, enjoying the fire that burned. She rode him hard and fast until she felt him tighten his entire body. Caylin stopped in her tracks and leaned over to kiss him on the mouth. His lips were like fire, as the wild man beneath her was pushed to the point from which she knew he would not be able to return. At this point, she didn't care.

Waving her hand, the ropes disappeared, and she looked deep into his desire filled eyes. "You can move now."

"Thank god," his voice gritted out as his hands wrapped around her ass and held her tight. "God, you feel so good, Caylin."

She smiled in a desire laded haze as she rode him slowly. He kept the pace slow until he sensed the orgasm that eluded her. His mouth came up to lick her nipple, and Caylin nearly fell over. When he started to suck on it, as his cock slammed harder into her, Caylin needed no further encouragement. She trembled around him, her smoothness swallowing his heat as he drove into her.

"That's it, Caylin. Yes. Take it."

She was nearly ready to collapse when her release was over, but his hands reached for hers. He kept her steady as he slowed his pace, controlling every inch of his movements. Caylin realized she had lost control over the situation, and her eyes flashed open.

"What are you doing, Griffin?"

"Taking care of you," he answered with a mischievous look on his face.

He must have known those words would make her angry, for she forced his hands over his head. "Stop doing that."

"Or what?" He was clearly waiting to see what she would

do next.

Caylin did the only thing left to do. She held his hands over his head and slammed herself down on top of him. His breath caught in his throat, and his eyes closed as the pleasure shook through him. She could tell he enjoyed it, and that made her want to push it that much farther. She rode him hard and fast, his hips rising to meet every motion, and yet Caylin could still sense he was holding himself back.

She brought her face down to his and let her mouth ravage his. Her tongue plunged into its depths, and they fought for control over the moment. When his body bucked beneath hers, Caylin reveled in his defeat. As he came inside her, her own traitorous body followed suit. Slumping over on top of him, Caylin yelped when his teeth bit her shoulder.

"Ouch, what was that for?"

"You drive me crazy, woman." He was still panting beneath her.

"Good, it's about damn time." She tried to move herself away from him, but his hands held her tight. "What are you doing, Griffin?"

"Just enjoying the aftermath." He grinned at her.

Caylin squeezed herself around him and saw his stomach bunch in reflex. She pushed away from him and lay next to him. The power of control was something she needed in her life. Not that she minded yielding from time to time, but it was time he started treating her like an equal.

"I'm sorry, Caylin." He kissed her neck, and she sighed.

"I know you are, Griffin. No more kid gloves, okay?" she made him promise her.

"I promise." He yawned slightly, and Caylin realized it was almost two in the morning.

"Get some sleep," she ordered.

He chuckled at her commands. "Now look who's being bossy."

"Damn skippy. We're going to need our energy." She sighed when his arms pulled her against him. She fell asleep listening to the beat of his heart and the gentle breathing that reminded her that she was finally home at last.

Chapter 29

Caylin was having the most wonderful dream. She was floating in the air like a cloud without a care in the world. Her insides stirred around like a blissful flower waiting to open. As she opened her eyes, Caylin discovered the reason why she was feeling the way she as. Snuggled against Griffin, his arms were wrapped around her. One of them was moving against her clit, bringing her immense pleasure while she slept.

Desire coiled inside her as her brain caught up with the rest of her. His other hand moved up to her breast, where her nipple had already risen to attention. She sighed as his finger worked her over—her ass ground against him as she came close to her orgasm.

"Cum for me, Caylin. God, yes." His breath was hot against her ear, and she shuddered against him.

She tried to focus on the fire building in the pit of her stomach. The first pitch came, followed by a tremor that ripped through her entire body. She went tight against him as her body continued to shake. He gave her no quarter, his fingers moving even faster as she came around them. The pleasure and pain mixed together as the fever built inside her again. She wanted to push him away, to stay relaxed in her release, but he gave her no choice as his hands took what they wanted from her. When the next orgasm came, her toes curled painfully against his legs.

"There, Caylin. That's how bad I want you."

She shivered at his words, wondering what he was going to do next. He removed his hand and flipped her over on her backside. Her eyes searched his and saw the raw desire reflected inside them. She licked her lips and waited to see what would happen next.

He spread her legs and slid his finger inside her. "So wet for me."

Caylin whimpered when he leaned down and bit her nipple. Every inch of her was awake and ready for him. She would crumble away inside if he refused to finish what he started.

"Tell me what I want to hear, Caylin," he challenged her.

"I want you, Griffin." Her voice came out in a gasping whisper.

"That's not it." He punished her with another hard bite.

She writhed beneath him. "Please...."

"Please, what?"

"Take me." God, how she wanted him to bury himself deep inside her.

Those words seemed to work, for he removed his hand and moved over her. When he slammed into her hot juicy core, she trembled around him. With just one thrust, she had come undone beneath him.

"That's my girl. Yes, cum for me."

His cock continued to plummet inside her over and over until Caylin no longer knew what was up or down, left or right. Her hips rose to meet every thrust, pushing her to a plateau that was so close yet out of reach. His hands pulled her legs up in the air, and he slid even deeper inside her. Caylin nearly lost her mind when she felt him slamming against her. His balls seemed to be plastered against her, which was driving her wild beyond belief. Clearly, she would never get enough of his masterful moves. The fire rose inside her and burst before she could even second guess it. He was close behind her.

When he pulled out of her, his hand tweaked her nipple, which was already raw and tender. His mouth covered hers and his tongue plunged into her. She wrapped her hands around his head, attempting to pull him deeper inside her. Caylin would swallow him whole if she could. If she could bottle up the desire she felt for him, it would carry her for the rest of her life.

When he finally pulled away from her, Caylin sighed against him. "I see you're a man of your word."

"That I am." He gave her a cheeky grin.

"Good." She pushed up on the bed and stretched. "What time is it?"

"Time to get up," he teased her.

"Fine." She started to move away from the bed, and he smacked her ass. "Ouch, what was that for?"

"Later." He winked at her devilishly.

"Ooooh." She shivered slightly. "When is it later?"

"I'll let you know."

She giggled as she went to get ready for the day. As she ran the shower, she heard him enter the room behind her. His hands slipped around her as he pulled her back against him. "It's not later yet, is it?"

"If you're lucky."

She relaxed against him and sighed. If only there was just this in her life. But reality would set in before she had a chance to hold on to it. Caylin could sense it working its way into her consciousness. They still had a lot to do, and while she wished it was all within the confines of his apartment, the truth of the matter was they had to leave here soon. Tonight, if she could arrange it. The Revenant wouldn't be expecting it, nor would he be able to force his way into her consciousness ever again. She would not stop until he was completely decimated.

Griffin sensed her pulling away. "What is it, Caylin?"

"We have a job to do." She sighed and turned around to look up at him. "He's still out there, Griffin."

"Yes, but he's not here at the moment," Griffin reminded her. He reached for her hand and brought it down to his erection that had already started to reform.

"How in the hell did you manage that?" she asked him.

"It's been a long time," he answered her.

Yes, it had. Ever since she had returned, he had been living like a monk. Well, no more. They were two able-bodied people, ready and willing. Why not indulge whenever they could?

"Yes, it has." She licked her lips and thought about all the wicked things she was ready to do to him the minute they stepped into the shower. She crooked a finger at him and gestured for him to follow her. Caylin stepped into the shower and let the hot steamy water fall around her.

As he stepped in behind her, Caylin reached for the soap. Lathering it in her hand, she ran her hands all over his chest, down his stomach, until she reached the part of him that held most of her attention. She collected more soap in her hands and slid it up and down the length of him.

He moaned softly. "You're so good to me."

"You keep thinking that. I'm really only thinking about what I want right now." Her eyes met his, and she felt a spark ignite between them.

"I see...and what is it you want, Caylin?"

"Wouldn't you like to know?" she teased him as she slowly lowered to her knees. Taking the bar of soap with her, she was now eye level with his cock that seemed to prance in front of her, begging for her attention.

Running the soap along the length of his right leg, Caylin licked the tip of his shaft. He clearly had not been expecting that, as her hands had distracted him from her goal. She continued to lather his legs as she opened her mouth wide to accept him. Her tongue continued to bathe him as she sucked him in further. Reaching around, Caylin started to run the soap along his ass. She let it slip from her fingers and gripped his cheeks with her hands. As she took him into her mouth, she teased him with her tongue. Caylin felt him grow harder, and she relished the control she had over him. When he was near the brink, she pulled away and stood up.

"You dropped the soap," he pointed out.

"So I did." She wrinkled her nose at him.

"Are you going to get it?" he asked her.

She looked down at the bottom of the tub and saw the way his dick twitched. Caylin knew exactly what he wanted. Leaning over, she bent to pick the soap up from the bottom. She felt his hands grab her ass and slide her cheeks apart. His fingers slid into her, and she moaned softly. She throbbed for him, knowing she would never get enough of him.

"Grab your legs," he ordered her.

Caylin was happy to comply. She spread her legs wide open and reached down to grab herself to keep her balance. When he slid into her, Caylin was half afraid she would fall over, but Griffin held her steady as he slowly moved in and out of her. Her breath caught in her chest as the heat from the shower slid down her back. His slow, steady ride was making her wilder by the second. She wanted him to slam into her to take every inch of her until she was begging for more.

"Faster, Griffin," she demanded.

He was happy to comply. No longer holding back, Griffin took every inch of her over and over until both of them were ready to explode. When the rapture took them, they both shook to their core. Griffin slid out of her and pulled her up against him. He retrieved the soap from her hands and started to tenderly wash her body in the aftermath. She sighed against him and wondered if every shower could be just like this. She'd be wrinkled and pruny if it was, for Caylin would never want to leave.

Griffin gently toweled her off when they were finished, and she was smiling from ear to ear. "That was delicious."

"Yes, but I think you've seriously depleted me, woman." His mouth came down to hers, and kissed her gently.

She sighed against him. "It was worth it."

"We've got to get moving," he cautioned her, for the tattoos on their arms were telling them their presence was required.

"I'll be down in a minute."

Caylin sighed and went to retrieve her clothes. Reality was coming closer to the forefront of her mind. Tonight, everything would change. That she was sure of.

Chapter 30

When they gathered down at the table, Caylin found herself greeted with a few surprised glances. It had been a while since she had sat among them. Caylin had felt like she was letting them down, but today was different. She was resolved and ready.

"Caylin, nice to see you." Lia smiled her welcome.

"Good to really be back," Caylin replied. "What's going on?"

"Take a look for yourself." Campbell showed her the globe before them.

Caylin looked down and saw the globe was lit up with many red dots. "What's going on? I've never seen so many portals at once."

"Neither have we. That's what we're worried about." Devon shook her head as she continued to look at them.

Caylin rested her head against her fist and debated what their next plan of action should be. With all this activity, it was entirely possible that this was, in fact, the perfect time to act. The Revenant's goons were out to play, and the more of those that were distracted, the easier it would be to get to him.

"You're up to something," Griffin interrupted her thoughts.

She smirked at him. "Yes, as a matter of fact."

"Caylin," he cautioned her.

"Don't worry. It's actually not as hair-brained as you think." Caylin pointed to the dots. "See those?"

"Well, duh, of course, we do." Devon rolled her eyes as she twisted one of her braids in her fingers. "You sure you're up for this?"

Caylin smiled. "I'm better than ever. In fact, I'm ready to bring my end game."

"That sounds dangerous." Bryce grinned at her. "Count me in."

"You don't even know what she's got planned." Devon rolled her eyes at him.

Caylin smirked. It was clear to her now that something was definitely going on between the two of them. Their hidden glances were much like the ones she shared with Griffin. The fire that rose between them was easy to spot, now that her eyes were open. She cleared her throat. "Ahem...can I continue?"

Campbell nodded at her. "What did you have in mind?"

"The Revenant is not expecting an attack. If he were, he wouldn't be sending all these shadows through the portals. For whatever reason, he has left himself open to attack." Caylin pointed at the newest portals that were popping up as she spoke.

"So, you're suggesting the Watch Tower heads in?"

"No. I'm not." Caylin nibbled on her bottom lip.

"What are you saying, Caylin?" Griffin's voice was almost cold.

"I'm suggesting we use the other Guardians as a distraction. Send them to attack the other portals, while — "

"You're not going by yourself." Griffin cut her off before she could finish.

"Let me finish, jackass," she threw at him. He had the decency to close his mouth, even though he was grinning at her. "I thought we could work together."

"Now, that is something I can get in on." Lia's purple hair seemed to shake with each nod of her head.

"Good. What about the rest of you?" Caylin's eyes met Griffin's as she waited for his reply.

"I say, bring it on." Griffin rose to the occasion, his mouth set and determined.

This didn't surprise Caylin much, because she knew he was not going to let her out of his sight. That suited her just fine because she didn't want to lose sight of him either. "Good. Anyone else?"

"All in?" Campbell asked with a curious raise of his brow. In a matter of seconds, it was unanimous.

"So, what do you have in mind?" Campbell asked her.

"I know where he is." Caylin was pretty confident she could reach him if they made their way into the vortex. There was a reason she had dreamt of that path so many times before. It was her map to him. Whether he knew it or not, the Revenant had been drawing her to him all these years. Tonight, he would regret that.

"Why do I have a bad feeling about this?" asked Lia.

"Because it's not a pleasant place." Caylin knew it would be a disservice to sugar coat it. "The last time we went in, we almost didn't make it out."

"The vortex?" Griffin asked her. His eyes told her that he wanted to go anywhere but there. That was where he had lost her last time. She wanted to soothe his feelings over, but life was not filled with guarantees or warranties. Anything could happen at any time. That was chance.

"Yes," she confirmed and watched the others settle into the

idea. "If you enter afraid, it will come to no good."

"I'm not afraid." Bryce nodded to her. "We've got the stalker."

Great. No pressure at all, of course. She scanned the table and found that all of them were looking at her with renewed determination. "Good. The fact that he is activating these portals in the daylight means he will send his minions through tonight. Can you speak to the others?" she asked Campbell.

"That I can do. Should we bring the Walker?" he asked her.

"If she's free. We could use her help." Caylin had a lot of respect for Lyssa. She had walked in her shoes several times over before Caylin had even begun to fight. With her help, they might actually bring down the entity that was tearing their world apart piece by piece.

"Let's get to it then." Campbell waved his hand as if to tell them they were dismissed.

"Get your rest, it's going to be a long night," Caylin warned them.

As they moved away from the table, Griffin reached for her hand. He didn't seem to care that the others were watching him. His eyes were tender when he looked down into hers. "You are not leaving my sight."

Caylin smiled. "You're worried."

"Hell yeah, I'm worried. The last time we went into that portal, I nearly lost you."

"I know," she whispered. She couldn't meet his eyes, for she knew they would try to talk her out of what she knew they had to do.

"We'll go in, Caylin. We'll fight until there's nothing left to give. But when we get home...." He paused for a moment.

"What?" Caylin asked him.

"We'll have a lot to talk about."

She looked up into his eyes and saw the tender love reflected there. The magnetic pull that kept them ripping each other's clothes off was merely an aftershock for the love that was woven into every inch of their bodies. Caylin knew that, but to see it so clear in front of her made her wish she never had to push herself forward to fight. It was this love that she was fighting for, this love that would help her realize her full potential and end the reign of terror that had been ransacking her world.

"Yes, we will." Caylin wasn't sure where the conversation would lead, because the more they talked, the more she imagined herself ripping his clothes off. She nibbled on her bottom lip, and Griffin squeezed her hand.

"I said *talk*," he teased her.

"Like hell, we will," she taunted him. Caylin turned to look around her and realized that they were now alone. "Did we scare them off?"

"Not likely. I'm pretty sure Bryce and Devon have plans of their own." He grinned at her.

"And what about us?" Caylin asked him.

"We need to get our rest."

Caylin pouted. Rest. She was too wound up for rest. "Fine. We need to save our energy, but I can't go back to sleep."

"What do you suggest then?" he asked her in all seriousness.

"I'm going to spend the day in the library."

"The library?" Griffin looked at her like she was sick. "Why?"

"There's some magic I wanted to read about it." Not that he needed to know. Caylin wanted to double-check her thoughts on how to bring the Revenant to his knees. She planned on bringing the one thing he had no defense against.

"I'll join you." Clearly, Griffin was afraid to let her out of his sight.

Caylin wrinkled her nose. "If you must."

"Oh, I must." He followed her into the library and plopped down in one of the chairs.

Caylin went to the shelves and started to pull out a few of the journals she had looked over before. She placed one in front of Griffin and sat down next to him. "Time to read."

"What am I looking for?" Griffin asked her.

"Rose quartz, healing energy, the effects on dark energy when the light bleeds into it."

"That's a pretty wide net. What are you planning?" Griffin asked her.

"To kill him with kindness." Her answer was matter-of-fact.

"Kindness?" He looked at her as if she had lost her mind.

"Not exactly." Caylin knew it was going to be hard to explain, so she sat down next to him and reached for his hand. She placed it on her chest and took a deep breath. "A wise woman once told me that love was the highest power of all. I didn't believe her then, but now I know it's true."

"Love?" He smiled at her.

"Yes. I never felt its touch before I knew you. But now that I have, I know it's there with every breath I take. It was the one thing he could not take from me, even though he tried. When he became you there, he was trying to manipulate the way I felt, but in the end, he couldn't even begin to understand the depths of the emotion."

"It is definitely complicated," he agreed.

"But worthwhile," she reminded him.

"Worth fighting for too." He brought her hand to his mouth and kissed it gently. "I'd fight through the gates of hell for you."

"I'm afraid you may have to do just that."

"Bring it on." Griffin pulled her into his lap and kissed her softly.

When his lips left hers, she snuggled into his embrace. She felt the white light surround her, the peaceful balm that had been her saving grace long before she recognized it. Anyone who turned that feeling away was a damned fool. No matter how hot and furious she was with him, she knew she would always remember how much she loved him. The trick to it all was making sure to not lose herself in the process. She had to hold on to the anger that fueled her, but not when she was in his arms. Later she would unleash her fury, and the Revenant would regret the day he had walked into her life.

Chapter 31

They had spent the day together, researching in between snuggles, taking as much time as they could to just be present in the moment, something that was incredibly difficult for Caylin. The time together only strengthened her resolve.

Now that night had fallen over the world, it was time to get started. They gathered together in the meeting room. Caylin looked at all of them and was honored that they put so much trust in her. She wasn't quite sure how to put it into words. It was a good thing she didn't have to.

"Are you ready?" Campbell asked her. His eyes were even more serious than before.

"As ready as I'm going to be." Which was the truth. No amount of training could really prepare them for the unknown world they were about to venture into.

"That sounds about right," a new voice echoed around them.

"Walker!" Caylin's face lit up. She was glad to have Lyssa at her side again.

"Wouldn't miss it for the world." Lyssa nodded to her. "Let's go take down some shadow scum."

"Let's move." Caylin waved her hand in front of her, and the world shifted around her. She was flying in the air, determined to find the vortex portal that would lead her to the one being she hated more than any other creature in this universe.

As she landed near the grove of trees, she stepped aside to make way for the others. They were right behind her in seconds, each one wearing their game faces. They all knew the dangers inside, but when they joined the Watch Tower, they knew their lives could be forfeit. The one who had the most to lose was the Shadow Walker, whose family counted on her to return. Caylin would make sure she did.

"I'm surprised there aren't any guards to the portal this time." Lia seemed disappointed.

"Don't worry. I'm sure you'll get your chance to lay into a few by the time this is over," Caylin assured her.

"Good. It's smashing time." Lia ground her hand into her fist, and small blue sparks shot out when she pounded them harder.

Caylin was glad she was on their side. She hadn't seen the Guardian in action much, seeing as her own stint here seemed short-lived. "When we go in, we're taking the red portal. After we get inside, I will be porting to the road on the other side of the oasis."

"Some oasis," whistled Bryce.

"I wish we could set those souls free." Devon's face was filled with sorrow for the souls that were being tortured inside the deadly waters.

"Another day," Campbell assured her.

"You can port directly to me. I'll send a burst of light so you can find me, like a flare." Caylin knew that would be the easiest way for them to find her without teleporting into the depths of the poisonous waters.

"Got it," Bryce assured her.

Caylin looked over at Griffin and didn't need a verbal affirmation. She knew he was not going to let her out of his sight for too long. He would be right behind her. Heaven help the being that tried to take her away from him again. She felt the same about him. Nothing was going to keep them apart. "Let's move then. No time like the present."

Stepping through the portal, Caylin closed her eyes against the icy blast that hit her. She remembered this free fall, so she mentally prepared herself for the landing. As she hit the ground, this time, she held her body tight so that she wouldn't roll into the burning sands beneath her. Sidestepping, she made room for the others. As they appeared one after the other, she nodded at them before heading to her mark.

Once she made her way to the dirt road, she pulled out Asodio and sent a purple stream of light into the air. Not even seconds later, Griffin was right by her side, the first to arrive. His eyes met hers, and she tried not to smirk at him. "Worried?"

"Always." He smiled softly at her.

The others came right after, each one ready to go. Caylin nodded to them and pointed to the road in front of them. "I've dreamt about this road, this path, every day for the past few years. It's like he was calling me."

"He probably was," Lyssa added.

"Joke's on him, though. I'm not as corruptible as he thought. In the end, he's only led me directly to him." In a way. The only problem was Caylin knew this road forked a little further ahead. She had to make a choice, and Caylin was still trying to find the information in her head that would lead her in the right direction. They had a fifty-fifty chance at this point.

Looking behind her, she saw the bright desert sun beating down on the ground below. She knew they were about to run into bitter darkness. "It's darker than pitch where we're going.

Be ready for anything."

Turning back around, Caylin started the trek down the road. Griffin was at her side, his hand holding a wand in front of him, its white glow a constant reminder of everything he was to her. She would hold onto that feeling no matter what it took. The trees that had always lined the path were present, and even more pointed and brittle than she remembered. Their branches seemed to be long talons that scraped against each other with small little shrieks. A shiver ran up her spine as a black fog settled around them.

Griffin's wand was barely able to keep up with the darkness that surrounded them. His eyes met hers. "Something wicked...."

"Always comes," she finished for him. Holding up Asodio in front of her, she wasn't surprised to see the athame glowed vibrant purple against the darkness surrounding them.

Shadows started to rise from the ground, one right after the other. They turned, so they were back to back, ready to take on the shadows one at a time.

When the first one came at Caylin, she sent a burst of light into it. She was surprised to see it still stood from her attack. The shadows were becoming more resilient as if they were immune to her magic. As much as that irritated her, it wasn't enough to deter her. Caylin leapt at it with Asodio, striking from the head down to the ground. The shadow split in two and burst into a dark flame before it sizzled to the ground.

She turned to find Griffin plunging his wand into the heart of the creature, and it gave a cry like a banshee before he sent a large burst of light through it, causing it to explode into dust. Caylin went to help the others, knowing that Griffin was more than capable of holding his own. Slicing into one right after the other, Caylin did not stop until the last one exploded before her. When they were done, she wiped the sweat from her brow.

"We have to keep moving." Caylin gestured to the road, and the others followed after her.

They continued down the road together, as silent as they could be in a world that seemed devoid of its own sounds. Their steps seemed amplified around her, and Caylin knew that was only because no other sounds could be heard. When they came to the fork in the road, Caylin stopped. She knew all eyes were on her. Closing her eyes, she tried to think of all the times she had visited this place and the outcomes that resulted. She knew the left road was a metaphor for her life. Messy and unruly, it was the harder road to travel, the one she often tried to avoid. It would not lead her to the Revenant. The right path had always brought her to more shadows. She remembered the prism, and the Revenant's voice had echoed all around her there.

"We're going to the right."

"Are you sure?" Campbell asked her from behind.

"Yes." And she was sure. Without waiting for anyone else, Caylin started down the path, determined to face the evil at the end.

The path turned into the city she remembered from before. The buildings jutted out of the ground in jagged shapes that seemed to curl toward the sky menacingly. Their shapes were still unusual to her. She could see dark shadows looking out from the windows, but none of them came their way. Caylin was actually thankful for that at this point.

"There will be another intersection ahead of us," cautioned Caylin. Asodio glowed brightly in her hand, and its hum warned her that danger was all around them. She moved to the closest building and slid against the wall. She gestured for the others to follow suit. Moving her head slowly around the side of the building, she looked out into the streets to scan for anything that could impede their progress. Once again, she saw wicked shadows making their way slowly across the broken pavements.

"Be careful. Make sure to use your cloaks," Lyssa warned them.

Caylin nodded to the Shadow Walker and took a deep breath, focusing on retracting as much of her energy into herself as she could. When she was ready, she stepped away from the building. She wasn't surprised to find Griffin right at her side. He would be her fiercest protector, and for once, she didn't take it personally. His love wasn't something that second-guessed her abilities. It only enhanced her in ways she never expected it to. With him, she actually felt anything could be possible.

"They are constantly drawn to the park," Caylin whispered. "There's a prism there that seems to power everything."

"Oooh, this could be a two for," Lia exclaimed.

Caylin looked over at Griffin. "What?"

He grinned at her. "Two for one."

"Oh. Right." She rolled her eyes and nodded to the shadows ahead. "We need to not be detected by them." She wasn't sure how many there were, but Caylin wasn't too worried about her odds. After their last encounter, it was clear that all the Guardians were in their prime and able to handle whatever the shadows threw at them.

Caylin followed behind the dark figures, with the other Guardians behind her, each of them blending almost too easily into the background. The large group of fir trees was just ahead, letting Caylin know they were almost at their target. As they moved past the tree line, the trees became shriveled before they opened to a small clearing.

The shadows were now pooling around the prism. Caylin felt it call to her, and she turned to look at Griffin. "I know you're not going to understand this, but I have to do this myself."

"Like hell you do," his voice bit out.

"You have to let me do my job, Griffin." Her jaw jutted out fiercely as she tried to make her point. "When he's gone, then you can have my undivided attention."

"And adoration?" His mouth turned up into a small smile.

"And a few other things." She winked at him.

"What do you need me to do?" he asked her, even though she could tell he was reluctant.

"Love me." Caylin wrinkled her nose at him before stepping toward the prism.

"What is she doing?" Campbell asked curiously.

"Her job, apparently. Our job is to keep her protected. Let's clear these bozos out." Griffin waved to the shadows that had started to recognize them.

"On it." Devon had already started to take some of them down.

Caylin gripped Asodio and prepared for what would come next. As she neared the prism, her head started to hurt again. She knew the pain well — it was a remnant of what she had felt over the past year — the Revenant.

The prism was not just a prism; it was his castle, where he dwelt among the souls he had trapped inside it. This was where he had begun, and it would be where he ended. Caylin leapt at the prism with Asodio, its purple flames ripping into the stone beneath. The rip grew in size, creating enough room for her to push herself through. She turned to look at Griffin one last time and was surprised to see his face was not covered in fear for her. Instead, he nodded to her and continued to fight the shadows around her. They both knew this mission was more important than either one of them.

Come back to me. His words floated across the void between them.

I plan on it. And she did plan on it. Before the end of the night, this horrible dream would no longer plague her.

Caylin entered the prism, sliding through the dark crack. When she pushed all the way through, she was surprised to find it was not completely saturated in the oily residue she had seen from the outside. In fact, that had merely been trapped on the outside of the stone like a haunting projection that soaked every inch of its exterior. Inside, she was surrounded by black obsidian walls and a set of stairs that seemed to lead up to the sky.

Caylin took a deep breath and started the climb the stairs. The air was thick and cold as she made her way up. She kept her footsteps as quiet as possible, but she knew the Revenant sensed her presence. He was waiting for her. At least if he were here, he could not hurt her sector below. Caylin was confident her team would be able to dispatch the majority of the shadows.

When she made it to the top, she took a small look around her, but barely had the chance to look, as a strong hand gripped her from behind. Caylin sucked in her breath and waited to see what he would do.

"So you've come back to me." His voice was dripping with a sinister rasp that grated on her ears.

Caylin shivered slightly against him. He was already trying to infect her with his magic, but she resisted. "You're going to want to let me go."

"Never," he cackled. "You're mine, Stalker. Don't you remember?"

He sent thousands of images into her head. Him posing as Griffin as he kissed her cares away while she was trapped inside his world. His hands slid up her stomach as if implying there had been more intimacy than she remembered. "Don't you remember how good it was, Stalker?"

Caylin fought the revulsion that came to the forefront. His implication made her skin crawl, and that was his intention. Caylin closed her eyes and focused on the sound of her heart beating inside her chest. Anything he had done to her was not her fault, and it was nothing more than she'd been through before. It did *not* define her. She relaxed against him, knowing she only had one hand to play. Her time on the street had taught her that she could be anything she needed to be, especially with men who thought they could control anything they wanted. The Revenant was clearly male — she could feel his excitement behind her.

"That's it, Caylin. You know you want to give in to me." His voice was right at her ear.

Caylin sighed against him, pretending to be weaker than she was. As his hand slid up her chest, Caylin reminded herself to stay in the moment. The further she let this go, the easier her task would be. His hands were flesh — she could feel their warmth as he slid his hands under her shirt to dip over her nipple.

She turned in his arms and put her hands on his face. Her eyes were filled with a manufactured desire as she looked into his glowing red ones. The dark marbled skin seemed to ripple under her fingers. So, he was no longer human — or he was a manufactured one. All she knew was right now, she had him right where she wanted him.

"I'll give it to you." She licked her lips and waited to see if he would take the bait.

His body seemed to tremble in anticipation. "I knew I could master you eventually, Stalker."

With him thoroughly distracted, Caylin still held Asodio firmly in her hands. She knew it would not be enough to do him in. First, she had to weaken him. When his mouth came down to her, she turned her thoughts to the love that swirled through her. Her thoughts turned to Griffin and the joy he had brought to her life. As the Revenant tried to pull away from the white light growing inside her, she reached one hand up and pulled him closer. His mouth parted, and she sent the light into him. Like a snake, it burrowed inside him, looking for its way out. It grew larger and larger until it was pushing his insides almost out.

He pulled away from her and gripped his stomach painfully. "What have you done?"

"Given you everything you asked for." Caylin waved her free hand in front of her and sent more white light into him until he was struggling for the very air he breathed.

"You bitch! This isn't the end. When one falls, the other rises."

"Then, we'll take that one out too." Caylin was about to plunge Asodio into his depths when he cackled loudly in front of her.

"As long as you don't have the Master, the cycle will continue on for eternity." His whole body rippled and distorted as the darkness inside was devoured by the light.

"We're not going anywhere. When you get to the hell you came from, tell them the Stalker sent you." Caylin held Asodio over her head and plunged it deep into his chest. The white light joined with the purple, and a blast shot from his open pores. Small cracks formed in his skin as his flesh eroded painfully. Caylin took no joy in his death, not when she knew it was yet another beginning. When it was all over, the prism around her started to shake furiously. She knew implosion was imminent.

Get everyone out of here right now! she warned Griffin.

On it. And you? His voice was filled with worry.

I'll meet you there. Now go!

Caylin did not wait to see if he would reply. There was no time to spare. She put Asodio back in its sheath and quickly teleported back to Sector Fifteen.

Caylin was almost light-hearted when she traveled through the air. She knew this wasn't the end game for all of them, but she had learned enough to know that the Revenants were not as powerful as they first thought. When she made her way into the meeting room, she was about to tell them first thing, but Griffin walked over to her and pulled her into his arms.

"Don't ever do that again." His whole body seemed to be shaking.

"I told you I would be here." Caylin stroked his head and pulled him down to comfort him against her own. She ignored the others standing in the room. She knew she had not been the only one to suffer when she was gone. He had truly worried for her safety, and when she hadn't come back, he had forced himself to move on, believing she had died far away from here. If it had been him missing, she would feel the exact same way.

"Yes, but that hasn't always gone to plan." His eyes rose to meet hers. "Are you okay?"

Caylin smirked. "Well, it wasn't pretty. But I'm a tough cookie."

"What happened?" he asked her.

Caylin looked away from him and tried to figure out what she should tell him and what he didn't really need to know. When her eyes met his, she settled for the one thing that wouldn't hurt him. He didn't need to know the truths the Revenant had shared with her. To know that thing had done those things to her made her want to scour her body from top to bottom, inside out. "He thought I was coming back to him. I let him believe it."

"And?" He was not going to let this drop.

Caylin looked at the others apologetically; as they were witnessing drama they did not have to be privy to. "I waited for my chance to attack. When he kissed me, I sent the only power into him that he never saw coming."

Griffin stiffened slightly. "He kissed you? I'll kill him."

Caylin giggled. "You're a little late for that. He's dead. Never saw it coming."

"What did you use?" Lyssa asked her from across the room.

"Love, of course." Caylin winked at her. "A wise woman once told me it was the most powerful magic in the universe. He had no idea what hit him until it was too late."

"That's my girl." Lyssa grinned at her. "But—"

"It's not over," Caylin finished for her.

"What comes next?" Campbell asked her.

"He said when one falls, another rises. I expect there will be another Revenant before long. I also think he's not as inhuman as we thought. He was human at one point, so my guess is one of the Craven might replace him." Caylin knew there were hundreds of Craven willing to take his place, but she had no idea how or when it would happen.

"Anything else?" Lyssa asked her intuitively.

"He said until we find the Master, they will continue to control the shadows." Caylin wasn't entirely sure what that meant.

"Master?" Campbell asked curiously.

"Ah, sounds like we have another search on our hands." Lyssa smiled. "Perhaps when we bring a strong triad together, we can take control of the situation and restore the proper order to our world."

"Three is a magic number," agreed Lia. "We should tell the council."

"Agreed. I'll get right on that." Lyssa waved her hands and

disappeared from the room.

Triad? The Walker, Stalker, and Master? Caylin wondered where in the world they would find the third piece to their puzzle. She looked up at Griffin and saw the worry cover his face. "Don't worry. I'm not going anywhere any time soon."

"Oh? You sure about that?" He nodded to the others as he wrapped his arms around her. He moved one arm to whisk them away.

Caylin felt the air blast past her face as she snuggled against him. When they landed in his room, she looked up at him. "What are you doing, Griffin?"

"I'm going to wipe his memory from your brain." He kissed her face gently. "One...." Another kiss. "Kiss...." His mouth covered hers and her hands reached up to pull him closer. "At a...."

He never finished his next word, for Caylin took his breath away with the love pouring through her. For the next hours, maybe even days, she planned to prove just how much she loved every inch of him. They may not have the happily ever after she craved, but at least they had this moment filled with enough love to keep them whole until it was time to fight again.

About the Author

Ever since childhood, Elissa Daye has enjoyed reading stories as an escape from life. When she was a teenager, she started to write her own stories that kept her entertained when she ran out of books to read. When she was accepted into Illinois Summer School for the Arts in her Junior year of High School, she knew she wanted to become a writer. Elissa graduated from Illinois State University in December 1999 with a Bachelor of Science in Elementary Education and began her teaching career, hoping to find moments to write in her free time. After seven years of teaching, Elissa decided to focus on her writing and made the decision to put her teaching years behind her so that she could create the stories she had always dreamed of. She is now happily married and a stay at home mom who writes in every spare moment she can find, doing her best to master the art of multitasking to get everything accomplished.

Acknowledgements

The world is constantly plagued with shadows, as we try to find our humanity. To the people who have held me up during that time, I will forever be thankful. I encourage you all to the light that's soft glow will change the world. We can and will overcome the darkness, one light at a time.

www.ingramcontent.com/pod-product-compliance
Lightning Source LLC
Chambersburg PA
CBHW071852220626
47052CB00002B/77